Former Rain

Vanessa Miller

Butterfly Press
Dayton, Ohio

Published by Butterfly Press

Butterfly Press
5145 Salem Avenue
PMB 257
Dayton, OH. 45426-2041

Library of Congress Card Catalogue Number: 2003090473
ISBN 0-9728850-0-5

PUBLISHER'S NOTE
This novel is a work of fiction. Names, characters, places, and incidents
either are the product of the author's healthy imagination or are used
fictitiously, and any resemblance to actual persons, living or deceased,
business establishment, event, or location is entirely coincidental.

Cover design by Jeff Hurst
Author photo by Melvin Williams

For my precious daughter, Erin,
my life would not have been complete without your love.

Acknowledgments

It is beyond my understanding, but for some reason the Lord has chosen to bless me. I still remember saying, "I'm too young to serve the Lord," and telling God that I wanted to write a few books before I committed my life to Him. But God's call was so strong, I couldn't continue to fight against it. I turned my life over to the Lord, and gave up my dream of writing.

Some time after I joined my church, Revival Center Ministries, International, Bishop Marva Mitchell preached a message entitled, 'Hold On To Your Dreams.' I truly believe that You had her deliver that message that Wednesday night, just for me. That was the night I discovered that You could use novelists in the Kingdom, just as effectively as You use preachers. I began to dream again.

Bishop Marva, thank you for being obedient to God. Your wisdom and counsel have truly been a blessing. I also want to thank Pastors Paul and Keisha Mitchell for preaching and living the Word of God. You challenge me to go higher in God, from glory to glory. I'm on my way to my good land – and it's all God. I cannot forget to mention Pastors Arthur and Charlotte McGuire. Once these two beautiful people knew about my dream, they would always ask me, "How's the book coming? You know that's your ministry, right?" I am so grateful that you never let me forget my dream.

Before I go any further, I have to acknowledge my mother, Patricia Harding. She has always believed in me. Thank you, Mama. Your unconditional love has meant more to me than you'll ever know.

You are blessed if you meet one person whom you can call a true friend. I, however, have two such people in my life; one life long friend, Rhonda Bogan and one new life friend, Valerie Coleman. You two are the best in my book. During this project, Valerie served as my constant encourager, editor, reviewer and study guide question provider. Rhonda became my biggest cheerleader, reviewer and publicist. I also have to give a shout out to Bobby Joe Bogan and Craig Coleman for putting up with the crazy hours their wives put in to make sure that FORMER RAIN would be a success.

My sister Debra Clark, cousin Kim Ivy, friend Renee Martin and my daughter Erin Miller were awesome in getting the word out about the book. I appreciate everything you did, don't ever doubt that. Every writer needs a few honest reviewers. Seana Reeves, Lucinda Greene, Andy Zavakos, and Deborah Birdsong provided valuable feedback about the actions of the characters in FORMER RAIN. Their input was right on time, and helped me to view my characters through the eyes of the reader. Also, my cousins, Tina and Mark Smith were such an inspiration when I visited them last summer, that I added them in the book. Hey Tina, I had Elizabeth and Kenneth visit New Orleans just so I could show the world how wonderful you and Mark are. Thanks for being beautiful people!

My editor, Susan Malone, of Malone Editorial Services is second to none. Thank you Susan for having the guts to tell it like it is. I am a much better writer for your candidness. A special thanks to Pia and Anita of Wilson-Body Communications for working so hard to make sure the Let It Rain book tour is a great success!

Lillian Thornton is a woman that would give you the shirt off her back. Now, she might tell you off after she gives it to you, but she will make sure that you are good and warm before you get told about yourself! I love you, grandmother. I have to send some love out to my great aunt, Ruby Knox, my aunt Geraldine St. Amant and my nephew Eric Leon Epps, Jr. Keep on keeping it real.

Finally, I have to acknowledge two people who were very instrumental in my life. My natural father, Chester Ward, and my spiritual father, Bishop Willie E. Mitchell Sr., are both deceased, but their memory lives on.

My dad was an old school hustler with big ideals and a beautiful mind. I remember sitting on my grandmother's porch listening to him recite poems and tell masterful stories. It was in those formative years when I discovered that I was born to write, and that I would probably die with pen in hand.

Under the tutelage of Bishop Willie E. Mitchell Sr., I learned how to live for Christ. Words can't express how grateful I am to this man. As a tribute to his ministry and the many people he discipled, Bishop Mitchell is the focal point for the heaven scene in this book.

May the Grace of God forever rest with you and yours,

Prologue

July, 1998

Nina Lewis had the key in the lock of Marguerite's 1990 Chevy Cavalier when she noticed the white Cadillac with tinted windows parked a few feet away. She squinted in the thick darkness of the night as she tried to read the license plate number. The street light in front of Joe's Carryout had been broken for several weeks. A sign tacked to a raggedy old fence across the street read, "Tax dollars, hard at work."

The Cadillac's door swung open. The key jammed in the lock of the Cavalier and refused to yield. She frantically searched for any sign of help. A leg stretched out of the Cadillac and touched the ground. Fear clenched Nina's heart. She dropped the grocery bag. The dozen eggs Marguerite needed to bake that sweet potato cheesecake splattered in the street. The Reese's she had been craving for a week violently connected with the ground and her heel, as she ran like the wind. Tears streamed down her face, as she thought, so this is my destiny; to die like a dog in the street.

***

The ringing of the telephone cheated Elizabeth out of much needed sleep. She turned over in bed and glared at it. "Somebody better be dead!" she growled, reaching for the receiver. Then again, at one in the morning, if someone were dead, she could do nothing about it. So she turned back over in bed and as her shoulder-length hair swished across her mocha-chocolate face, she resolved to let the answering machine pick up the call.

The salutation seemed a bit long this morning, and the beep was a tad loud. But the noise that bellowed from that little box on her night table was the most annoying of all. "Hi Liz, it's your big brother. You've been so heavy on my mind I couldn't get to sleep… Where are you?"

"Lying right here listening to you, bonehead!"

"Well, call me when you get in. Let's do lunch or something, okay kiddo?" He hung up.

"Not if I can help it," Elizabeth grabbed Kenneth's pillow and covered her face. Ever since Michael became a minister he was always preaching, always telling her that she was a sinner. The way he talked you'd think she was a complete heathen who never set foot in a church building a day in her life. Didn't she take her kids to church almost every Sunday? Didn't she sing in the choir and lead most of the songs? Hadn't her pastor told her that he was glad she was a member of his church? As far as Elizabeth was concerned, she was all right, and there was no way she was going to lunch with Michael to have him tell her everything she was doing wrong. Hmmph, no way! Mister Holier-than-thou could just find someone else to preach to!

The phone rang again. Elizabeth sank deeper into her bed and screamed, "Why me?" The answering machine picked that one up also. "It's one in the morning, Elizabeth," a sultry woman's voice announced. "Do you know where your husband is?"

As the line went dead, Elizabeth looked over at Kenneth's side of the bed. It was empty.

***

"He's out there!" Nina screamed. She ran the entire two blocks from Joe's Carryout. A gallon of two-percent milk was on the hood of the car, which was still in the grocer's parking lot. "I saw him! He followed me."

Marguerite Barrow quickly opened the screen door and peeped around the corner. It was so dark she could barely see past her porch. The street was quiet and full of inactivity. That was one thing for which she could praise God. The neighborhood dope pushers must have checked in early tonight. "There's nobody out here." Marguerite grabbed Nina's shoulders and turned her around to face the emptiness of the night. "See, you're safe, baby. Nobody's following you."

Marguerite's comforting voice was not enough to reassure Nina. She fell down at Marguerite's thin ankles and wrapped her arms around her as if her life depended on the tightness of her grip. "He's gonna kill me, Marguerite. He thinks I betrayed him. He said that nobody gets away with what I did to him." His exact words were more along the lines of, *I believe in an eye for an eye, Nina. You aborted my baby – you gon' wish you were aborted.*

"You're here now Nina. You're safe -- stop worrying. Lord Jesus, give me the strength to help this child," she prayed as she lifted Nina's limp body from the ground. Marguerite had been Nina's caregiver and protector for several weeks now. "Come on in here and sit down."

Nina dragged her frail, shaken body over to the couch as Marguerite closed the door and sat down in the chair opposite her. Watching as Nina stared off into space, she asked, "Can I get something for you, honey?"

Nina jumped. *A quick death is too good for baby killers like you, Nina. When I'm done you gon' be the feature story on Unsolved Mysteries.* "No, nothing."

Marguerite's eyes misted over as she watched this young woman battle her demons. She clasped her hands together and asked, "So, did you have any luck finding a job today?"

"No, ma'am."

"Don't give up, Nina. I know you'll find something soon."

Nina looked up this time. A pained smile crossed her face. Her voice was whisper soft. "Yes, ma'am. Thanks for letting me use your car. I'll get it back here in the morning. I promise."

"Don't worry about the car. I'll go get it myself." Marguerite rose and walked into the kitchen mumbling something about washing the dinner dishes. Just as she entered the kitchen, Nina heard her say, "I just wish that child could find some peace."

But peace was inconceivable to Nina as she sat on the couch rocking back and forth. Scared to die, yet at the age of twenty-five she could only think of one reason to keep on living. Life is really funny, she thought. A few years ago she was just three-quarters shy of graduating from Wilberforce University, with a degree in Journalism. She was going to become a world-famous novelist. And out of nowhere, in stepped Isaac Walker.

Sweet-talking, million-dollar Isaac. He had it all, or so she thought, and he promised her the world. Only trouble was she didn't find out until later that it was *his* world he was promising. His world, with his rules and his game board. Isaac always had the checkmate, while the rest of the players stood around as pawns, waiting to be plucked out of the game.

In the beginning, he took special care of her. Dressing her in designer clothes, expensive purses and Italian leather shoes. He even took her to nice restaurants. Not like those college bums she dated. They loved to talk about their future payday, while eating in any old greasy spoon they could find. Nina was sick to death of the "I have a dream" brothers she had been dating. That was one reason she fell so quickly for Isaac. The first time she saw him he was wearing a cream-colored Armani suit that hung on his body like it was made strictly for his frame – and what a frame. Make a sistah wanna SCREAM!

Nina and some of her friends decided to leave the college scene and check out a party on the West side. She had worn her black leather jumpsuit that fit like a second skin and accentuated the curves of her voluptuous boom-boom bootie. The two-inch heel on her black leather knee high boots added extra depth to her five-foot frame. The strobe lights moved over her olive skin as she stepped into the crowded room. The men and women turned to stare as her hazel eyes glistened in the light. Her friends headed toward the dance floor. Nina sat at the bar and ordered a Long Island Iced Tea. Cigar smoke assaulted her nostrils as King Puff seated next to her blew cancer into the air.

Mr. Armani inched his way toward her. His diamond bedecked hands glittered in the air as he sauntered. His suit jacket curved nicely over his muscles, "Mmmh, mmh, mh." Running her French manicured fingers through her short-layered hair, she turned slightly in his direction to put out the welcome mat. His pace quickened and before long he stood looking down at her.

Honey oozed out of his chocolate-coated mouth as he asked, "Have you been waiting long?"

She looked into those deep chestnut eyes. Eyes that seemed to read her every thought and intent. *Lord, have mercy.* "Waiting for what?"

"A man. Someone to take care of you, like you deserve."

Although a little too bold for Nina's taste, he spoke just the right words to appease her vanity. Most guys never seemed very appreciative. She deserved better. Yeah, she thought, I have been waiting a long time. "So are you here to rescue me?"

"Why don't we get to know each other a little better first." He pulled up a seat next to her. "Then we'll see if you're worth rescuing." He flashed a dimpled smile.

Nina thought that smile of his must have driven countless women wild. And she was no different.

"If only I had known", she said as she sat lightly rubbing her belly, tears rolling down the side of her face. "What are we going to do? How am I going to take care of you?"

She rocked back and forth, trying to come up with an answer. When none came, she put her head in her hands. "If only I hadn't let myself get so caught up."

"Hush child," Marguerite said, walking back into the room. "No since wishing yesterday back when tomorrow has enough pain of its own."

1

"*D*id you drop my clothes off at the cleaners?" Isaac asked as he walked through his front door. Cynda told her man what he wanted to hear as she dutifully took the hat from his head and walked into the kitchen.

Isaac sat his solid one hundred and eighty-pound frame down on his sofa. Cynda walked back into the living room with a glass of lemonade and handed it to him. She was gorgeous, with long statuesque legs. Coal-black hair flowed down her back, and that skin of hers was oh-so-buttery-sweet. Not one pimple had ever dared to disgrace Cynda's amber face. He took a sip of lemonade and gave her one of those 'come here' looks. Cynda moved the newspaper off the sofa and squeezed in next to her man.

Trying to forget about the troubles with his business and Nina, Isaac pulled her closer.

"Oh, before I forget, Keith called. He said that you need to get in touch with him. It's important."

Isaac pushed her away and sat up.

"Wh-what did I do?"

"Nothing." Isaac put his head in his hands and shook it. He needed to clear his mind. It didn't work. "You can go on home tonight. I'll call you if I need anything else, okay?"

Cynda folded her arms across her chest, shifted her position on the sofa and stared at Isaac.

"Is something wrong?"

"Well, I've been here all day cleaning this house for you. I would think you'd want to spend a little time with me."

He waved a hand, dismissing her. "Not tonight, I'm bushed."

"But I..."

"Not tonight."

Cynda stood up, snatched her keys off the dining room table, and stomped over to the front door. She turned and glared at him as she opened the door. "I'm sick of your mess."

"If you slam my door, don't expect to walk back through it."

"When will I see you again?"

"I'll call you."

Cynda rolled her eyes and gave the door a strong, angry tug as she stepped onto the porch. Just before the door slammed, she stopped its motion and gently closed it.

Isaac unbuttoned his shirt, propped his feet on the coffee table, and leaned back. What did Keith want now? Hadn't he caused him enough grief with his last phone call? Keith was his boy and all, but Isaac could still hear his voice when he picked up the phone two weeks ago. "Man, I just dropped my girl off at that abortion clinic on Main Street, and guess whose car was in the lot?"

The fun wasn't in guessing for Isaac. He was a cut-to-the-chase, kick-butt ask questions later kind of man. "Who?"

"Nina. Man, I thought y'all was gon' have the baby. When did you decide to get rid of it?"

"We didn't. I got to let you go." Isaac never dressed so fast in his life. He threw on a pair of FUBU jeans and a rumpled baseball shirt, and hopped around trying to find a pair of matching socks. He gave up, and put his Nikes on without them. He didn't take time to rein in his wavy hair. He had a baby to save, and not just any baby, his baby.

Isaac wasn't the baddest hustler in Dayton, but he was so notorious that even the baddest didn't mess with him. Other hustlers speculated if that fact alone didn't make Isaac the baddest hustler on the street. Isaac didn't much care how he was dubbed. As a matter of fact, whenever the subject came up, he would growl, "I never laid a hand on nobody that didn't have it coming to 'em." Actually, it wasn't his hands that caused them to dub him the 'baddest hustler on the street.' It was all those bullets to the head he doled out like Christmas presents, that winter he was establishing himself as the HNIC (Head Nigga In Charge).

Isaac was no fool. He knew that while many kids wanted to be like Mike, some also wanted to be like Ike. But the thing those kids didn't understand was that one day, someone smarter, faster, and more notorious than he would come. That would be the day he would be required to pay for all his transgressions. This certainty caused him to yearn for a son all the more. In Isaac's mind, even if an executioner's bullet did take him out of the game, he would live on – through his son. But Nina was trying to take that away from him. It wasn't enough that she was always complaining, always unhappy about something. Now she wanted to take his child, his future, his immortality.

He made it to the clinic in twenty minutes flat. The right-to-lifers were across the street carrying picket signs. A heavy-set Black woman held a sign that read "A life is a terrible thing to waste." Isaac didn't know if that slogan was universally correct. He had known quite a few brothers that made the world a better place -- when they exited this life. But, for his seed, he wholeheartedly agreed with the slogan. He wanted to grab the sign from that woman, march right in this God forsaken clinic and shove it down Nina's baby killing throat. How could she do such a thing? He knew she was mad about the weekend he spent in Chicago with Valerie, but to kill her own child because of it…

The back door opened and Nina stepped out of the clinic. She stood there for a moment; head bent, hands on her stomach. A couple months back Isaac swore that he would never lay a hand on Nina again. But when he saw her, he knew his future, his immortality had just been sucked out of her body. A rage boiled up in him the likes of which he had never known. Too late for regrets, Isaac thought, as he advanced on his prey. Nina looked up. Her eyes bucked as she saw Isaac and the murderous rage exuding from his body. She turned and tried to open the clinic door. It was locked. She banged on the glass and assaulted the buzzer, "Help! Help!"

Isaac grabbed her arm and drug her down the concrete steps. "You had no right!" he yelled at her as he smacked her hard with his left hand, then connected his right fist to her jaw.

The old one-two punch knocked Nina to the ground faster than Ali or Tyson ever dealt with an opponent. She sat there stunned, shaking her head, when she saw Isaac raise his foot. She put her arms around her stomach protectively and curled up into a ball. His foot connected with her back and then the side of her stomach. Nina screamed. "No! Oh, God, please, no."

"I'm going to kill you," he growled. Nina saw an opening between two cars in the parking lot and hurriedly crawled in between them.

"Isaac, please wait. Listen to me…"

"You don't have nothing to say to me." He grabbed her hair and started dragging her from between the parked cars. Nina held on to one of the tires. "I believe in an eye for an eye Nina. You aborted my baby, you gon' wish you were aborted." He took his fist and jabbed it into her arms trying to make her release her hold on the tire.

The right-to-lifers put their picket signs down and ran over to the scene. A six-foot, 240-pound man grabbed Isaac. Another, who was just as big with bright red hair, put Isaac in a bear hug and moved him away from Nina. "This is not the way, man," the red head told him.

"Get off me!" Isaac angrily struggled against them. "She's getting what she deserves."

The woman who had been carrying the "A life is a terrible thing to waste" sign, helped Nina up. Blood dripped from her lip, her arms were black and blue. There was already a visible bruise on her left cheek. "It'll be alright honey. You're safe now." Nina put her hands to her face and sobbed, the woman hugged her. "That's right, go ahead and cry."

Isaac felt no sympathy. "Give me my house key," he said between clenched teeth. "You can find yourself someplace else to live."

Nina sobbed harder.

"I said give me my keys, tramp." Isaac's upper lip curled as his eyes sent piercing volts through her.

Nina brought her hands down from her face and looked around. Her purse was on the ground in front of one of the cars she had been sandwiched between. She picked it up and fumbled around for her keys. Her eyes were blurry from crying – and her right eye was closing. The woman grabbed her purse and pulled the keys out. She handed them to Isaac. "Wait," Nina said, "I need to get my car key off the ring."

"Oh, no you don't. Do you think I'm gon' let you drive out of here in the BMW I paid for? When they pulled my baby out of your belly, they must'a took part of your brain too." Isaac pushed the two men off of him. "Don't show your face at my house. Don't ask me for nothing." Nina opened her mouth. "Nothing!" Isaac repeated. He ignored the crowd that had gathered around them as he walked over to her BMW, opened the door and looked back at her. "A quick death is too good for baby killers like you, Nina. When I'm done, you gon' be the feature story on unsolved mysteries." He got in the car and sped off.

Nina was really stupid, Isaac thought as he rubbed his chin with his index finger and his thumb. Whenever he needed to think something through – develop a plan of action, he would rub his chin. How simple it would be to dispose of her in any way he saw fit. He could have taken care of her tonight when he saw her at that convenience store, but that would have ended the game too soon.

Isaac frowned. He would have given her anything she wanted. All he asked was that she accept his lifestyle. But no, Nina was a reformer, always trying to get him to change, see things her way. None of his other women complained about their competition. They had no reason to complain. He took good care of them all. He assigned each one of his girls certain tasks -- cleaning his house, holding and transporting his drugs, waitressing at his bootleg joints, or managing his laundromat. He even had a girl who knew how to pick pockets. Hustling wasn't easy, but Isaac did his best.

He would have to make an example of Nina. He didn't want his other girls thinking they could betray him without facing the consequences for their actions. That was his baby. He slammed his fist on the coffee table. "She had no right to discard what belonged to me. Oh, she'll pay, and she'll pay big."

The last time he had to make an example of someone was five years ago. When he closed his eyes he could still see the savage beating he gave Renee. She spent weeks in the hospital. Her once beautiful face was still slightly twisted when they released her.

Messing up that striking face of Nina's, that had previously dazzled him was something Isaac almost couldn't bear to think about. "Oh Nina, why are you forcing me to hurt you?" Isaac growled through his empty house.

2

"Sorry ma'am. We're not accepting resumes today."

So what's new? Elizabeth thought as she turned to walk out the door. She'd been hearing the same song all week. By now, Elizabeth pretty much knew what the receptionist's response would be by her expression. If she frowned, it was, 'Sorry, no applications accepted today.' If she looked disapprovingly at Elizabeth's colorful attire or her deep ebony skin, it was, 'We don't have anything for you.' If the woman smiled at Elizabeth, it was only to say, 'We don't have anything right now. Come back in a month or two.'

Elizabeth hated the last response most! If she didn't find a job within a month, she and her children would starve to death.

Kenneth C. Underwood's unfaithful, stank-behind made her stomach turn. It was his fault she was in this predicament. He forced her to quit her job and help him get his technical consulting business off the ground, but she was far from an equal partner. No, all Kenneth wanted was an administrative assistant. As if she struggled through graduate school to sit in his office saying, "Mr. Underwood's office. Can I take a message please?" Every time one of his lousy customers talked down to her, she wanted to tell them that they were dealing with a bonafide sistah with an MBA, not a GED – thought ya knew. But like a sucka for love, she took the abuse and did every one of the menial tasks Kenneth assigned to her. The real truth was that Kenneth couldn't deal with an educated Black woman, making educated decisions, and passing him on the way up the corporate ladder.

He promised to love, honor and cherish her, but he preferred to beat, neglect and misuse her. The beatings weren't so much physical as emotional. Okay they weren't physical at all, but the treatment she received was worse than any physical beating. If someone gives you a black eye, won't that eye heal? But how does one heal from being verbally tormented night and day? Constantly told you are too fat, when you only weigh one hundred and twenty-three pounds; told that you're too dark, so you wear your foundation two shades lighter for a month, knowing that you look like a clown! And if that wasn't bad enough, brother-man had to go and flip the script by cheating on her with blonde hair and blue eyes.

Elizabeth thrust the key into the ignition. What in the world made Kenneth think she would remain with him? Did he think that just because he no longer found her attractive that no one else would?

As she drove down the street, she mouthed, "Kenneth is on a serious sistah-free fast." But Elizabeth knew all too well what his White man's trophy would soon discover. Not only was the grass not greener on the other side of Kenneth C. Underwood, it didn't even grow.

Elizabeth slammed on the brakes and was almost rear-ended. Did she read that sign right? She turned into the shopping plaza and sped up to get in front of the building. Yep. A sign posted in the window read, 'Position available, apply within.' Elizabeth walked toward the building smiling. Near the building, two women shook hands, then one of the ladies walked toward the window.

. Elizabeth screamed internally.

woman grabbed the sign out of the window. Elizabeth just
ed around and walked back to the car.

All the way home she kept telling herself, "I won't cry. My
children won't starve, and I won't cry!" She violently shook her
head as a disobedient tear rolled down her face. She wiped the tear
from her cheek as she pulled up to her home. That's right, this
two story, five-bedroom, three and a half bath - and don't forget
the weight room in the basement -- $350,000 house in the suburbs
belonged to a sistah. She could still see the surprised looked on
Kenneth's face when she told him to get his stuff and get out. All
she needed to do now was find a way to pay for this place.

As she walked toward the front porch she didn't need Les
Brown or Zig Ziggler, she became her own motivational speaker.
"You will not let this break you. You are a strong Black woman –
and you will survive."

"Elizabeth."

She looked up and cursed. Standing in front of her with his
hands on his hips, got the nerve to have an attitude, was that light-
bright-just-know-he-wishes-he-was-White-no-good-freckle-faced-
adulterous husband of hers. "What do you want?"

"Where are my kids Elizabeth?"

Her head started bobbing, lip got ta' twitching. Can't nobody
do attitude like a mad Black woman, and Elizabeth intended to
give him plenty of it. "Funny how you remember you have kids
now. Maybe you should have told that strumpet you've been
laying up with that you have kids."

He took his hands off his hips. "Look Elizabeth, I don't want to
fight with you. I just want my kids. You put me out, I didn't want
to leave, and I sure didn't want to leave my kids -- they need me."

"The kids need you!" Her hands started flailing in the air.
"Why you good for nothing ##%@!." The wind blew, dust flew
up; there was definitely a chill in the air. It did nothing to cool the

fierce heat from the anger Elizabeth felt at this very moment. "What about me, huh, Kenneth? Did you ever stop to think for one second that I might have needed you – or was that irrelevant?"

He looked down at the cracks in the concrete, then over at the leaves as they fell off that big oak tree in front of their house. "Oh, so now you can't even look at me. Come on Kenneth. What's the matter, cat got your tongue?"

He still said nothing.

"Well maybe snow flake has your tongue. Do I have to call your woman and ask her to give you permission to speak to your wife?"

He shoved his hands deep in his pockets. "I don't want to fight with you Elizabeth, I just want to see Erin and Danae – that's all."

"Oh really? Well people with visitation rights pay child support. Did you know that Mister Adultery Committing man?"

He pulled his wallet out of his back pants pocket, counted out two hundred dollars and handed it to her. "Is that enough?"

"What, wasn't I a good *enough* wife to receive a little alimony?"

He counted out another two hundred and handed it to her. "Look, I'll put your name back on our joint account, you can take whatever you want. Now can I see my children?"

She threw the money at him. "No!" she said, and walked away.

Kenneth grabbed Elizabeth's arm to turn her around to face him. She immediately balled her fist and struck out. He ducked, she slipped, and her bottom hit the concrete with full force. "I don't want to fight with you. Will you please stop?" He bent down to help her up.

Elizabeth jerked away from him and pushed on the ground as she stood up. "Tell me why you did it. Why did you do this to us?" The tears were out now, and she hated him for it. Neighbors were peeking out their windows. Then they had the nerve to come outside, taking half-full trash bags to their trashcans. Elizabeth didn't care. She wiped at her face and those disobedient eyes and stood toe to toe with her husband. "Why? Tell me why."

He backed up, shoulders slumped. "The last couple of years haven't been our best."

She stepped to him again. "In other words, after I had *your* kids," she was so close to him, so angry, that spit smacked him in the face as she said the word 'kids.' "You had no more use for me."

He wiped at the spit on his reddening face. "Look Elizabeth, you know as well as I do that we haven't been happy for a while now."

She started strutting up and down the walkway. "I knew no such thing!" She turned to face some of her nosey neighbors that had the nerve to be standing in the street watching them. "Mind your own business! Matter-of-fact, where's your husband right now, huh? That's what your nosey butts need to be figuring out." She turned back to Kenneth, "How was I supposed to know something like that, Kenneth?" She looked him dead in the face. "Am I a mind reader or something? Cause you sure never opened your mouth to tell me you were unhappy."

His shoulders slumped again, his knee bent and his eyes slowly glazed over, as they became cold and withdrawn. The look in his eyes sent a chill through Elizabeth.

"If you cared anything about me, you should have been able to tell how I was feeling. You should have been able to read my body language."

Oh she was good and mad now. Read it in his body language. Ha! Okay, she wasn't blind. Yeah, she could see he was unhappy. Matter-of-fact, he looked more than unhappy. Kenneth quite nicely projected the image of a poor, rejected, freckle-faced stepchild. But she was always so busy with the kids, the house, the bills, the dog, and oh my goodness, when she finally got around to his needs - that didn't take any thinking, no mind reading. What did he want from her? Forget it. She threw up her hands and walked away from him. He didn't try to grab her this time, but as she reached the top step, he called out to her again.

She spun around to face him, all the while thinking, *you are a strong Black woman, you will get through this.*

"I miss Erin and Danae. When can I see them?"

She struck a pose for him and said, "Read it in my body language."

3

*I*saac was at his favorite Chinese restaurant on the corner of Main and Jefferson with Valerie Middle. Although the menu offered a myriad of delicacies, he always ordered shrimp fried rice. It was as if he believed the stories about the cats and the dogs, but still had an uncontrollable hunger for Chinese.

Dimly lit chandeliers hung over small round tables. Soft music played as most of the patrons gazed into the eyes of their partners, enjoying light-hearted conversation. Isaac gazed into his shrimp fried rice and ate in silence.

Valerie leaned forward and put her hand over Isaac's. "Baby, why haven't you returned any of my calls? Have I done something wrong?"

He moved his hand. "Oh, you know exactly what you did!"

"Wait a minute, baby." She hunched her shoulders, a look of pure innocence on her face as she added, "I'm not following you."

At that moment, Isaac contemplated slapping that innocent-as-a-three-day-old-baby expression off her face. She knew exactly what had happened, and that she caused it. He wanted to get up and tell her 'Don't call me. Naw, better yet, forget you ever knew me!' But what could he do? Valerie was an essential part of his business. To leave her now would be like cutting off his nose to spite his face. So in the final analysis, he simply asked, "Why did you tell Nina that we went to Chicago together?"

Her skillfully arched eyebrows flew up and that sinful red painted mouth dropped in shock. "Why would I do something like that?"

"You tell me!"

She leaned in closer and reclaimed his hand. "Look, all I want is for you and me to be happy again. And baby, believe me, I'm not going to do anything to jeopardize that. So why would I tell Nina that we were in Chicago, when I know that's the last thing you want her to know?"

"You tell me why you did it."

"I didn't do it!" she shouted.

"I know you! You did it – you need to quit playing games!" He shoved a shrimp in his mouth as he stared right through her.

She leaned back slightly in her seat and gazed at him. "You know, there was a time when I didn't have to worry about you throwing other women in my face."

"Just keepin' it real, baby. You know how things are with us."

"Yeah, I know. But I can't forget how you used to smile at me. Seeing those dimples would just about drive me out of my mind." She lightly brushed her hand against his cheek. "In those moments, my heart only beat because there was you." She looked away from him for a moment. "Did you ever love me?"

"What's all this love stuff?"

"Just tell me, I need to know."

"Honestly, Valerie, I don't think I know what love is."

Her eyes misted over a bit, but she managed to give him a half smile. "You used to tell me that it was just you and me against the world."

Isaac looked at Valerie for a brief moment. It was a soft, endearing moment, and he had few of those. Yeah, he did tell her that. And at the time, he meant it. He had also told Nina the same thing less than two months ago. And he meant it then too. Women, Isaac thought, either they hang around too long and make you wish they were gone, or they leave too soon, and make you chase them all over again.

4

*T*here are two things in life that you can count on.

No, not a man or a woman, and certainly not love or promises. But you can always be sure that the thick darkness of the night will caress you while you sleep, and the boldness of the morning light will creep right into your bedroom louder than any rooster's crow.

Nina sometimes wished that the light would simply fade back into night. But it never did. So this morning, she stretched her tired body across her pillow-top bed, grateful that she could stretch without wrenching from the pain of the horrible beating Isaac had given her a couple of weeks ago. She reached for a pen and some paper. She had started a poem yesterday and the ending was dancing in her head. She wanted to write it down before it got lost and jumbled in the turmoil of her mind. She lay across her bed and started reading.

> *I ache from the pain of never feeling loved,*
> *I ache from the sorrow of much wasted time.*
> *Some mornings just before I wake I dream of lying very still,*
> *So still that I can't feel the gentleness of a summer's breeze.*

And on those mornings the world seems so peaceful,

She picked up her pen and tapped it on the paper a few times. Her thoughts weren't always as clear as they used to be, but she knew she could finish this poem. It was in her head. She just needed to pull it out. The pen tapped the paper once more. "Yeah, that's it."

> *And I have the answer to it all.*
> *If I never move again, if I just stay in this very spot,*
> *Friends won't forsake me,*
> > *Love can't deny me, and family disappointments won't*
> > *even matter.*
> *Now I smile, until the fear of dying alone sets in---*
> > *And I ache once more.*
> > ### *Nina Lewis*

She set down the pen and paper, slowly peeled back the rumpled covers, and got out of bed. A piercing pain shot through her. She crumpled over and sucked in her breath until the pain subsided.

She stood in front of the mirror and grimaced. Nina had always taken great pride in keeping her hair cut and styled just right. Nina's hairstyle normally accented her caramel skin, and brought emphasis to her high cheekbones. But today, as her hair lay matted to her head, those same cheekbones made her look like a hungry Cambodian refugee.

She dutifully took her shower and put those same scraggly old plaid pajamas back on. She then took her regular spot on the couch in front of the television, which she rarely turned on.

Every once in a while, as if she could feel the presence of her hunter, she would get off the couch, creep real easy over to the window, and peek out of the red-velvet curtains. This morning, on her third trip to the window, Sheila and Lisa walked into the living room. "Girl, you missed your calling. You should be a detective, acting like I spy and carrying on," Sheila said.

"Take it from me, that man ain't thinking 'bout you. He's off playing footsy with some other woman. One that isn't stupid enough to get herself knocked up." Lisa rubbed her protruding belly. "I mean, look at me. I'm six months pregnant and haven't heard word one from a single guy I slept with. They're all just in it for the fun."

"They're probably drawing straws, trying to see who's going to get the short end of the stick. Someone will be around, just give 'em time," Sheila told her with a smirk.

"Shut up Sheila, at least none of the guys I slept with are in jail. Once I have a blood test done, I'll be able to collect child support. What you gon' collect from a bum in jail, huh?"

Sheila started bobbing her head back and forth. She was eight months pregnant and huge. She could barely move without wobbling, but she could bob that head. "You keep your mouth off my man. He loves his family, and we're going to be together. My man takes care of…"

"Excuse me, I hate to interrupt, but I really wanted to be by myself. Do you two think you could find somewhere else to hold this conversation?"

Sheila wobbled around to face Nina. "Look here Queen Bee, this living room is community property, so if you want to be alone, go somewhere else. We're getting ready to watch TV."

Nina got up and walked out the room. Arguing with those two just wasn't worth it. Hopefully the deck was quiet and empty so she could sit and think. It was cool out this morning. Nina pulled her sleeves over her hands as she walked over to the edge of the deck. She looked up at the sky. She wanted to ask God what she should do, but she felt a little silly. She wasn't really sure if there was a God in the sky. If God truly exists, would He have allowed her birth mother to give her up for adoption? Would He have allowed her adoptive parents to both be killed in a senseless traffic accident? "Why does everybody leave me?" She looked down at the plaid pajama top that covered her ever-fattening belly. Nina was glad she hadn't gone through with that abortion. Not this time.

No one was ever going to rip life out of her body again. Walking into that abortion clinic brought all the memories back. She was seventeen again. Her first love, Dwayne, might as well have been standing in that clinic telling her she was too young to be stuck with some snot nose brat.

"What about your dream of going to college and making something of yourself?" he asked her.

At the time, Nina thought Dwayne made good sense. After all, it wasn't a baby, yet. It was just a mistake. Dwayne convinced her, "When you make a mistake, you erase it," he said. So that's what they did. But no one told her how empty and heart broken she would feel. No one told her that she would lie awake at night consumed by guilt. Eight years later she still thought about her baby. Still mourned its murder.

She gently touched her stomach. "Five months to go." A tear rolled down her cheek. "I can't wait to see your face." Her voice broke as more tears came. "I know I've made a mess of things, but if I live through it, I'll make this up to you – somehow."

"Nina, come sit over here with me."

Startled, Nina turned to see Marguerite. She had a glass of water and two tiny pills in her hand. At Nina's questioning gaze, Marguerite lifted the glass in the air and said, "For my heart." She put the pills in her mouth and gulped down the water.

"What's wrong with your heart?"

Marguerite sat the glass down. "The doctor says I've got a murmur – but hey," she smiled, "I'm not dead yet."

"Don't joke about things like that." This woman had been her savior. Marguerite had stood by her the day Isaac beat her senseless in the parking lot of the abortion clinic. And when Isaac left her destitute with no place to go, Marguerite had brought her here. She sat down on the swing next to Marguerite, folded her hands on her lap and slumped in her seat. "What made you open your home to pregnant women who have no way to repay you?"

Marguerite shrugged. "I just wanted to help women, give them an alternative."

"You've been so good to me, Marguerite. But sometimes I feel like my presence here puts you in danger."

"You're in no danger, you just need to rest."

Nina lifted her hand to silence Marguerite's protest. "I've seen his car parked outside your house."

"But he hasn't knocked on the door. He'll get over his anger and move on."

"No he won't," Nina looked up at Marguerite. "You know what hurts most?"

"What?"

"He didn't love me enough to change, but he now hates me so much that he would kill me."

"Hush child. That boy ain't gon' kill nobody."

Nina's head cocked as she looked at Marguerite. This woman had been so kind to her, as kind as her adoptive mother had been before she died. She could tell that this woman would really miss her. Nina's eyes welled up. "I'm so sorry, Marguerite."

Shaking, Marguerite released herself from Nina's embrace and said, "Honey, I know you didn't have any extra clothes when you came here, I hope you don't mind, but I… I bought you a real nice dress yesterday. I laid it on your bed. Did you look at it?"

"Yes ma'am. It's nice."

"Well, I was wondering…" Don't push, she reminded herself. "You know that I go to church on Sundays… I was just wondering if you'd like to come with me tomorrow?"

It would be nice to see the house of the Lord one more time, but not right now. "Let me think about it."

5

*E*lizabeth needed a change.

She put the kids in the car and drove over to Lowes. "What are we going to get, Mama?" Erin asked, while Danae was lifted out of her car seat.

"Mommy's going to get some paint, and maybe some curtains so I can change a few things in my bedroom."

"What about Daddy, Mama? Does he want you to change the room?"

At five, Erin was the most curious child Elizabeth had ever known. She had a question, and sometimes an answer, for just about everything. Elizabeth rubbed Danae's back as she carried her into the store. She was thankful that Danae was only two and not yet aware of the goings on at the Underwood house.

"Is Daddy okay with the change, Mama?" Erin repeated.

"He's okay with it, baby." Then Elizabeth mumbled to herself, "Your Daddy don't run *my* show." The way her mood was, she could paint her bedroom black and call it a day. But as she concentrated on the task at hand, she ignored her dark mood, and became inspired by some colors in the red family. It's bold and dramatic, like me. Yep, she definitely liked it. Kenneth always wanted everything so neutral; the change will do me good. She held the card out so Erin could see it. "What do you think, honey?"

Erin crinkled her nose. "It's too loud, Mama. Nobody could look at that everyday without going blind."

Elizabeth tried to constrain her bruised feelings as she pulled the card back and looked at it again. It is a little bright, but she wouldn't say it was *too loud*. Erin was just like her father, so reserved. *Maybe that's what Kenneth thought about me. Maybe he chased after other women because I was too loud, too bold for him.* She p ut the paint card back in its slot and moved down the aisle. She stopped to look at some browns and oranges. She caught a glimpse of a high-yellow, muscle-bound brother as Danae scrambled out of her arms and ran over to Erin. He caught more than a glimpse of her, the brother was flat out staring. "So what are you going to paint?" He asked.

Elizabeth looked up again. She saw something in his eyes that had been missing from Kenneth's for quite a while. Desire. For her. Erin must have noticed it too, because she came running back with a paint card in her hand. "Look Mama. What do you think about this one?"

Elizabeth took the card out of the little blocker's hand. The color was olive green. It was soft and inviting, without being too bland. Maybe this is what I need. "I like it honey. Let's get it."

"Need any help painting?"

He gazed down on her with hungry eyes. "Why don't you give me your number? I'll let you know."

He pulled pen and paper out of his pants pocket. "My name's Terrence – and yours?"

"I'm Elizabeth," she looked down at the kids, feeling a little guilty. "And this is Danae and Erin."

"How do you do?" Terrence asked them as he handed his digits to Elizabeth.

"We're fine," Erin answered for the both of them. "But my Daddy probably wouldn't like you helping Mommy paint."

"Thank you," Elizabeth said, taking his number. A smile brightened her face. She remembered what her father said when she was sixteen and Mr. All-American threw her over for a red-bone, pee-brained pom-pom girl: One man's trash is another man's treasure. "I'll give you a call." She walked away from Terrence, and went to the paint counter to get the paint mixed, found a pair of matching curtains and was in the check out line waiting for the clerk to process her purchase. Why was it taking so long? The clerk looked up at Elizabeth and then back at the credit card machine. "I'm sorry," she said, hesitantly. "Your account has been closed."

"What do you mean, *my account has been closed?*" she mimicked the clerk. Just as she was about to snatch her card out of the clerk's hand, she realized exactly what had happened. "Why that low-down, good for..." Danae started crying and rubbing her eyes. "I don't believe this."

"What's the matter Mama?"

She was fuming. "Your Daddy ain't worth the time it took to hatch his sorry behind. That's what's wrong." She pulled out her checkbook, scribbled out the amount, tore the check from its holder and threw it at the clerk. "Just give me my receipt, so I can get out of here." Not five minutes later, as Elizabeth pulled out of the parking lot, she angrily picked up her cell phone and dialed Kenneth's office.

His secretary didn't have a chance to finish her greeting before Elizabeth yelled, "Put my husband on the phone!"

"What's up?" Kenneth asked when he picked up the line a few seconds later.

"How dare you? Y–you no good, low down... In all my life, I never met such a – a ---"

"Calm down Elizabeth. What's wrong now?"

She pulled up to a red light and slammed on the brakes. "Sleep-around-Sam, what do you think is wrong? You cancelled my credit card!"

"Let me speak to Daddy. Let me speak to Daddy." Erin unlocked her seatbelt and tried to pry the phone away from her mother's ear.

"No!" Elizabeth spanked her hand moving her away from the phone. "I'm speaking to your ol' no good, lying, cheating Daddy right now."

"Elizabeth! Please don't say things like that to my children." He let out a long exasperated sigh. "What kind of a mother would tell her kids something like that about their father?"

"Kenneth, you act like your mess don't stink. Well I'm here to tell the world, you are one wrong Black man. And if you don't want me telling your kids the truth about their precious Daddy, I suggest you stop giving me so much truth to tell!" She hung the phone up and threw it in the passenger seat.

"Mommy, are you okay?" Erin asked.

"I'm okay baby. Your iniquitous Daddy don't know who he's messing with. I'm tired of taking his crap." Danae started crying again. Elizabeth reached her hand in the back and rubbed her tummy. "I didn't mean to scare you baby. Mommy's sorry."

Her cell phone started ringing. Elizabeth snatched it up. "What is it?"

"Look Liz, I only closed the no-limit credit card account. I didn't want you to go crazy and charge up more than I can afford."

Silence.

"Use any of the other cards you want, just let me know before you purchase anything substantial, okay?"

"I'm not a child Kenneth. You don't run me like you run your company."

"Whatever. Look, I'll be over this evening. I need to pick up some more of my clothes." And he hung up.

No he didn't hang up on me. So he wants to come and get his clothes huh? I'll give him his clothes all right. "Guess what?" Elizabeth said, exuding excitement she didn't feel.

"What Mama?"

"Daddy's coming over today."

"Yea!" They both sang in unison, and clapped their hands.

"Guess what else? We're going to have a barbecue today." The backseat was full of 'yeas' again. "I think I'll see if Uncle Mike would like to come over too. How 'bout that?"

"Can we play volleyball too?"

"Yeah, why not."

***

An hour-and-a-half later, Elizabeth and the kids were in the backyard. The hot dogs, hamburgers, baked beans and potato salad were done and ready to be served. She told the kids to close their eyes so she could put a surprise on the grill. Just as she closed the lid on her surprise, Michael walked through the back yard. His hands were flattened to the side of his pants, head straight, knees erect. The military must have taught him to walk like that, Elizabeth thought for the hundredth time, as she watched this incredibly composed specimen come toward her.

"Hey you," Elizabeth smiled.

Erin and Danae ran over to him yelling, "Uncle Mike, Uncle Mike. Pick me up." "No, pick me up." He bent down and picked both girls up in one swoop.

"Hey Sis, how's it going?"

"Not too bad," she told him as she put the paper plates and utensils on the picnic table. "Come on you guys, let's eat. You can wrestle Uncle Mike down later." She fixed the plates and sat them around the table.

Michael sat down, and looked around the expansive back yard. It was immaculate. "I have to commend you Sis. This yard is well maintained."

"I can't take credit for it. Kenneth made me get a gardener about a year ago."

Michael swallowed a spoonful of baked beans, then asked, "So how have you been? Any luck finding a job?"

Elizabeth smiled, bubbling over with excitement. "I have an interview with a non-profit organization next week. But I received a job offer yesterday, so I'm trying to decide what I want to do!"

"Oh, yeah? Where at?"

"Tommy Brooks asked me to be the lead singer at this new nightclub downtown. It sounds exciting, I'm really thinking about it."

"That's nice, Elizabeth."

The smile left her face, and her hands went directly to her hips. "But…"

He raised his hands in mock surrender. "Don't misunderstand me Elizabeth, I'm proud of you."

"But…"

His body stiffened as he directed concerned eyes to her. "I just hoped that you would use your God-given talents for the Lord, rather than for the secular world."

"What *secular world*? What are you talking about? I sing in the choir, don't I?" Her head did a sistah-sistah motion. "How else am I going to support my family? I sure can't depend on Kenneth's cheating behind."

"Mommy, what does 'cheating' mean?" Erin asked.

Elizabeth picked up a napkin and wiped the mustard from the side of Erin's mouth. "It means, your Daddy likes to date other women."

"Elizabeth!"

She gave Michael a hard cold stare. "My children have a right to know what kind of father they have." She looked up and saw Kenneth walking toward them. "Speak of the devil and in he walks."

Erin and Danae jumped off the bench and ran over to their father, as if he were bread to a starving refugee. "Daddy, Daddy!" Kenneth, in all his wonderfulness, picked up his children, gave them a huge bear hug, then swung them around. "Swing us again, Daddy."

Kenneth swung his children around in circles a couple more times, then kissed both of them on the cheek. "I've missed you two so much."

"We missed you too, Daddy," Erin said, beaming up at Mr. Wonderful with those light brown eyes of hers.

"Dadda cheat," Danae said.

Kenneth turned to his youngest daughter. "What did you say baby?"

"Dadda cheat."

"She means you like to date other women," Erin told him matter-of-factly.

Kenneth put his children down and glared at his wife. "How could you tell them such a thing?"

Elizabeth smiled ever so sweetly at Kenneth. Her eyes portrayed none of the hatred she felt at that moment. Wide-eyed innocence overflowed as she said, "Oh, was I supposed to lie to them, the way you lie to me?"

Michael jumped in. "Hey Kenneth, man, long time no see. How's it going?"

Kenneth stopped glaring at his wife to respond to Michael. "Things could be better. How's everything with you?"

"Pretty good, I can't complain. Come on over here and sit down. Get some food in your stomach."

"I just stopped by to pick up a few things. I don't want to bother you guys."

Elizabeth stood up. "Kenneth, you're not bothering anyone. After all, you do pay the mortgage," she said sweetly. "Sit on down. As a matter-of-fact, I made something especially for you."

"You did, huh?" he smiled and joined Michael at the picnic table.

Elizabeth grabbed a plate, took the lid off the grill and scooped up a plate full of Kenneth's clothes. She walked back over to the picnic area, stared at Kenneth for a moment, then put the plate in front of him.

"What's this?" Kenneth asked dumbfounded.

"Aw, man. No she didn't," Michael interjected.

"Oh, I'm sorry, you need a fork." She pulled a plastic fork out of the box and put it in front of his plate. "Eat up."

Kenneth put his hands over his face and rubbed his temples. He looked up at this woman he called Wife. "Why'd you do this Liz? You charbroiled some of my six and seven hundred dollar suits."

She hunched her shoulders. "You know what they say about a woman scorned." She sat down and just stared at him, daring him to make the next move.

"You are one sick, twisted---"

"No. I'm one mad Black woman. And I'm sick and tired of taking your crap."

He stood up. "Psychotic ---"

"What?"

Kenneth picked up his daughters, whispered something in their ears and kissed them goodbye. He put them down, then turned to Michael. "It was nice seeing you, man. But, I've got to get out of here before I do a slam dunk upside your sister's empty head." He turned to walk away, but Elizabeth wasn't going to be put off so easily.

"You didn't eat your food. What's the matter, Kenneth? I've never known you to be so unsociable."

He gave her the hand. "Get therapy."

"While I'm getting therapy, you can get another family. Cause this one's off limits to you. You hear me?"

He turned, and his eyes bore into her. "I have had it up to the high heavens with your crazy behind."

She stretched out her arms, puffed up her chest. "If you feel froggy – leap."

He walked back to the picnic table, braced his hands on it, and leaned in to face her. "You've been begging for a fight. I've decided to give you what you want."

"Good, bring it on! Can't wait."

He straightened back up, feet straddled, but firmly planted on the ground. His lip curled into a smirk. "There's just one thing about a fight you don't seem to understand, *my dear wife.*"

Elizabeth had seen that smirk before. It was the same look Kenneth had given a former business associate who had mistaken his kindness for weakness. It was a mistake that proved very costly. "What's that?" Elizabeth asked, a slight tremor in her voice.

"You can't quit when *you* want to," he said, and walked out.

Michael had completely lost his composure when Elizabeth served up Kenneth's clothes to him. He was finally getting himself together. But pure anger was rushing through him now. "So this is why you invited me over here. You needed me to protect you from Kenneth's wrath."

"Hush Michael," she picked up Kenneth's plate and threw it in the trash. "I didn't need you to protect me from Kenneth. He's never laid a hand on me in his life."

Michael shook his head and stood up, "He must be a candidate for sainthood." He brushed off his pants. "I'm outta here."

"Oh, so you're going to leave me too? Well, go ahead then. I don't need either one of you. Just wait and see, once I start my singing career, I'm going to make a name for myself."

"When will you get it through your thick head, your name doesn't have anything to do with secular music? As a matter of fact, do you know the name Elizabeth means 'She worships the Lord'? Do you think it's some sort of coincidence that God gave you the singing voice of an angel and Mama gave you a name that means 'She worships the Lord'?" He walked out of the yard toward his car.

Elizabeth sat on the bench feeling no satisfaction whatsoever. What was she doing wrong? Why is it that nothing ever turned out the way she planned it? A fly buzzed around the table. She picked up her fly swatter and lunged at it, missed and gave up. What she really wanted was a big human-sized swatter so she could knock Kenneth and Michael upside the head. "Mmph, mmph, mmph. The more I deal with the nigga, the more I like the fly."

6

*N*ina was bleeding.

Doctor Hanson told her that her placenta was torn. He said that the complications with her pregnancy were more than likely a result of the beating Isaac gave her a little over two weeks ago and the stress she had been under.

Nina was cramping.

One minute she lay stretched out in her hospital bed and the next she was in a fetal position screaming, "Aaaaaaarh!"

"What's wrong with her?" Marguerite asked the doctor after witnessing Nina's third cry of pain.

"She's having contractions. She'll lose the baby before the night's out." The doctor told Marguerite, then turned to Nina and said, "If I take the baby now, it will save you hours of pain."

Nina gripped her belly tightly and shook her head. "No, no."

"Miss Lewis, I don't think you understand the severity of the situation. You're only sixteen weeks out. If you were further along I could give you some magnesium to stop the contractions, but I can't do anything to help you this early on."

Sweat drizzled from Nina's forehead. She grabbed the doctor's arm, as she told him, "I can't lose my baby."

"You could lose more than this baby Miss Lewis. If you bleed any harder, you could lose your own life."

Nina turned her face from Dr. Hanson and thought about the baby she had aborted. Oh, how she longed to hold that child. She ached as her mind replayed Isaac's cruel words, *"A quick death is too good for baby killers like you, Nina."* Maybe he was right. Maybe she did deserve a slow agonizing death.

A steely determination over took Nina as she looked back at her doctor. "If I must die, then let me die. But I will not take the life of my unborn child."

Dr. Hanson turned imploring eyes on Marguerite. "Maybe you can talk some sense into her," he said, glancing at his watch. "I'll be back in an hour."

Marguerite watched the doctor leave. Then she lowered the railing on the right side of Nina's hospital bed and began rubbing her back.

Another pain ripped through Nina's small body. Tears welled in her eyes as she turned to heaven and asked, *"Why are you against me?"*

"Hush child," Marguerite told her. "God's not against you. He'll come through for you, just wait and see."

Nina turned her face into her pillow and sobbed.

Marguerite tried to stop the tears that threatened to spill from her eyes. She rubbed Nina's back and sang:

"I got a feelin' everything's gonna be alright,
o-o-o-ooh, I got a feelin' everything's gonna be alright,
be alright
be alright
be alright."

Nina turned her face from her pillow and looked at this woman who had shown her more compassion than she'd ever known. She'd been more than a friend, more than a caregiver. Marguerite

Barrow had some how replaced the mother that threw her away, and the adoptive mother that died before she could fully raise her. Nina loved Marguerite, she trusted her. "Why do you do that?" Nina asked while wiping the tears from her eyes and grabbing some Kleenex to blow her nose.

"Do what, honey?"

"Act like God is this super being who can do anything?"

Marguerite gently touched Nina's face, then put a wayward string of Nina's hair back in place. "He is," was all she said in answer to Nina's question.

"Then why has so much happened to me? Why have I lost so much?"

"Ah, Nina. Child, don't you know that life is full of love and loss?"

Nina balled her fist and struck the mattress. "I'm tired of losing." She said through tears.

Marguerite wrapped Nina in her arms and rocked her as another contraction shot through her body. Nina cried out. Marguerite rubbed her back and prayed. When she was done communing with the Lord concerning Nina's situation, she turned back to Nina and said, "It's going to be alright."

7

*C*ounting money was a pain.

But if you let somebody else count it, you might as well let 'em spend it too.

That must be how Leonard felt about the situation, or that down-on-his-luck simpleton never would've had the nerve to take Isaac's money.

"Want me to take care of him?" Keith asked.

"Naw." Isaac rubbed his chin for a moment. "Leonard may be one of the stupidest brothers alive, but he's a friend of mine. I'll take care of him."

"What you gon' do?"

"He stole a hundred thou from me. What you think I'm gon' do?"

Keith turned away from Isaac and finished counting the stack of green back in his hands. The house they were in, as well as several others had been grafted into what Isaac lovingly referred to as 'The Promised Land.'

Ten years ago, Isaac's mentor relocated him from the mean streets of Chicago to Dayton, Ohio to help a street hustler name Ton-Ton with his war for drugs. Six months after Isaac arrived, Ton-Ton executed four young hoodlums who foolishly thought they could come up on his turf. The neighborhood always-in-somebody's-business watchers, sickened by the viciousness of the executions, made sure there would be no advance to Park Place or Boardwalk for Ton-Ton. No, that Negro went straight to jail on a serious do not pass go felony.

Isaac had already decided he wasn't going back to Chicago. He was twenty-one years old and itching to be his own boss. He spied out the land left vacant by executions and neighborhood-do-gooders.

He had no doubt that he would be able to claim it for himself. He had already shown them what he was capable of while working with Ton-Ton. No one would challenge him, he was certain of that. Standing on the corner of Riverview and Broadway, he stretched out his arms, leaned his head back and bellowed, "Welcome to The Promised Land!" Taking the land had been easy, keeping it had been work, but Isaac paid his dues, and earned respect one beat down at a time. He held up a stack of money. "Is this all we collected from Williams Street?"

"Yeah, man. It's been slim pickings for a couple of weeks."

"Why?"

Just as Keith parted his big lips to respond someone pounded on the door. Keith blew out some hot air and relaxed a bit as Isaac stood up.

Isaac snatched the door open and glowered at the crack-head in front of him. "We're closed. Come back later."

"Come on man, I need to score now." He lifted his hands to show Isaac the hotter than a day in July, fresh-out-the-back-door-of-somebody's-house DVD player. "One of your lady friends would love this – brand new, man."

"I said we're closed! Go find one of my runners. What you think they're on the streets for?" He slammed the door. He wasn't 'bout to spend one day behind bars for selling a ten dollar piece of rock. That's how hustlers get caught up all the time. Isaac turned his attention back to Keith. "Put that money in a bag and let's bounce."

"Where we headed?"

"Williams Street. Where you think, fool?" He snatched up his Nine and shoved it in the side of his pants. "We gon' find out why my money's short."

Keith chauffeured Isaac through the desecrated streets of West Dayton in his two-seater candy apple red Corvette. The music was thumping louder than a Saturday night at the Silver Fox, when all the fly girls backed that thang up, hoping to become some dope man's woman. Heck, some of 'em settled for being the 'play thing.' Isaac leaned back as they drove down the Strip. He watched the inhabitants of the jungle. As they passed by, weave flowed heavy and thick down the backs of yellow, brown and dark blue sistahs. The electricity and telephone might get cut off, but never let a sistah be accused of having a bad hair day. Bling, bling weighed down the necks and arms of brothers in the game. Lexus, Mercedes, Cadillac, you name it, and it was flashed, ghetto-fab in full effect in the jungle. Keith turned down James H. McGee and kept rolling until he pulled into the parking lot of some carry-out that had changed owners, as well as names too many times to keep track.

"I'll be right back – gotta buy my lotto ticket."

Rain or shine, Keith was gon' play the lotto. Winning must not have been part of his strategy, 'cause that brother never collected one green-back from his felonious gambling habit. Just another scam backed by the government, as far as Isaac was concerned. Keith went into the name-change-a-lot store and Isaac leaned back in his seat, content to keep his money in his pocket where it could make a difference.

"Hey Boo!"

Isaac turned and saw Rochelle Bozeman trotting her hourglass frame in front of him. She shook her head and Mr. Ed's mane danced in the air, until it landed just above her Black woman's glory. "Hey you," Isaac said as he eyed Rochelle.

She cozied up next to the car. "Heard you and Nina broke up."

"Nothing lasts forever."

"That's too bad. I always liked Nina."

"Is that a fact?"

She swung Mr. Ed's mane again, softened her eyes and her voice as she stared at Isaac. "Yeah, but I like you better. I'm in the phone book, you know."

Isaac looked at her. Body tight, face wasn't bad to look at either, but right now he was playing daddy to four women too many. He just didn't have the energy to add number five to the list. "Not taking applications right now."

"If you say so." She started walking toward the store, then turned back. "Give me a call anyway – never know, you just might find an opening I can fill."

Keith was back in the car. "Did you get them digits?"

"Naw, not interested."

Keith started the car. "Let's roll."

They pulled up to their spot on Williams Street. Isaac jumped out of the car and greeted his boys.

Lou, Mickey, and Johnny high five'd and 'what up'd' Isaac and Keith. They chitchatted for a few minutes. "How's your girl?" "She's fine." "Hey, did your mom get out the hospital?" And then Isaac was ready to get down to business.

"Money's been slow over here Lou, what's going on?"

Lou looked to Mickey and Johnny hoping one of them would speak up, neither did. "Man, Ray-Ray moved a couple of his boys in the alley right behind us."

"Yeah, them cats done took half our biz, just like that." Johnny snapped his fingers.

Isaac confronted Keith. "I know you knew about this, Keith. How you gon' let them take from The Promised Land?"

Keith opened his mouth to answer. Isaac lifted his hand. "Forget it, let's just go take care of this. Mickey, follow me." Mickey stepped in line behind Isaac and Keith as they pounced upon the unsuspecting runners in the alley.

***

"Aaah yeah, baby needs a new pair of shoes." He blew on the dice, threw them out and watched as they rolled through the alleyway. His snaggletooth mouth filled with curses as a foot stomped on one of his die.

"Now is that any way to talk to the man who holds life and death in the palm of his hands?" Isaac asked while showing off his gun.

The four men scrambled to get off their knees, crap game completely forgotten. A guy in a Nike jogging suit held out his hand. "What's up Isaac?"

Isaac shook his proffered hand. "Nothing much. I'm just trying to figure out how y'all set up for business in The Promised Land, and I didn't know nothing about it."

Snaggletooth raised his hands. "No – no disrespect Isaac. Ray-Ray told us that your turf ended at Williams Street."

"I just moved it over dog. Y'all taking money out my pocket."

Nike suit looked at snaggletooth. "Ray-Ray ain't gon' like this."

Keith bent down, picked up the dice, and handed them to Nike suit. "Take this game on down the street somewhere. You are officially off duty."

Isaac pointed at Mickey. "This is your turf, get a couple boys to help you run it." Isaac and Keith headed back to the car, both had only one thought: find Ray-Ray.

"Got any idea where Ray-Ray might be?" Keith asked Isaac as they drove away.

"You know that fat simpleton is at Fish & More, inhaling all the catfish he can eat."

***

Isaac stepped into Fish & More. Ray-Ray was on his cell phone when he and Isaac's eyes locked. Sweat dripped from his cornrows, as he watched Isaac and Keith descend on him. Isaac wasn't sure if Ray-Ray was nervous or if all that sweat came from being 120 pounds overweight. The one thing he was sure of was that Ray-Ray was on the line with one of the cats from the alley. Good, Isaac thought. Now I don't have to explain nothin' to him.

Since there were no explanations needed, Isaac swooped down on Ray-Ray like a bad dream. He whipped the gun out of his pants, and slapped Ray-Ray upside the head. The impact knocked his victim to the ground. Ray-Ray lifted up his hands trying to cover his head. "You got a problem with me taking what belongs to me, Ray-Ray?"

"Man, that alley ain't part of your turf."

"Everywhere my feet shall tread, boy. That's The Promised Land, you got it? Everywhere my feet shall tread."

Ray-Ray glared at Isaac and said. "That alley is mine. Go to He…"

Isaac put his gun to Ray-Ray's temple. "I got a better idea, Ray-Ray. You go to Hell – right now. I'll meet you there later. Okay?"

"Isaac, man don't do it." Keith looked back and forth at all the stunned faces in the restaurant. "Not with all these witnesses."

Isaac didn't look up. He pushed his gun further into Ray-Ray's temple. "So what's it gon' be Ray-Ray?"

"All right, take it. Just take it!"

Isaac smirked at Keith then extended his hand to help Ray-Ray up. "Thanks man, I like doing business with reasonable brothers."

8

*E*lizabeth's car was missing.

She had dropped the kids off at her mother's house last night. Good thing, since she was already running late for her three o'clock meeting with her new boss at the Belante' Club. Intuition told her that raggedy ol' Kenneth had something to do with it. As soon as she was seated in the back seat of that yellow cab, she was on the phone with Kenneth. "Where's my Lexus?"

"Who pays the car note on that Lexus?"

"You do, or have you stopped paying?"

Kenneth leaned back in his leather chair. "Oh, I'm still paying the bill. But I figured, since I'm the only one paying for that car, then I should be the only one driving it."

"What am I supposed to do for a car? How am I supposed to get the kids where they need to go?"

He tapped his pen on his desk. "Well you don't need to worry about that. I'm moving back to *my* house on Monday. I'll be able to take Erin and Danae wherever they need to go."

Elizabeth sat up in her seat. "Kenneth, you can't be serious. We agreed that you needed to move out."

"I changed my mind. Why should I keep paying hotel bills, when I've got a perfectly good house on Rahn Road?" He smirked, "If you don't like it, you move out."

Elizabeth started chewing on her lip. "Look, Kenneth, I know you're still upset about your clothes, but that's no reason to act all nasty."

"You started this fight Elizabeth. And I warned you that you couldn't quit when you wanted to." He ruffled some papers on his desk. "Be out of my house by noon on Monday, feel free to leave my kids."

"Why you..." Mr. Dial Tone blared in her ear. She pulled the phone away and stared at it. "Oooh! I hate him."

***

Elizabeth tried to put Kenneth's no good self out of her mind. But when she wasn't thinking about Kenneth, she was forced to remember what her worthless brother said about her name meaning 'She worships the Lord.' It kept repeating itself in her head. "Ooh, Michael, you make me so sick!"

Elizabeth paid the cab driver and went inside the Belante' Club. The smoke from the night before still lingered in the air; half-filled glasses were scattered all over the top of the bar. As she walked across the triangular-shaped dance floor, she wondered for the hundredth time, how so many people could fit on such a small space. This was the place of illusions. A little drink, a little dance, and those colorful lights above the dance floor made everybody beautiful. That is, until the next morning. Or, until seven years roll by, and he stomped on your heart, closed-out your credit accounts and repossessed your Lexus. Next morning, seven years, whatever.

Tommy Brooks smiled and gave her a standing ovation as she walked closer to his table. He was a handsome man. Athletic, GQ perfect. She found little comfort in his looks or applause. "From this moment on, you'll get nothing but standing ovations." As Elizabeth and Tommy sat down he said, "I'm telling you, Elizabeth, you sing like an angel."

She worships the Lord. "So what did you want to discuss with me, Tommy?"

Tommy took a pen out of his jacket pocket and laid it next to the piece of paper on the table. "I wanted to talk to you about your singing career." He picked up the pen. "I think you have a shot at being a real superstar, and I'd like the opportunity to manage your career."

Secular music. "Sure Tommy, whatever you want."

He smiled, pushed the contract in front of her, and began talking about his plans for her future.

Elizabeth stopped him in mid sentence. "Tommy, what do you think the word secular means?"

Tommy leaned back in his seat, his brow lifted, as he stared at her. "I don't know, why?"

"I think it means, without God."

9

"*I*saac, man, please don't do this."

Leonard was on his knees. Isaac stood over him, gun in hand.

"Come on man, we been through too much together."

"Guess you should have thought about that before you stole my money."

Leonard closed his eyes. Sweat ran down his forehead. His hands were shaking like a newborn crack baby. "You're my son's Godfather. Come on man, Lenny Jr. needs me."

Isaac thought about that for a second. He was Godfather to this man's son. He promised to look after the little tyke. And that was serious business. "Tell me where my money is, and I'll put it in a trust fund for my Godson."

"I spent it, man. I spent it." Leonard started crying. Seriously, he was crying like a little girl with a sprained ankle.

"What could you have spent a hundred thousand dollars on in a month's time?"

Leonard wiped some of the sweat and tears off his face and bent his head and cried some more.

Isaac cold cocked him with the handle of the gun. "Stop all that crying!" Leonard may be a no good thief, but he and Isaac had been friends. He could at least help this man go out with some dignity. "What'd you do with my money?"

"I bought Tanya a house."

"You did what?" Isaac couldn't believe it. He just absolutely couldn't believe that he was Godfather to the Lollypop Man's son. "You bought a house for Tanya – that trick who is right now, laid up with Keith in her new house?"

Leonard shook his head back and forth. "I didn't know, man. I thought she loved me."

Yep, the Lollypop Man. If he kept this fool around, Lord knows how much of his hard earned grip would come up missing. "Good night, man. I'm sure I'll see you soon." Isaac squeezed the trigger and snuffed out a life-long friendship.

Bang!

Isaac was jolted up in bed. He shook his head and checked out his surroundings. He wasn't with Leonard. He was home. This was the second night in a row he dreamed about his former friend. Why wouldn't the memories leave him be? He put his hands to his head. Something or somebody was always invading his sleep, making him remember.

Bang… Clang.

Isaac stretched and yawned in his massive oak four-poster bed. Sunday mornings were generally a lazy time for him. He would lie in bed for hours, trying to drive the demons from his head, while Nina waited on him hand and foot. But this Sunday morning, as well as the three that preceded it, Cynda was in his kitchen, clanging pots and pans and waking him up well before he was ready to greet a new day. The food was never quite as good as the clang or smell promised, so Isaac decided that it was time to end Cynda's reign as Queen Bee.

But there was something else he had to take care of first. He picked up the phone and dialed Keith's cell.

Ring, ring. "What up?"

"Did that trick sign the house over to you yet?"

"Yeah. But she was crying so hard, I doubt that Tanya will ever speak to me again."

"Look at it this way. I just saved you a trip to the doctor and a shot of penicillin – put the house on the market." Isaac instructed Keith, then hung up the phone.

"Cynda!" he yelled.

She stepped into the doorway of the bedroom. "Hey baby, I'm just whipping up a lil' sumin'- sumin'."

He lifted himself up in bed and put another pillow behind his head. Even in the morning Cynda was breathtaking. She always wore candy-apple-red lipstick, and when she talked, her lips looked so luscious he just had to have a taste of all that red. As pretty as Nina was, Cynda still outdid her. But Spoony, Isaac's mentor, told him a long time ago, "It's all right to have a pretty woman, but after you get done looking at her, make sure she can handle your other needs." Cynda couldn't.

"I'm not hungry and it's time for you to go." He got out of bed, opened up his closet door, and tossed out some of Cynda's clothes. "Get your stuff, and take it home. I don't want to see anything of yours left behind."

"What's wrong? Isaac, why you trippin'?"

"Ain't nobody trippin'. It's just time for you to go," he said, as he slipped on his robe and walked out of the room. Walking papers served.

"You're just upset about Nina. Isaac, why won't you just let that go and, --"

"That's enough!" Isaac swung back around to face her. "I don't want to hear another word about Nina! Is that clear?"

She submissively answered, "Yes."

He was tired of Cynda. She was constantly reminding him of Nina's wrongdoing. Well, he would show her. Today he would show them all. No woman, man or child would betray him and live to tell about it.

Isaac Walker was nobody's push over. Schooled on the streets of Chicago, where every penny-ante hustler dreamed of becoming the next Al Capone. Hustler 101 was taught daily on Michigan Avenue. And at the age of twelve, Isaac became a student of Spoony Davidson.

Spoony got his shoes shined every Tuesday morning like clockwork at the corner of Michigan and State Streets. Rumor was, Spoony had to get his shoes shined on Tuesdays, because his Monday evenings were spent kicking the living daylights out of his women who failed to meet their weekend quota. Spoony was a pimp, a gambler, and a dope pusher.

As Spoony put one of his shoes on the rack for shining, Isaac came barreling out of the small candy store directly behind the shoe shine stand, and ran into Spoony. The owner of the store ran out behind Isaac, yelling, "Stop, thief! Stop, thief!"

Spoony grabbed Isaac and held onto him tightly. "What's the matter with you, boy? You almost knocked me down."

Isaac stared straight through Spoony, but said nothing.

"That's good, keep holding him, Mr. Spoony, and I'll call the police."

"Wait a minute," Spoony told the storeowner, then pulled out a fifty-dollar bill. "This should cover whatever he took. Okay?" The storeowner smiled and walked back inside.

"What's your name, kid?" Spoony asked as he released his hold.

"What's it to you?" he asked defiantly.

Spoony folded his arms across his chest, stood real still, stared down at the kid in front of him, and waited.

"Isaac, okay. It's Isaac."

"Well Isaac, why ain't you in school?"

"School's for chumps."

Spoony took the stolen candy out of Isaac's hand, "No, stealin's for chumps; school's for learning."

"School can't teach me nothing. I'm a hustler, just like Al Capone." Isaac tried to stand a little taller as he added, "One day this city is gon' know my name."

Spoony smiled. "My friend, you don't know the first thing about hustling. Stick with me, I'll teach you."

Years later, driving down the streets of Dayton; he picked up his car phone and dialed Valerie. "I want you at the house when I get home. About five, okay?"

Valerie didn't ask any questions. "I'll be there, baby."

Isaac opened his glove compartment and took out his Glock. He no longer lived in Chicago, but as far as he was concerned, the rules in Dayton were no different. "Get ready, Nina. Today you will meet your Maker."

10

It was not a common thing to hear of people beating a path to the house of God, at least, not this new generation of people. But The Rock Christian Fellowship was, by no means, a traditional church. Greeters were assigned to every door to welcome the congregation with a hug, a smile, and a word of encouragement as they walked inside. The sanctuary could seat about five hundred people; however, The Rock had a membership of about twelve hundred. Hence, the need for two services, and extra chairs placed in the aisles every Sunday morning. No, The Rock did not have a huge church building, or a ministry of thousands as did TV evangelists such as Bishop T.D. Jakes or Creflo Dollar. But there was something different about this church that had caught the very ear of God. The power in the prayers could be felt throughout the sanctuary and the worship could only be compared to that of angels. The honey came out of The Rock, when praise and worship went forth to God.

Elizabeth felt the difference the moment she stepped into the church. She immediately noticed the banner that hung over the doorway of the fellowship hall: "Enter at your own risk. Holy Ghost at work." She took Erin and Danae to the children's church then entered the sanctuary. Her two-inch heels were swallowed up in the thick rich burgundy carpet that covered the entire sanctuary floor. Gold chandeliers hung over the cushioned pews. Directly behind the pulpit, a gold cross hung above the baptismal pool. The sanctuary itself, although tastefully decorated, would not have been the standard by which sanctuaries were measured. A smile crossed her face, which she quickly tried to conceal.

As they walked down the middle aisle of the sanctuary, Michael said, "I'm glad you decided to come to church with me. I just wish I could sit with you." They stopped at a pew five rows from the front of the sanctuary.

"I'll be all right Michael, don't worry."

Her tall handsome brother did his military walk as he entered the pulpit and joined the other elders. Besides the pastor and co-pastor, The Rock had three elders. The elders were varied in their gifts and abilities. Michael Edwards was the well known and loved youth pastor. The teenagers to whom he ministered respected him, not just because he walked the talk, but he was down to earth, and related to them. He understood that people make mistakes. He also understood grace. Michael had been at The Rock for six years.

At sixty-two, Marvel Hardison, a warm-hearted faithful man, was the oldest of the three elders. Many of the saints felt at ease bringing their problems to him. He had a knack for helping people accept the grace of God. Elder Hardison was head of the Senior Saints Group. Every first and third Sunday, this group of saints marched off to several nursing homes to minister to the sick and shut in. They encouraged young married couples. The retired members of his group traveled the globe like there wasn't nothing to it, but to do it. The Senior Saints did more for the cause of Christ, and just plain ol' experienced life more than some of the twenty and thirty year old saints in the congregation.

Jonathan Woodlow was the most dynamic of the elders at The Rock. The old cliche 'tall, dark, and handsome' was manifested on him. Elder Woodlow oversaw the Mission's Ministry. He had also just recently been appointed over the Evangelistic Ministry at The Rock. After that appointment, single sisters joined the Evangelistic Team at ten times the rate they had joined in the seven years the ministry had been in existence. If Jonathan noticed, he never said a word. He just kept seeking God's will for his life.

Elder Woodlow stood behind the podium to welcome the congregation into the second service of the day. "Everyone, please take your seats."

***

The time had come.

Isaac would soon have his revenge. It was so close he could taste it. He would soon be rid of Nina and her defiance. He was sick of her I-can't-live-your-life attitude, as if her life was so much better. Her scared-straight behind hadn't left the house in over a month, and Isaac should know. He drove up and down Elmhurst Avenue everyday since the night he almost cornered her at Joe's Carryout.

This morning as he parked Keith's Bonneville three doors down from Nina's place, he thought, today, I will set you free, Nina.

With Nina's freedom, also came Isaac's. As long as Nina was alive her betrayal dogged him. But once she was dead, he could forget what she had done to him, and remember the good times. And with Nina, it was all-good, until she cold-bloodedly murdered his child.

Isaac put his Glock inside his jacket pocket. He couldn't wait, as a matter of fact, he was tired of waiting. Nina would never come out of that house, she had turned herself into some kind of hermit.

"What's taking them so long?" Isaac asked. He knew that the woman who owned this women's shelter went to church every Sunday with a trail of fatsoes behind her. He still couldn't understand why the same woman who carried that "A life is a terrible thing to waste" sign, allowed Nina to stay in her house. The woman saw Nina come out of that abortion clinic, knew what she had done, and still she took pity on her.

Well, Isaac had no pity for that lying betraying tramp. His plan was a simple one. He had driven over to wait for the house to empty. He was then going to sneak inside the house and blow Nina's don't-want-your-baby-no-more brains out.

But that woman just wouldn't come out of the house. He looked at his watch. 11:00 A.M.

11:05… What time did these people go to church?

11:08… His stomach growled. Did they cook anything, any breakfast left for ol' Isaac?

11:10… Forget it, he would just kill 'em all. He hated the thought of bringing innocent bystanders into this, but hey, that's what they get for harboring a baby-killer.

As he started to get out of the car, the door to another house opened. A young man, about twenty-two, walked out, dressed head to toe in Tommy Hilfiger. The youngster came out of his yard, turned in the direction of Nina's house, and began walking down the sidewalk.

Just as Hilfiger man was about to walk past the house, Nina's door opened. Isaac sat up. Out walked the right-to-lifer, two other fatsoes, and Nina. "No, no, no," Isaac said. "Stay in the house, Nina!"

But Nina kept walking despite Isaac's pleading. Then Hilfiger man started talking to Nina. Isaac growled, "Why is he smiling?"

Isaac looked around. Nobody else was on the street, except for that guy, smiling down at Nina, and he deserved what he was about to get. Him, and anybody else that would smile down on somebody else's woman, showing all his long yellow teeth, as if to devour her right where she stood. Yeah, he would gladly put two bullets in him.

Isaac opened his door. His black leather shoes touched the gravel. A red Grand Am pulled up right across from him. The woman behind the wheel honked her horn.

Nina turned, and Isaac caught her profile. Nina was a fatso too. He closed the door and sat back in his seat stunned, as his mind replayed the blows he dealt Nina in the back lot of that abortion clinic. "I could have killed my baby."

Nina said goodbye to her friend and jumped in the back seat of the car.

The woman across from Isaac honked her horn again. And as Nina drove away, Isaac said words that cannot be repeated.

11

*N*ina walked into the sanctuary.

Her gaze moved toward the pulpit. She stood in the aisle for a moment looking at the marble pillars behind the pulpit. Those pillars reminded Nina of the story of Samson and Delilah. Her adoptive mother told her how Samson took hold of two pillars, and prayed that God would give him back his strength. The Philistines stood around waiting to make sport of him. What was it that the Bible said? Something about, in his death, he killed more Philistines than in his lifetime. Nina tried to imagine Samson holding up the pillars in this church, rather than bringing them down. The thought made her feel safe, and right now, she needed that.

She spent the last three weeks lying on her back. The doctors couldn't explain it, but somehow her placenta wasn't torn anymore. Her baby was still alive, and Dr. Hanson took her off bed rest.

The doctor's might not be able to explain it, but Nina knew that her baby was still alive because of the many nights Marguerite walked the living room floor praying.

"Come on, Nina. We need to get a seat," Marguerite whispered into her ear as praise and worship began.

"Oh, sorry, I guess I was day-dreaming," Nina told her as they started down the aisle to find a seat.

***

Isaac walked into the church a few minutes after Nina. He stood at the door of the sanctuary and looked around for her. Everyone was standing, singing some type of song that had the word 'Jesus' in it so many times that Isaac shook himself. What am I doing in here? he wondered. Years ago he had vowed never to set foot in another church. He turned to rush out of this 'Jesus' place when someone tapped him on the shoulder.

"Man, what you doing in here?"

Isaac's hand went inside his jacket as he turned around. "Um, I was just looking for someone."

"Man, I thought you had turned into a Jesus freak or something." The young man began to laugh. Isaac's eyes widened.

"Jimmy?"

"Yeah, man, who else?"

"Boy what *you* doing here?" Isaac asked.

"Didn't you know?" He snapped his finger, then shook his head. "That's right, how would you know? My father is one of the elders of this church. I come every now and then. You know, just to give him reason to keep hope alive."

Now it was Isaac's turn to laugh.

"Well, see you later man. I got to grab a seat."

"Yeah, all right." Having found Nina, he said, "I think I'll take a seat too." An empty seat in the back of the sanctuary called Isaac's name. He hurriedly grabbed it, then focused on his prey. Okay Nina, I'll wait. But I want answers.

Pastor McKinley took his place behind the podium. He stood there for a moment, silently worshipping God. Then he led the congregation in prayer. "Lord, I thank You for this time You have allowed for me to share Your Word. We bind the enemy and give him no place in this assembly. And Father God, my prayer, as always, is that not one unbeliever leave this place without knowing You as their Lord and Savior. I ask all of this in the mighty Name of Jesus, Amen."

A few people said, "Hallelujah" and "Amen."

"Turn in your Bibles to Isaiah 65:1-3." The Pastor paused, then read the verse. "*I was sought by those who did not ask for Me; I was found by those who did not seek Me. I said, 'Here I am, here I am.'*" He looked up, and stared at the congregation before returning to his text. "*I have stretched out My hands all day long to a rebellious people, who walk in a way that is not good. According to their own thoughts; a people who provoke Me to anger continually to My face.*

"Turn to Jeremiah 5:22-24." He watched as the parishioners turned the pages of their Bibles, then bent his head and started reading. "*Do you not fear Me? Says the Lord. Will you not tremble at My presence. Who have placed the sand as the bound of the sea, by a perpetual decree, that it cannot pass beyond it? And though its waves toss to and fro, yet they cannot prevail; though they roar, yet they cannot pass over it. But this people has a defiant and rebellious heart; they have revolted and departed. They do not say in their heart, let us now fear the Lord our God, who gives rain, both the former and the latter, in its season.*"

Pastor McKinley looked at his congregation and declared. "I am always amazed by how surprised people are about the rain that comes into their lives because of the choices they have made. You choose to fornicate, and then you look sad and surprised when you have a baby out of wedlock. You rob, cheat, murder, and steal – then have the nerve to cover your head in shame when you get carted off to jail." He shook his head at the people. "You know what I believe the former rain is? It's the problems that rain down thunderstorms in your life because of the bad decisions you made." Pastor McKinley raised his voice and declared. "But there is One who can wash away the former rain – it is He who brings the latter rain. But you still refuse to give honor to the One who not only can bring the rain, but also has the power of life and death in His hands.

"You've chosen to fear man and his ability to rob you of your life. But the Bible has already told you that it is foolish to fear the one who can only take your life, rather fear the One who can take your life and cast you into hell for eternity."

Nina fidgeted in her seat and threw an accusing glance at Marguerite. The woman had been telling her business to this preacher.

As Pastor McKinley continued to preach with the anointing of God on him, Isaac looked around the room. These people were really eating up every word this man said; some sat up in their seats and leaned in a little closer. Others were hollering "Amen," and "That's right," as this man told them about all their sins, told them how no good they all were. Don't these people have anything better to do with their time? "What a bunch of losers, they deserve to be treated like this," Isaac mumbled under his breath.

A woman in the seventh pew from the front stood up and yelled, "Holy, holy, holy!" A man a few rows back jumped out of his seat and started running around the sanctuary. As Isaac watched, he became convinced that his usually-wrong daddy had been right about one thing; Christians are coocoo for cocoa puffs.

Being in church brought back a lot of unwanted memories. Like the last day he and his brother Donavan went to church with their mother. The service had been all right. And even though he was thirteen and pretty good at hustling, he was considering joining the drama team.

But when they arrived home from church that day, Isaac's usually-wrong daddy started in on his mother.

It was just barely one o'clock on a Sunday afternoon, but that no-job having mug had a beer in his hand talkin' 'bout, "Where's my dinner? Do I have to do everything around here?"

How doing nothing but lying on your lazy behind had turned into '*doing everything around here*,' Isaac didn't know. Nor did he have time to ponder it. He headed upstairs to change out of his Sunday best, and get away from the drama. He opened his top drawer to put away his tie and socks. His thick red sock that held his money had been moved from its normal spot at the left corner of his drawer. The sock had also depreciated since he last checked it. "That bum robbed me again."

That's when he heard his mother scream.

Isaac swore under his breath and slammed his dresser drawer shut. "That's it. He is getting outta here." He opened his bedroom door and stormed down the stairs.

Slam! Boom! Crash!

By the time Isaac made it to the living room, Donavan was on the phone dialing 9-1-1. Usually-wrong was standing over his Mama yelling, "Get up, girl! Ain't nothing wrong with you."

Isaac looked at his Mama. She was stretched out on the floor, on top of the glass that used to be the coffee table. Blood was everywhere. Mama wasn't moving.

"What did you do to my Mama?"

"Boy, don't question me." He waved his hand. "Go on back upstairs."

"Nigga, I said, what did you do to my Mama?"

Isaac's daddy turned to face him. "Oh, so you smelling yourself now, huh? You want a piece a me, boy?"

Isaac looked at the still form of his mother. His lip curled, as he balled his fist. "Yeah, that's exactly what I want."

Donavan interrupted. "Come on, Isaac. Don't do this. The ambulance is on its way."

Usually-wrong rubbed his fist in his palm. "Come on, boy. I'm gon' give you the whuppin' of your life."

A savage rage boiled in Isaac that he could not contain. When it exploded, his dad was pummeled with the residue of Isaac's violence, but he still didn't win. When the ambulance and police arrived on the scene, they carried his sweet Mama out in a body bag. Usually-wrong went to the hospital. Isaac went to juvee.

He stopped believing in God when they sat him in the backseat of that police car.

Two years later, when his brother was in an alley shooting dice and a bullet exploded in his head, Isaac wished for the existence of God.

He wanted to track God down, and curse Him to His ain't-never-looked-out-for-nobody face, but it was useless. Nobody was going to come out of the sky to see about him, to hear his cries. Only the rain came.

So at thirty-one, when he finally returned to church he had a gun in his jacket pocket, ill-gotten gain in his wallet, and malice in his heart.

***

Pastor McKinley gripped the pulpit with both hands and leaned his body forward as he continued his message, "Because you did not fear God, you've committed every sin known to man. You've lied, cheated, fornicated, and murdered. You've been a back biter, and I pity the man or woman that has to deal with your attitude and your unforgiving heart."

Elizabeth felt a jab. My knucklehead brother had no right to talk about me like that to his pastor! Attitude, unforgiving heart, indeed!

Pastor McKinley said to the people, "I've tried to convince you today that God is to be feared. And the One that you should fear hates sin. So if you are deep in sin, you might ask, 'How do I come to such a powerful God?'"

Pastor McKinley got excited. He started jumping around the pulpit. "That's where grace comes in my friends. Oh, I know that many of you think you were saved because you were so good, so deserving of salvation. You sing your 'All day long, no sin have I done' song, and look down your pious noses at the rest of us.

"But I came to tell you this morning, all have sinned. And we are all saved by grace. It is a gift from God, lest any one of us should boast and take credit for His work. God lets no man instruct Him on who to bestow His grace upon. He is sovereign.

"I'm ready to meet Jesus when He returns. I have accepted His grace, have you? Don't sit there thinking about all the evil you've done in your life. God isn't concerned with how many times you have done somebody wrong or how many times someone has wronged you. As a matter of fact, God loves you just the way you are; but He also loves you too much to let you stay that way."

Isaac smirked, there was always a catch.

Pastor McKinley continued, "God is concerned with your heart. Are you ready to be forgiven of all your sins?"

Pastor McKinley delivered the Lord's message for about ten more minutes. The congregation amened, and high-fived each other every time he hit a nerve. Pastor McKinley didn't believe in sugar coating the Gospel. He called sin, sin. And he called truth, the Word of God. Just as his mentor and founder of the Rock, Bishop Willie E. Mitchell Sr. had done.

As Elizabeth continued to listen, she understood why her brother liked the church so well. She thought, I like it here. I just might join this church.

Pastor McKinley finished his sermon, and as he closed the Bible he said, "During this message God revealed to me that many backsliders here today, repented in their seats, while I was preaching. I want the congregation to applaud you for your wise decision. Don't turn back again." The congregation rose and began to clap. Pastor McKinley spoke again. "But right now, I would like to make a call for salvation. If God has flashed your life before you today and you realize that you need the kind of help that only Jesus can give, I want you to come down to the altar right now, so we can pray with you."

Tears streamed down Nina's face, as she thought about her life. How mixed up it had all become. Could this Jesus really deliver her? Does God forgive people who have abortions? Could He help her raise the child she now carried? She had tried just about everything else -- men, cars, school, clothes. Nothing worked. She had sunk so low and lost so much. Maybe there was only one way to go from here. Maybe she needed Jesus, and the people in this church. "God, I sure hope You can forgive me for the way I've lived my life – I need somebody, Lord. I, I need You." She stepped into the aisle. Each step she took brought her closer to the altar. Closer to forgiveness -- acceptance. By the time Nina stood in front of the altar, tears were streaming down her face. Her body was tingling. Though she'd never be able to describe what peace or joy looked like, at that moment she felt it – bubbling up inside her. Someone asked her to raise her hands and repeat the sinner's prayer.

Nina repeated the prayer, then stood at the altar completely dazed. Her body was shaking, and she couldn't stop it. "God's glory. That's what this is," she said to no one in particular. Then she smiled. For the first time in months – maybe years, she actually felt safe.

Isaac was shaking his head and smirking. "That's alright, Nina. Run to Jesus. He didn't save my Mama and He won't save you."

Elizabeth was still in her seat. She couldn't believe the ushers didn't sit chairs out in front of the altar and announce that the doors of the church were open.

She stayed in her seat looking down at the empty seat next to her. The man that had occupied it was now down at the altar. She looked around at the different faces in the crowd. They all seemed to have something she was missing. Right then she decided that she would have to return to this church. At her current church, she was one of the lead singers in the choir. She was asked to sing just about every Sunday. She liked the feeling she received when the congregation applauded after one of her songs, but she had never felt such soul-stirring conviction at her church. Not like she was feeling right now. She shook her head and smiled, already deciding to let her choir director know that she planned to attend The Rock more often.

12

*E*verything looked different to Nina as she left the church.

The leaves were falling from the trees. Their crisp brown edges danced in the air, then elegantly floated down to the softness of the glistening, greenish-yellow grass. Nina quickly stopped, wanting, needing to view this precious sight once more. Leaves had fallen from the branches of trees since the earth had been in existence, but she had never taken the time to notice the beauty of it. Why had she gone through life never seeing or noticing how beautiful this all was?

Marguerite prodded her toward the car, and as Nina hopped in the back seat, she glanced back at the finely crafted oak tree one last time. Another brown leaf danced in the air and fell in a thick bed of grass. Nina smiled, grateful that she hadn't missed the leaf's final performance. As she rode down the street, Nina told Marguerite, "I feel a hundred pounds lighter."

Marguerite smiled back at her. "That's because your burdens have been lifted, baby."

When they reached the house, Nina ran straight for the bathroom on the second floor. She stood there for a moment, looking at her reflection in the mirror. Same reflection from this morning, no noticeable change. Nina peered into the mirror, her eyes brightened and a smile seeped through. "That's what peace looks like, isn't it?"

Nina thought back to all the things she'd done in her life. The lying, the cheating, the men. She had never been able to forget about having that abortion. That pain would probably be with her for the rest of her life, but at least now she was forgiven. There wasn't much in her past that was worth writing about. Much of her life had been one big embarrassment after another.

She sat on the edge of the tub and remembered some ugly times, when she had wronged others. Like the time, about two years ago, when she convinced a crack-head named Rose to steal some clothes out of Dillard's Department Store. She promised Rose five dollars for each stolen outfit. Nina didn't think she was hurting anybody, she was just getting some much-needed clothes to wear around campus. Most of the girls at Wilberforce dressed nicely. She didn't want anyone to think that she came from a poor family, or worse yet, an adoptive family that couldn't even afford to put decent clothes on her back.

Things didn't go as smoothly as Nina had hoped. Rose was arrested and thrown in jail for six months. She had two children, and both were remanded to Children's Services. The woman had been out of jail for eighteen months now, but had not been able to get her children back home.

Tears streamed down Nina's face as sobs escaped from somewhere deep inside her soul and she bellowed, "Lord, please forgive me. Please deliver Rose from her drug addiction and unite her with her children again." More sobs escaped her mouth. "I'm so sorry."

Nina sat on the edge of the tub until she felt the sweet forgiveness of the Lord caress her very soul and loosen the shackles of her life. She was free. Free from the past, free from doubt and fear. But most of all, she was free from Isaac, and his tormenting grip.

She fell on her knees on the bathroom floor. She was newly saved, but beginning to understand something it took many Christians years to grasp. The altar does not only reside in the sanctuary of a church building, but in the sanctuary of your heart. Wherever you fall down and pray, wherever you meet Jesus; that, is your altar. So, surrounded by Charmin toilet paper and Dial soap, Nina lifted her arms to the Lord and declared, "I will serve You, Lord. Show me how."

13

" *T*hanks for taking us to church today, Michael. I really enjoyed it."

"I'm glad," he pulled the car in Elizabeth's driveway.

Elizabeth turned to Erin and Danae in the back seat. "Tell Uncle Mike bye-bye."

"Bye, Uncle Mike," they said in unison.

Elizabeth got out of the car and helped Erin and Danae out. She looked back at her brother as she headed up the walkway. "Can you pick me up for church next Sunday?"

He smiled. "Sure can. I'll wait for you to get in the house."

Elizabeth lifted her door key. "Not necessary. See you later. Give Char a hug for me."

"I will. I have to pick her up from the airport right now." He backed out of the driveway.

The girls ran up the walkway. Danae did more falling than running. Elizabeth smiled. It was so cute to watch her. She put the key in the lock and tried to turn it. The key didn't fit.

That's strange. She looked at the key. "Mmmh, it's the right key." She shrugged her shoulders and put the key in the lock again. Still didn't work. Dread swept over her, the likes of which she had not known in many years. She rang the doorbell, no answer. She banged on the door and screamed, "Kenneth I know you're in there. You better open this door."

Kenneth walked into the foyer and spoke through the window. "You don't live here anymore, Elizabeth. I told you that."

"You said you were moving in on Monday."

"The locksmith was available today."

Elizabeth balled her fist. "Oooh, Kenneth, you better open this door!"

"Leave my children here and go find yourself a place to stay," he told her as he pulled back the curtain.

Elizabeth was hot. She stumped up and down the pathway trying to figure out what to do about this situation. That's when she spotted the decorative red bricks. Bricks she'd laid around the flowerbed when their love was in full bloom. "You think you can just put me out of my own house, huh?" She grabbed one of the bricks and threw it through the bottom pane of the window.

Kenneth opened the front door and menacingly moved toward Elizabeth.

"Daddy... Daddy," the girls screamed.

Kenneth ran past them as Elizabeth picked up her second brick. "You lunatic. Only a fool destroys her own property."

She shook the brick in her hand. "I don't live here anymore, remember?" She reared back, ready to send another brick sailing through the foyer window.

Kenneth grabbed her arm and pulled the brick out of her hand. "You are the most selfish woman I have ever met. God, I can't stand the sight of you!" He moved back, trying to put some distance between them. He'd grown-up believing that only weak men beat their women. His father told him that it was easy to smack a woman around, but a real man takes time to talk things over with his woman – help her understand why things are the way they are. Real men loved their wives into submission, rather than beating a 'yes sir' out of them.

His dad took a hard stance against men who beat on their wives. He should have stood just as firm against extra marital affairs, of which he had many. When he was a kid, Kenneth vowed never to take the easy way out. He would never beat or cheat on his wife. He had already broken one of his vows, now this woman was making him rethink the other. Kenneth wanted to smack the taste out of her mouth, but he didn't want to stop there. He wanted to keep on pounding until she was dead. Distance, that's what he needed.

Sirens could be heard afar off.

"Don't you walk away from me." She strutted up to him and put her finger in his face. "I bet you feel like a big man today, don't you? Put your wife and defenseless kids out on the street with no place to go."

Sirens were blaring on their street.

"Get out of my face, Elizabeth." More distance, that's what he needed. But Elizabeth grabbed his arm. Her hand balled into a fist and she bust Kenneth in the mouth.

Erin and Danae were sitting on the steps crying. That's it, he'd had enough. Kenneth stepped back and raised his fist to retaliate.

"Don't do it, sir."

A White, heavy-set police officer approached as Elizabeth advanced on Kenneth like a tiger. Her claws dug into his skin. "Ouch!" Kenneth screamed.

The police officer grabbed Elizabeth and pulled her off Kenneth. "Sir, we received a call about a domestic disturbance. Is this your wife?" he asked Kenneth as he held Elizabeth's struggling form.

"Let me go!" Elizabeth screamed.

Kenneth nursed the scratches on his face. "She's my wife."

"Do you want to press charges, sir?"

Kenneth watched Elizabeth struggle to free herself. Her eyes were ablaze with fury. He turned toward his children. They were huddled up together on the porch, crying their eyes out. "No, I don't want to press charges. I just want her off my property."

"Off *your* property?" Elizabeth broke free from the officer and lunged at Kenneth.

The police officer regained his hold on Elizabeth. "That's it. You're going to take a little ride with me." He took his cuffs out and put them on Elizabeth.

"No!" Erin shouted and ran to her mother's aid. She grabbed hold of Elizabeth's waist. "Leave my Mama alone."

"Officer," Kenneth lifted his hands. "Please… I'm not pressing charges."

"You two are disturbing the peace. One of you has got to go." The officer looked at Elizabeth. "Since this one appears to have anger problems -- she should be the one to go."

Erin ran to Kenneth and pleaded, "Don't let him take Mama, Daddy."

The officer started walking to his car dragging Elizabeth with him. She was huffing and puffing all the way. Kenneth sat Erin down on the porch and ran after them. "Look," he said to the officer. "This is the first time you've ever come out to our house. My wife and I lead a normal life, we've just been having a few – problems lately." Kenneth couldn't tell if he was getting through to the officer or not, but he continued anyway. "Man, don't do this." He pointed toward Erin and Danae. "My kids… they don't deserve this."

The officer stopped, he looked back at the little girls on the porch. He let out a heavy sigh. "Okay, but if I let her go, you've got to get her into some anger management classes."

He looked at Elizabeth. She was practically foaming at the mouth. He didn't know how he would get her inside, let alone to anger management classes, but he would say anything to minimize the drama for his children. "Will do."

The officer unlocked the cuffs, took them off Elizabeth, then turned her around to face him. "If I get another call about a disturbance at this house, I'm taking you to jail. Do you understand?"

She rubbed her wrist, and shook her head. "I understand."

"Good." The officer left and the Underwood family walked inside the house. Kenneth went to get the broom and dustpan to clean up the mess from the broken window.

Elizabeth was tired and weary from the struggle. She stood with her back against the door holding onto the knob.

Kenneth started sweeping up the glass. Erin and Danae ran to him. Erin, the spokesperson for the duo said, "Daddy, please don't put Mama out. She didn't mean to break the window."

Kenneth moved his girls away from the glass. "Go play. I need to clean this mess up." Kenneth watched his girls run into the family room and sit in the entryway, peeking into the foyer. He turned cold, unyielding eyes on Elizabeth and whispered. "You take the master suite. I'll sleep in one of the guest rooms."

She rolled her eyes. "Your generosity overwhelms me."

"I'm not being generous to you." Kenneth peered around the corner and saw that Erin and Danae had scooted into the hall. "My children have been through enough. Just find a place to stay, Liz. I'll pay for it until you can get on your feet."

"Oh, you'll be paying long after I'm on my feet."

He kept his voice low, but his tone held purpose. "I don't care, Liz. Whatever it takes to get rid of you, I'm willing to do it."

"Who do you think you are?" She pushed herself off the door and got in his face again.

"Lower your voice."

She looked into the hallway and saw Erin watching her. She turned back to Kenneth and whispered, "I made you. Without me, you'd still be in middle management – somewhere being told what to do and when to do it. But look at you." She waved her hand up and down his physique and sneered, "Mr. CEO – top dog. You think you've gotten big enough to forget the bridge that carried your country-behind over?"

"Liz, I'm not going to tell you again, you need to back off me."

Elizabeth was not intimidated. She pointed her index finger in his face. "If you think I'm going to let another woman come in here and enjoy the fruits of my labor, you've got another thought coming."

A bitter laugh escaped his lips. "If you think I'm divorcing you so I can have another woman, you're crazier than I thought." He sat the broom and dustpan against the wall and stood to his full height. He looked down on Elizabeth. "You, my dear wife, have cursed the institution of marriage. It'll be a long time before I can even think about putting a ring on a woman's finger without vomiting." He turned away from her and walked into the kitchen.

Elizabeth screamed at his departing form. "If you hadn't cheated on me, we---"

Kenneth turned on her. "I guess everything didn't go the way you planned it, after all. Must been a real shock to your system, huh?"

14

"She's pregnant!"

Isaac slammed his fist on the steering wheel. "Why didn't she say something?" But he knew exactly why she didn't tell him. He never gave her a chance. His 'kick-butt-first, ask questions later' motto could have cost him his son.

His immortality!

Isaac tortured himself with questions as he sat outside the group home where Nina stayed. He kept seeing Nina rolling on the ground holding her stomach while he kicked her. What if his actions had caused damage to the baby? He had to know.

He got out of his car, walked up to Nina's safe house and banged on the door.

"Keep your pants on!" Lisa yelled as she slowly made her way. She opened the door wide and glared at Isaac. "What's the emergency?"

Isaac brushed past her, and strutted through the house like his name was on the deed. "Nina! Nina! Where are you, Nina?" He opened the door on the left and walked into the bedroom. It was empty. He headed toward another door, but was cut off by the right-to-life lady. "Look mister, I don't know what you want, but you got about two seconds to get out of here."

"I'll leave, just as soon as I get what I came for."

"You'll leave now, or I'll call the police!"

Isaac glared at the rigid woman in front of him as he said, "You gon' be calling on God, if Nina don't get out here right now."

"Look, we don't need no mess started up in here." Lisa told Isaac as she stepped in between Isaac and Marguerite.

"Shut up Lisa – go sit down," Marguerite told her.

"Oh no. I'm not about to be up in no drama, just to save Miss *Thang*." Lisa pointed toward the back of the house. "She's in the last bedroom on the right."

"Lisa! How could you?"

"Whew, I need to sit down." Lisa pressed her hands in the middle of her back and wobbled her way into the living room. "Way too much drama for me."

Isaac headed toward the back. Marguerite headed toward the kitchen. "I'm calling the police."

Isaac opened the bedroom door and found Nina on her knees, head bowed, lips moving, but no sound exited her mouth. For a brief moment, he was struck dumb by the sight of *his* Nina, on the floor, bowed down, obviously praying. He had never seen her do this before. Never, not once in the entire year they lived together, did Nina ever bow down to anyone but him. He hated to admit it, but he was jealous. "You're gonna have to pray a long time, if you're asking God to save you from my wrath."

Nina stood up and turned to face Isaac.

Isaac looked at her stomach. "Why didn't you tell me you didn't have an abortion?"

She bent her head and touched her stomach, but remained silent.

"Nina, didn't you think I would find out about *my* baby?"

She looked up at him. One small tear escaped her sad brown eyes. "I thought you'd kill me before you found out the truth."

Isaac blushed. "I'm sorry about that, baby." He reached out to touch her, but she stepped back.

"I'll never put my hands on you again. You've got my word on that. *My* child will never see his mother battered and bruised."

She didn't say anything.

"Get your stuff, let's go."

Nina put her hand on her belly and backed away from Isaac. "I can't go with you."

"What do you mean *you can't go with me?*" he mimicked.

No response.

"Nina, get your stuff."

She flopped down on the bed and looked at Isaac. He had been everything to her, but not anymore. Jesus had revealed Himself, and showed her that He was the only living God, and He alone was worthy of her worship. "I cannot live in sin with you, Isaac."

"We ain't living in sin! Stop trippin' girl, we live in Dayton."

Nina was not amused.

"You're carrying my baby – you belong with me."

She looked down at her hands. "We're not married."

Isaac opened the closet and threw her clothes onto the bed. "I don't know what these people have been filling your head with, but," pointing at her belly, "That's mine. And that makes you and me family."

Nina didn't know where her strength came from, but she opened her mouth and said. "I will not live with you."

Isaac kneeled down in front of her. He tilted her head toward him so he could look into her eyes. She was sad, he could tell that right off. But there was something else in those eyes, something he hadn't noticed before. Was it peace? No, no, maybe it was conviction he saw. Or maybe it was both. He couldn't be sure, but there was definitely something different about her. "You know I don't want nobody but you." He rubbed her shoulders. "It's you and me against the world. Come on baby, come home with me. Please."

She put her hands to her face as another tear fell to her cheek. "I can't live in your world anymore. I don't belong there."

He jumped up, agitated now. Beg mode over. "Where do you belong, if not with me, huh?"

Nina flinched, but said nothing.

"Girl, who do you think will treat you better than I have? Look around." He grabbed the clothes off the bed and flung them on the floor. "You happy in these Salvation Army rags? I kept you in Gucci and St. John's. Whatever you wanted, all you had to do was ask. What other man do you think can afford you? Shoot, truth be told, Nina, I barely can."

Silence.

He was strutting around the room now. Anger magnified. "I've done everything you asked me to do, so what's the problem?"

No matter what he had done to her through the years – no matter how angry he made her, he could always look into her eyes and see how much she loved him. But as she looked at him now, and their eyes locked, he found no love for him there. "Nina, don't you know how much I care about you?"

Nina softly said, "If you care for me, let me go."

He was a man. He could take just about anything, but to look into those sad eyes everyday and know that she had stopped loving him was more than he ever wanted to endure. He turned away from those unloving eyes and surrendered. "Fine, stay here. Rot here if you like, I don't care."

15

*L*ate into the night, Elizabeth lay in bed, disheartened and disillusioned. Earlier that day, as she sat in Michael's church listening to his pastor, she thought her life could be different. That she could make a change.

But when she arrived home and found that Kenneth had changed the locks, she went ballistic. She shivered at the thought that she almost went to jail. And, to think, she had considered going back to The Rock next Sunday. She actually thought there was something special about that church. Well, enough of this weak-kneed-using-church-as-a-crutch stuff. She needed to stand on her own two feet again. Not only would she never return to The Rock, she was getting out of the choir at her own church also. What was the use anyway? God wasn't interested in helping her out. Her life was a living testimony of that.

Kenneth claimed she was selfish and always had to have everything her way. That just wasn't true. Kenneth got plenty of things he wanted. If she thought hard enough, she knew she could come up with something.

She sat up in bed, thinking over their life together. Sure Kenneth wanted to get married right after he graduated from Howard University, but she had another year to go. No way was she getting married without spending at least a year in Corporate America. Why did she work so hard getting her MBA if she wasn't going to use it? So, two and a half years after Kenneth graduated, he and Elizabeth said 'I do.'

Kenneth wanted a house full of kids. Elizabeth had her tubes tied after Danae was born. When Kenneth came to visit her in the hospital, with his face all broke, Elizabeth told him flat out, "You might as well pick your face up. There's no way I'm getting all fat having a half dozen kids, so you can run off with some skinny twenty year old, claiming I've gotten too fat for you."

A tear ran down the crook of her nose. Ironically, even though Elizabeth didn't get fat, Kenneth still cheated. Since she was a teenager, men had always looked past her to get to the next woman in line. She had never been that 'someone special' to any man she dated. Somehow, with Kenneth she thought things would be different, but he too, had just used and discarded her like all the rest.

What was wrong with her? Why was she always left with the short end of the stick? Was she really selfish like Kenneth said? Is that why men ran out of her life like they were running from hell?

"What did I do that was so wrong?" Okay, she was willing to admit that she had made a few decisions that Kenneth didn't agree with. Like when she and Kenneth were looking for a house. Kenneth wanted to buy a smaller home so he could send more money to his mother in New Orleans. Since his father passed, his Mama was having a tough time making ends meet.

But Elizabeth wasn't having that. Mama Rosa couldn't stand her from day one - and didn't make any bones about that fact. So if she thought Elizabeth was going to lose square footage over her hunger pangs, she had another thought coming. Elizabeth fussed and cussed, but Kenneth still wouldn't listen. One day as they were eating breakfast, she told Kenneth that she was going back to work unless he bought her the house she wanted. That did the trick. Kenneth didn't want his kids raised by a babysitter. So Elizabeth won, and that wicked witch he called Mama, lost.

Hmmph, she wasn't about to let Kenneth play her second to his Mama – or any other woman for that matter. If she had, she wouldn't be in this house now, would she? Elizabeth put her head in her hands, as she wondered how much longer she would have her beautiful home. "How could he do this to me?"

She looked up to heaven and asked, "Why are You letting this happen?" She wiped some tears from her face. "Why don't You help me?"

She looked around for her Bible and found it in the drawer of her nightstand, hidden under some old magazines. She picked it up and flipped the pages. Stopping at the sixth chapter of Luke, she read:

"Whoever comes to Me, and hears My sayings and does them, I will show you whom he is like:

He is like a man building a house, who dug deep and laid the foundation on the rock. And when the flood arose, the rain beat vehemently against that house, and could not shake it, for it was founded on the rock.

But he who heard and did nothing is like a man who built a house on the earth without a foundation, against which the rain beat vehemently; and immediately it fell. And the ruin of that house was great."

Sounds like my house, she thought. No doubt she had built her home without a foundation. It had been tumbling down around her for years. *"Lord help me. My family is falling apart. Kenneth... Oh God, he hurt me, b-but I don't want to lose him."* The tears fell on the pages of her Bible as she curled up on her bed and moaned out the sorrows of her unfulfilled life. No one knew her pain. No one wanted to help her through her times of trouble. She laid in her bed, long into the night thinking about how she had ruined her marriage – all hope was lost. But something deep within her wouldn't let go of Pastor McKinley's words from this morning.

She remembered that he said the former rain comes into our lives because of the choices we make. "But there is One who can wash away the former rain – it is He who brings the latter rain."

Elizabeth got out of bed. She needed the rain that God could bring into her life. On her knees she prayed, "Oh, Lord, I need You. Come into my life and remove the problems Kenneth and I have created." Just then Elizabeth felt something sweep into her room. She looked around thinking Kenneth had opened her bedroom door. It was still closed. She got off her knees and walked around the room. She felt that sweeping wind again, but this time it enveloped her. She closed her eyes and exhaled. Tears escaped her closed lids, but these were not sorrowful tears. Right now, all she felt was comfort. It relaxed her, and loved on her. She softly cried, for she had finally found a love so strong, it satisfied the thirst of her soul.

She wrapped her arms around herself and smiled as she laid back in bed. Sleep would be easy now. Everything would be all right. She could feel it. "Thank You, Lord."

Elizabeth woke refreshed and ready to roll away the stone of her past and resurrect a new life for her family. She smiled as she got out of bed. She could hardly believe what happened to her last night. But it was true. She, Elizabeth Underwood, a confirmed finger popper and Saturday night bar-hopper, Sunday go-to-meeting choir singer, had finally been touched by Jesus. She was saved.

There was a new pep in her step, as she opened her door and walked out of her bedroom. Kenneth opened the door of the guestroom down the hall. Elizabeth smiled, everything would be okay. *Lord, I'll tell him that I'm sorry for the way I've been acting, and we'll sit down and talk about it.* "Kenneth, I---"

Kenneth put the five-finger disconnect in her face. "If it's not about Erin or Danae, don't say nothing to me."

"B-but I need to tell you something."

"Tell it to my lawyer." He handed her a business card. "I'm on my way to see him before I go to work."

For one quick second, Elizabeth thought about going back into her bedroom and praying about this situation. But how could she pray when she was so, stinking mad? She ran behind Kenneth yelling, "I'll take everything you've got. No judge is going to let an adulterer push his wife aside, and keep his business and all his goods."

Kenneth turned around to face her, his lip curled in disgust. "If I have to sell my business, and live on the street, it will be well worth it, to be rid of you."

***

What does one do the day after finding love? Do you shout the good news to the world, or do you keep it to yourself?

The love Nina had found was special. It was nothing like the go fetch kind of love she had with Isaac, that left her panting and begging Isaac to throw her another bone. And when he threw her the bone of his affection or a piece of jewelry, she was obligated to do tricks for him. No, this love was enduring, it was kind, and unconditional with no strings attached. She wanted to let everyone know about this love she found with Jesus.

Nina felt so good she was willing to do whatever it took to keep this feeling of joy in her life. Never, never, never – no matter what she was doing, whom she was with – had she ever felt like this. Even when she was hot and heavy in love with loving Isaac, she didn't feel this good. On their best days, guilt would creep in and tell her that what she was doing wasn't right.

God had been trying to get her attention for a long time. She kept putting Him off. She just couldn't believe that God truly wanted her. But now, as she lay on her bed rubbing her stomach, she remembered driving in her car headed to a nightclub, and feeling that God was trying to pull her in another direction. She rejected God so many times in those days. "I'm too young," she remembered shouting at the Lord, the last time she felt that pull, "I'll serve You when I'm too old to have fun."

But fun turned into chaos. Now she was twenty-five years old, and five months pregnant. A soon to be single mom, with a drug dealer for her baby's daddy.

There was a knock on her bedroom door.

"Yes?"

Marguerite peeked her head in the room. "Do you feel like having a little company right now?"

Nina sat up in her bed. "Come in."

Marguerite carried a black leather bound Bible in her hand. She sat down on the bed next to Nina. "I thought you might need this," Marguerite told Nina as she held up the Bible.

Nina took the Bible from Marguerite and smiled. "It's got my name on it."

"I had it done first thing this morning."

Nina sat the Bible in her lap and gave Marguerite a hug. "Thank you." She started flipping through some of the pages. "I used to read the Bible all the time when I was a little girl. My adopted mother would sit with me and we'd find all kinds of stories in the Bible."

"It's not just a Bible, this is a study Bible. It will help with the questions you may have while reading some of the passages."

Nina's lip quivered as her eyes watered. "How will I ever repay you for what you have done for me?"

Marguerite shook her head. "There's nothing for you to repay. I believe God has had His hand on your life for a long time. All of the events that have occurred in your life were designed to bring you closer to Him."

Nina was about to ask Marguerite why so much had to occur in her life. Couldn't God have encouraged her to serve Him another way? But somebody was pounding on the front door.

"Who in the world?" Marguerite asked as she stood up.

Then they heard, "Open the door. I need to speak to Nina."

Nina sighed. "Wait. Sit back down, I'll get it." She stood up and put on the robe Marguerite had given her.

"Are you sure, honey? Do you want me to do anything?"

"Yeah," Nina told her as she walked to the door to let Isaac in. "Tell the Lord I want a drama-free life."

16

*K*enneth's emancipated descent on his household occurred seven days ago. He and Elizabeth weren't speaking. Erin and Danae followed suit and stopped talking to one another also. By Thursday, Kenneth claimed he had to go to New York. He had some financial matters to take care of at the World Trade Center, or at least that's what she heard him tell Erin. But Elizabeth knew his girlfriend was going to New York with him, spending money she should be spending. She fumed all week, until Sunday when she went to church and fell on the altar; pouring out her anxieties, frustrations and fears. On the drive home, Elizabeth felt so much better. No, not just better, she felt delivered.

When she opened the back door and saw Kenneth sitting at the kitchen table eating leftovers that she fixed for her children, she asked him about his unexpected trip to New York. When he gave her an offhanded response, Elizabeth cussed him out.

On Wednesday night, she dressed the girls and went to Bible study. The pastor preached on forgiveness and letting go of the long list of wrongs that people have done. Had this man been a fly on her wall this week? What is up with this?

Elizabeth found herself back on the altar again crying out to God for help and deliverance.

After service, she met another new convert. Her name was Nina. She was five months pregnant, no ring in sight. But it's cool. Elizabeth still thought she was the sweetest girl she'd met in a long time. Elizabeth pulled out a pen and piece of paper. She jotted down her telephone number and handed it to Nina. "Give me a call. We can do lunch or something."

Nina smiled as she wrote her number on the back of the church's weekly program and handed it to Elizabeth. "I'd like that." They walked to the parking lot together, making arrangements to get together some time during the week.

When Elizabeth got home from church, Kenneth asked her if she'd had any luck finding a place to stay. That cussing demon reared its ugly head in her house again. After that episode, she went to her bedroom and fell down on her knees. *"Lord, please help me. I don't like what I have become."*

The rest of the week was peaceful, like the calm before the storm. Kenneth and Elizabeth mastered the art of delivering messages through their five-year old. Erin was in the family room with her dad, when he pulled out some money and told her, "Give this to your mother. Tell her this is the grocery money."

When Erin handed the money and delivered the message to her mother, Elizabeth asked her daughter, "Is there anything special your dad wants from the store?"

Kenneth told Erin, "I would love some Granny Apples and Louis Rich bologna."

By 7:30 that evening, Erin was exhausted. Elizabeth put her and Danae to bed, then went to her bedroom to study the Word of God. Each night before she went to bed, she tore into Psalms, Proverbs, and Esther. Day after day she poured into those chapters. She discovered that a foolish woman tears down her house, but a wise woman builds it up, she took note of how David worshipped the Lord through the Psalms. Even the way Esther responded to the king ministered to her heart.

The next morning when Kenneth left for work, Elizabeth vowed to stop talking through Erin, and start trying to salvage her marriage. She was in the kitchen cooking dinner for Kenneth and the kids, when the phone rang. It was Tommy Brooks. Elizabeth had been so consumed with all the drama in her life that she'd forgotten about singing at the Belante' Club.

"So when are you coming back to the club? We need to get these papers signed."

Elizabeth's house of cards was tumbling down in front of her. There was no way she could put one more thing in the mix. "Tommy, I'm sorry, now's not a good time."

There was an awkward pause. Then Tommy told her, "You're making a big mistake," and hung up.

***

"Daddy, you're home!" Erin exclaimed as she ran toward him.

Kenneth put his briefcase down in the foyer and bent down to pull his daughter into a tight bear hug. "Yes, baby, daddy's home."

Elizabeth walked into the foyer wiping her hands on a dishcloth. She planted her feet by the stairway, a good three feet away from Kenneth and his one-child fan club. The foyer had always been one of her favorite areas in the house. The natural stone marble floor spoke of elegance. The off white plush carpet that flowed up the winding staircase said, "I have arrived." It was the very thing that made her beg Kenneth to buy this house. But now, in the very place that had always made her feel regal and important, she felt out of place and unnecessary. She smiled at her wayward husband. The joy that was in his eyes at the sight of Erin disappeared. Contempt took joy's place. "You still here?"

Elizabeth silently prayed, *Lord, please don't let me start trippin,'* "Yeah, I'm still here. I was hoping we could talk."

Kenneth put Erin down. "I'm through talking. I've tried to tell you to get a lawyer. I don't know what you're waiting on."

Elizabeth opened her mouth, then shut it.

"Come on Daddy, Mommy made chicken and dumplings for dinner." Erin grabbed and pulled at Kenneth.

Kenneth allowed himself to be pulled toward the kitchen. "Mmh, I love chicken and dumplings."

"That's what Mommy said."

"I made you a German Chocolate cake too." Elizabeth said as she followed behind her child and her husband.

Kenneth stopped and glared at Elizabeth. "What are you up to? Am I going to need a stomach pump after I eat this *wonderful* meal?"

Elizabeth knew she deserved his contempt and mistrust. Everything she had done to Kenneth during their seven-year marriage had brought them to this point. She was willing to forgive him for the hurt he had caused her, but Kenneth didn't seem to have any forgiveness left for her. Elizabeth sighed, "Why don't you fix the plates Kenneth? Erin and I will eat what you serve us."

"Where's Danae?"

"She's asleep, or she'd eat dinner with us too. Okay?"

When they had filled up on chicken and dumplings and started in on the chocolate cake, Elizabeth sent Erin to the family room to play with her dolls, so she could state her case. "I know you want me to leave, Kenneth, but I can't do that. I just can't give up on us and let you go as if you meant nothing to me." She saw the coldness creep back into his eyes as his body stiffened. She put her hand on top of his hand. "Kenneth, please don't divorce me." He pulled his hand from Elizabeth's grasp. "Give me a month – I know you don't want to, but let's try to make this marriage work."

Kenneth jumped up. "No! If you need a month to find a place to live, fine. But understand this Elizabeth, we are through." He stormed out of the kitchen, went to his bedroom and packed his suitcase. He stomped down the stairs with his bags.

Elizabeth was at the bottom of the stairs waiting for him. "Where are you going?"

"I'll be back in a couple of days," he told her as he walked past her and out the front door.

***

By Saturday morning, the kids had torn the house apart but Elizabeth barely noticed. She did however, notice that Danae wouldn't stop crying. Elizabeth picked up her baby and discovered that she was burning up with fever. She gave Danae some Infant Tylenol, a couple of popsicles and several glasses of ice water. Nothing worked. By early afternoon, Elizabeth had bathed and dressed the kids and was on her way out the door when the phone rang. Thinking it might be Kenneth she picked it up. "What do I have to do to get you to call me?" her mother asked.

"Mom, I'm sorry. There has been so much going on, I don't know where my head is at lately."

"Well you know you've only got one Mama, right?"

Danae started crying. "Mom, you're right. I should call more. I'll call you back tonight, and you can give me a big lecture. But right now I've got to get Danae to the hospital."

"Hospital? What's wrong?"

"Fever. Do me a favor and page Kenneth. Let him know that Danae is sick and I'm on my way to Good Samaritan Hospital." Elizabeth hung up and ran out of the house.

Elizabeth sat in the emergency waiting room for three hours, just so the doctor could tell her to give Danae some Infant Tylenol and plenty of liquids. Like she hadn't already tried all that. Whatever.

"If she's still sick tomorrow evening, you might want to make an appointment with your regular physician," the doctor informed her as she got her children together and went back home.

She took Danae out of her car seat as Kenneth pulled up. He jumped out of his car and grabbed Danae. "Oh my God. She's burning up!"

"The doctor said that she'll be fine. She just needs to sleep for awhile."

While Kenneth carried Danae in the house, Elizabeth picked up a sleepy Erin and trotted behind her husband.

"Look at this house. My God, what have you been doing all week?"

"You may have finally remembered where home is, but don't think that gives you the right to pick on me." Elizabeth brushed past Kenneth and took Erin upstairs.

Kenneth stepped over toys and clothes, as he took Danae upstairs. "Where do you want me to put her?"

"Put her in our room."

He looked at Elizabeth. The coldness was in his eyes again. "I'll put her in *your* bed. Hopefully, it's not filthy in there too."

"On second thought, Erin is going to sleep with me tonight. You can take Danae into the guest room with you." She turned her back to him, strutted into her bedroom and laid Erin on the bed.

He stood in the hallway, an exasperated look on his face. "Well what am I supposed to do with Danae all night?"

Elizabeth stomped over to the doorway of her bedroom. "Do what any decent father would – take care of her." As he opened his mouth to respond, she slammed the door in his face. She leaned up against the door and sighed. "I'm sorry Lord, but he makes me so mad."

17

Elizabeth and Nina were at Red Lobster grubbing during an all-you-can-eat crab-legs night. Elizabeth told her about an in-home Bible study group that her brother held monthly. Nina realized she needed something to do that involved the Lord and no drama. Isaac made his rounds to Marguerite's house once a week. Each time, he arrived with someone different. A realtor, a dressmaker, the manager of a children's store, anybody he could find to help make Nina's life easier. She knew he was trying to make up for beating her at the abortion clinic, but she had already forgiven him. All she wanted now was to be left alone. Nina refused to take anything from Isaac. She told him that the Lord would make a way for her. That finally did the trick. He stormed out of the house, vowing that he was through trying to help hardheaded, stubborn people like her.

"That sounds good. Is your brother a good teacher?"

"I've never attended one of his classes, but I think he knows his stuff."

Nina cracked open one of her crab legs and stuffed the meat in her mouth. "If he can help me make sense of what I've been reading, count me in," she told Elizabeth, as she cracked another leg and swallowed the succulent contents.

"Slow down, girl," Elizabeth said while laughing.

"Hey, I'm eating for two. I'm allowed to pig out."

By the time they finished eating and talking, Nina and Elizabeth were both convinced that they needed a break from the toil and trouble of their dramatic lives. They had a hunger to know more about the Lord, so they decided to join the study group.

The first month they attended, Elder Michael expounded on the book of Hebrews and Romans. "Turn in your Bible to the book of Hebrews chapter eleven, verse six." While the pages turned, Michael told the group, "I want to get you hooked on faith." They had only been attending The Rock for a month, but in that time, Elizabeth and Nina had discovered the location of quite a few books in the Bible. And if they couldn't easily find something, they knew how to locate the table of contents.

When the pages stopped turning, Michael read:

"But without faith it is impossible to please Him: for he that cometh to God must believe that He is, and that He is a rewarder of them that diligently seek Him."

One of the original members of the Bible study group lifted his head. "So you can't even believe in God without faith, huh?"

"Correct. That's why faith is so important to God." After a sufficient pause, Michael told the group, "Turn to Romans chapter ten verse seventeen, and we'll find out how we can obtain faith."

The pages started turning again. "Could you read this verse for us Elizabeth?" Elder Michael asked.

She looked at her brother. Why did he have to call on her? She had half a mind to tell him to read it himself, but he was not only her brother, he was an Elder in the church. She figured that his position entitled him to a little respect. So she bent her head and began reading. *"So then faith cometh by hearing, and hearing by the Word of God."*

"Okay, so far we've learned that faith is the most important thing to God and the only way to obtain faith is by listening to the Word of God." Their meeting continued in the same fashion for the next two hours. Whenever Nina, Elizabeth or any of the other group members didn't understand a certain concept, Elder Michael would break it down to their level of understanding. At the end of the two hours, Elder Michael told the group to read the entire books of Romans and Hebrews before their next meeting.

***

The next meeting Nina and Elizabeth came back with loads of questions. This faith thing was a lot to grab hold of. They were eager to devour and learn the Word, so they pressed Michael until he was all out of answers. "Okay," Elder Michael finally said, "I can see that you guys have really been studying the chapters I gave you last month. Do you feel like you've got a better understanding of faith now?"

Numerous nods of affirmation went around the small room.

"Good! Now I would like to introduce you to the man you have been reading about in Romans and Hebrews." He then had them turn to the book of Matthew and began reading: *"The book of the generations of Jesus Christ, the son of David, the son of Abraham..."* he continued reading the entire first chapter of Matthew. Michael then took time to explain how all of these people from generation to generation connected with each other. At the end of their second meeting, he assigned the reading of the book of Matthew.

They left the meeting full of fire. "This is awesome!" Nina told Elizabeth on their drive back to Marguerite's house.

"I know. I can hardly believe how good I feel."

Nina sat back in the passenger seat and smiled. "It's like I've got all this stuff stacked against me; I'm going to be a single mom,

I've got no place to stay, and my baby's daddy is a drug dealer – but it doesn't bother me. Somehow, I know that God can help me fix this mess."

They pulled up to a red light. Elizabeth looked at Nina and shook her head. "I wish I had your faith. I don't know if my husband is going to come home from one day to the next. I'm not so sure that God can fix my mess."

Nina put her hand on Elizabeth's shoulder. "It'll work out, just don't stop believing."

18

Elizabeth was in the kitchen cleaning the lunch dishes. Kenneth was in the family room playing with the girls, when the phone rang once, then stopped. Elizabeth looked over at Kenneth. He was still playing with the girls as if nothing was going on. Five minutes later the phone rang once and stopped again.

This time Kenneth got up and walked up the stairs. Elizabeth waited a few minutes then picked up the telephone in the family room. She heard a woman's voice say, "Am I going to see you today, baby?"

Kenneth whispered, "I don't know about today, Denise. I'm trying to spend some quality time with my kids."

Denise spat, "Is she there?"

"Yeah, Elizabeth's here. But she's doing her own thing so I can be with Erin and Danae." Kenneth let out an exhausted sigh. "For once, she's not tripping."

Elizabeth put her hand on her hip. "Oh, you're wrong about that, Kenneth. I am definitely tripping."

"Elizabeth!"

"Were you expecting someone else?"

"Hang up this phone right now! Do you hear me?"

The sistah-sistah head motion was going now. "You must have lost your mind---"

"Get off the phone."

"Do you think I'm going to let you keep disrespecting me like this? Your little tramp has got one more time to call my house playing the hang up game and I'm going---"

"What are you going to do?" Denise asked Elizabeth.

"You little home wrecker! Give me your address, and I'll come over there and show you what I do to no-good-men-stealing strumpets like you!"

"D-Denise, don't give her your address. Just hang up – I'll be over in a minute." Kenneth hung up the phone and came barreling down the stairs with keys in hand.

Elizabeth met him in the foyer. "Where do you think you're going?"

"Out."

"Kenneth, if you open that door, I'll... I'll ---"

"Elizabeth, why can't you accept the fact that we just don't work anymore?"

"There's nothing wrong with us. If you would quit sleeping around, you'd have time to work on your marriage."

Kenneth laughed. "Work on my marriage? Elizabeth, I don't want my marriage – I don't want *you*."

Now that hurt. But Elizabeth knew how to make him hurt too. She looked around the room trying to find something to lay her hands on. Her eyes feasted on the pedestal in the foyer. Atop it was a very expensive oriental vase Kenneth's mother gave them as a wedding present. "Well, guess what Kenneth, I don't want this," she told him as she pushed the vase to the floor and watched it shatter into numerous pieces.

"My mother gave that to us."

"Like I care. I never liked your mother anyway."

Kenneth released the knob and advanced on her.

"You want to know what else I don't want?" Her eyes were full of fury as she picked up the pedestal and flung it at Kenneth's head.

He moved out the way and the pedestal went through the window. Kenneth grabbed Elizabeth's arms and shook her. "Are you crazy?" He screamed at her. "I just had that window fixed!"

Her heart was filled with turmoil. She was going through this same drama, and she didn't know how to stop. Didn't know how to make it better. She lost all her resolve as she crumpled to the ground. "Why don't you want me?" She cried in a pitiful tone, "You're supposed to be different. You promised me you'd be different."

Kenneth looked into his wife's eyes. He saw the pain she carried. He had hurt her deeply, but what could he do? Their life was what they had made it.

Erin and Danae ran into the foyer. "Mommy, Daddy, what's wrong?"

Kenneth released Elizabeth and hugged his children. "Everything's okay. Don't worry."

Elizabeth looked at the mess she had caused. She saw the look of fear in her daughters' eyes. "Oh no," she said. "Not again – not again." She put her hand over her mouth. "Oh God, what is wrong with me?" She crawled back and forth on the floor until she ended up in a corner rubbing her hair. "I'm so sorry. I'm so sorry."

Kenneth put the kids down and went to her. "Liz, Liz."

She didn't respond. Just kept rubbing her face and hair. He picked her up and carried her upstairs. "Talk to me Liz," he said as he opened her bedroom door.

She looked at him as he laid her on the bed. He saw the tears and the regret in her eyes. Eyes that looked like his mother's had the many times she caught his father cheating. "Why are you doing this to me?" she asked him.

"I never meant to hurt you, Liz."

The tears blurred her vision, but he could still see her pain. It was as clear as if he were watching a Mac truck run him over. He backed away from her. "This was a mistake Liz. I shouldn't have moved back home. I'll pack my stuff and be out by morning," he told her, then left the room.

Elizabeth turned her back on the door. With tears soaking her pillow, she cried out to the Lord, *"Please help me, Lord. Please..."*

Long into the night she communed with God. His sweet presence overwhelmed her and filled her with peace. That is, until she heard the words **release your pride** spoken into her spirit. "What do you mean?" She demanded as she looked toward heaven. "I've lost everything. Now you want me to let go of my pride and fall down at Kenneth's feet?" She tossed and turned through the night unable to accept the gentle guidance of the Lord. "I can't do it," she finally told the Lord.

At 8:00 a.m. the next morning, Elizabeth lay in her bed as Kenneth took his belongings to his car and left. She wanted to run to the garage and beg him to stay – tell him how much she loved and needed him, but she'd never begged for anything, not one single thing in her entire adult life. How could she start now? Kenneth was trying to humiliate her. That was all there was to it, and there was no way she was going to let him get away with it. Let him leave, he'll be back. But the next time he walks his butt back into this house, it'll be on my terms, she thought to herself.

Elizabeth made her decision. Now she set her mind to concentrating on her children and forgetting about Kenneth, but the passing days were so lonely without her man. How could she make it through the day without remembering how things were between them when they first met at Howard University? In those days, Kenneth would hang on her every word. He made her feel important, like she mattered.

She thought about how Kenneth would laugh at her jokes, no matter how corny. Her mind traveled on the path of midnight love in Kenneth's dorm room. All at once, Elizabeth's passionate mind stroll stopped. Her hand flew to her mouth. "Oh my God, we were sinning." Erin and Danae were on the couch taking their afternoon nap. Elizabeth laid hands on both of them and prayed, "No sex before marriage, in Jesus' name I pray. Thank You God."

On Wednesday, she received a summons to appear at a preliminary divorce hearing the next morning. She picked up the phone to call Kenneth's office, dialed three digits, then hung up. She sat down on the couch. "I need to think."

***

As she drove to Bible study that night, she kept asking herself what she wanted out of life, and what she was willing to give up to get it. They were having testimony service this evening, which was rare for her church. Numerous people stood and declared the goodness of God. Elizabeth stood up and shouted, "I want my husband back!" She broke down in front of a crowd of three hundred people, and could care less. When she shared her tumultuous life, many saints agreed to fast and pray about the outcome of the divorce hearing she had to attend in the morning.

Morning came like ice water poured over a warm, unsuspecting body. Determined to get through this day, she pulled her tired body out of that comfortable bed, took a long hot shower and put on a beige linen pantsuit. She dropped the kids off at her mother's house. As she drove to Kenneth's lawyer's office, she remembered how Nina admonished her to never stop believing. Elizabeth also remembered the scripture in Hebrews that talked about faith being the substance of things hoped for. Then she thought, what if I dare to hope that things will work out? What if I just choose to believe that God can fix my mess?

"*Please go with me*," she said to the Lord as she got out of her car and walked into the lawyer's office.

When the secretary brought her into the conference room, Kenneth was already seated with his attorney. They looked at Elizabeth. "Gentlemen," she said with a slight nod of her head as she pulled up a chair and sat down.

"Where is your lawyer?" Kenneth asked her.

"I brought all the help I need," she told him. Then silently prayed, *Lord, please be with me.*

Kenneth's lawyer extended his hand. "I'm Mr. Massey. Sorry we're not meeting under better circumstances. Okay, well, let's get down to business, shall we?"

Kenneth lifted his hands to stall the proceeding. "Why didn't you bring a lawyer, Liz? This is serious business."

She folded her hands in her lap. "I don't need a lawyer. Just tell me what you want, Kenneth."

He loosened his tie. "Look, Liz, besides joint custody of the girls, all I want is to be able to keep my business. You can have everything else."

Mr. Massey shuffled a few papers. "Now that's fair, wouldn't you agree?" He asked Elizabeth.

Elizabeth ignored him. "Kenneth, I have no problem with your request. You want to keep your business and all I want is to keep my husband. I think we can help each other out, don't you?"

Kenneth shook his head. "No, Liz. You're not getting your way this time."

She was silent for a moment. Unable to look him in the eye, humbled and with a bowed head, she told him, "I need you, Kenneth. I can't live without you."

"You've got a problem then, because I *can* live without you."

"What did I do that was so wrong?" Elizabeth demanded.

Mr. Massey broke in, "The purpose of today's meeting is to go over a few preliminary issues. Nothing more."

"Please, Kenneth. I need to know."

He looked at his wife. Her eyes begged him to tell all; to help her understand. He owed her that much, didn't he? "It wasn't just one thing, Liz. It was seven years of things. Everything had to be your way. You constantly complained and ridiculed me." He ran his hands through his hair. "Maybe I shouldn't have cheated on you. I thought I would be a better man than my father, but I... I. Ah, forget it. Let's just get this over with."

Elizabeth stood up and pushed her chair under the table. "All right, do whatever you want. I don't have the energy to fight you. I just want to know one more thing."

"What's that?" Kenneth asked.

A single tear rolled down her cheek. "How did you stop loving me? I've loved you since the day we met. I don't know how to make it go away." Her shoulders slumped as she turned and walked out of the office. Despair enveloped her, but she was determined not to fall apart. She didn't know how all of this was going to turn out. But trying to hold on to a man who was ready to go, was like trying to catch the wind. *"Lord, I've got to let Kenneth go. I place my marriage in Your hands. Your will be done."*

19

" *W*hen can you and the baby go home?"

Lisa sunk into the hospital bed and pulled the covers against her body. "Home? Where is that?"

"You know what I mean," Nina corrected. "When will you and the baby be able to go back to Marguerite's house?"

Lisa clung to those covers and seemed to sink even deeper into bed. "You know how they say that new mothers feel joy when holding their baby for the first time? And how we're supposed to forget all the pain we went through bringing that baby into the world?"

"Yeah," Nina touched her belly. "I'm counting on that."

Lisa looked at Nina. "I didn't forget."

Nina could feel Lisa's emptiness by the sadness projecting from her eyes.

"I still remember every ounce of the pain. My little girl brought me no joy at all." She released the covers to wipe away the tears rolling down her cheeks. "Maybe my mother never forgot the pain either. Maybe that's why she treated me like dirt." Lisa scooted around in bed, and wiped away a few more tears. "When I was ten years old, a doctor fell in love with my mother. He was moving his practice to Nashville and wanted my mother to come with him.

Just one catch, though. No kids allowed. So Mommy dearest handed me over to my grandmother, and never looked back."

"I'm sorry that happened to you." Wanting desperately to say more, but not knowing what, she began to rub Lisa's back. Lisa might never forget the pain inflicted by her mother, but Nina knew that if she turned her life over to Jesus, in time, she would be able to forgive. Nina only wished she knew how to communicate this message to Lisa. Nina silently communicated with the Lord while she continued to rub Lisa's back. *I know Lisa needs You, but I don't know what to do.*

Pray.

Nina jumped. "Did you hear that?"

"Hear what?"

A nurse trotted into the room with Lisa's baby. She was grinning from ear to ear as she told the baby, "Here's Mama. Now you can stop all that fussing." She handed the baby to Lisa. "Mama's going to take real good care of you."

The baby made a gurgling sound, while she was being transferred from nurse to mother. Lisa looked down, just as her baby girl looked up at her. That's when the weeping and wailing really got started. Lisa looked at Nina, as she rocked her baby. Sorrow was embedded deep in her eyes. "You see, she can feel the pain too."

Tears rolled down Lisa's face. Nina started praying. *Lord, take away Lisa's pain and restore joy to her. Give her the joy that comes from knowing You. Lord, please help her to treat this baby right. Teach her how to love and care for what You have placed in her care.*

Nina rubbed the baby's back.

The baby cooed and gurgled.

Nina continued rubbing her back.

Lisa looked up. "She's calming down."

"See," Nina took Lisa's hand and put it on the baby's back. "Just keep rubbing."

Lisa smiled at Nina. "She stopped crying."

Nina pointed to the baby. "Smile at her, Lisa. Talk to her, let her know how much you care."

Lisa and the baby started interacting. Nina started feeling like a third wheel, so she grabbed her purse and backed out of the room. "I'll see you tomorrow," she told Lisa, then headed out of the hospital.

Nina was getting ready to walk to the bus stop, when Isaac pulled up beside her. "I called the house. They told me you were at the hospital. You alright?"

Nina stopped. "Lisa just had her baby. I came to visit."

"The girl that's always so nasty to you? What you visit her for?"

"God requires us to treat everybody right. Even the ones who don't treat us so nice."

"Whatever." Isaac got out of his truck and took Nina by the arm. "Come on, I'll take you home."

At first Nina thought to resist, but the tiredness within her body betrayed her. She sat down on the passenger side, and rubbed her legs. She desperately wanted to rub her feet too, but couldn't reach them.

Isaac looked over at Nina. Her stomach was so huge she couldn't get the seat belt on. "You've gotten bigger." Isaac informed her.

Nina laughed. "That's the way it works, Isaac. I keep getting bigger, until one day the baby just pops out."

He smiled, "I can't wait to see him."

Nina became mesmerized as Isaac's chocolate skin dipped into his cheeks. She shook herself, then turned to stare out the window. I'm sure there are plenty of saved men with deep dimpled cheeks and a heavenly smile to go along with it. Besides, this is not God's best for you, Nina reminded herself.

By the time they reached Marguerite's house, all she could think about was climbing into her bed and sleeping the day away.

Isaac put the car in park and grabbed Nina's arm before she could get out and run away from him. "I need to talk to you, Nina."

She looked at him.

"My baby is not going to live in no group home." He shifted in his seat. "There's plenty nuff room for the three of us at my house."

"I can't live in sin with you Isaac."

Isaac lifted his hands in frustration. Then, to keep his hands from going across Nina's face or throat he held on to the steering wheel with brute strength. "What difference does it make? You're already carrying my baby. My God, I'm supposed to take care of you."

Nina saw the way Isaac held onto that steering wheel, and truth be told, she was a little scared. The Lord is my Shepherd, she said to herself. To Isaac she said, "I have not seen the righteous forsaken, nor His seed begging bread."

"What?"

"God takes care of me Isaac. He will also take care of our child." She opened the door and started to step out of the truck, but her body disobeyed her. She looked over at Isaac. "Can you help me, please?"

"Mmh, ain't that 'bout nothing." Isaac opened the door and walked over to Nina's side of the truck. "Tell me, Nina, where is the good Lord when *you* need Him?"

20

*T*hank God for the prayers of the Saints. Kenneth came home two days after their meeting in his lawyer's office. Nothing much had changed, he was still sleeping in the guestroom and still grumpy and hard to get along with. He acted like he hadn't walked back in this house on his own two feet – like he was a prisoner or something.

"So what are your plans for today?" Kenneth asked Elizabeth as the family finished their breakfast.

Elizabeth twisted her lips as she opened her mouth to respond. It felt like molasses or super glue was in her mouth, holding it shut – trying to stop her from saying what she wanted to say. Michael told her that she needed to ask Kenneth's permission, or at least inform him, when she wanted to do something she knew he would be against. Michael said that good marriages worked better that way. He told her that there was no room for independence in marriage, but there was plenty of give and take. Communication and compromise. As far as Elizabeth was concerned, she might as well stand around her house in an apron with a big ol' Aunt Jemima biscuit-making hat on her head singing Swing Low, cause this sho' nuf felt like slave duty. Elizabeth massaged her jaw and opened her mouth. "I was thinking about applying for a job today. What do you think about that?"

Kenneth finished chewing the grits in his mouth, put his fork down and stared at Elizabeth. "Why do you need a job? As long as you're here, it's my responsibility to take care of you."

"Just for a little extra spending money. It would only be part-time, nothing major."

He pushed his plate away, wiped his mouth and threw the napkin on the plate. "What do you need spending money for? Don't I provide for everybody's needs?"

"Yes, you do." Problem is, she had a few wants. She knew Kenneth's money was strictly off limits when it came to her enjoyment.

"Mommy, where you work at?" Erin asked.

Elizabeth bent over and gave Erin a kiss on the forehead. "No where yet dear."

"What will you be doing?"

Elizabeth wiped some jelly from the corner of Erin's mouth. "The company has a need for a part-time receptionist."

"Isn't that beneath *you*?" Kenneth asked.

No he didn't. "Why would you say that?"

"Experience is a great teacher."

She knew he was thinking of her attitude toward working as a receptionist at his company. "That was different, Kenneth. I have an MBA, but all you would let me do was answer your phone and type your memos. It was degrading."

He sat up and pointed an accusatory finger at her. "You know, it's funny how you always remember things in a way that makes you look like the victim."

See, Lord, you can't even talk to this man without him getting an attitude.

"Funny how you just simply forgot," he continued. "That it was the marketing plan you put together that inspired Bank of

America to give me the business loan I needed to start the company."

"I didn't forget, but I thought you had."

"No, Elizabeth, I didn't forget. But silly me. I thought an MBA could develop the marketing plan for our business and my *wife* could answer a few telephones and type a few memos so I wouldn't go over my budget trying to hire an assistant. And guess what, I'd be able to stay in business another year."

Put that way, she sounded all petty and bouje'. "Okay, Kenneth, you're right. I should have been able to help you no matter what I was asked to do."

He didn't respond.

"I've changed, Kenneth. I think the job will be good for me."

"And just who do you think will watch my children while you go get your *spending money*?" He spat those words at her as he stood up.

No sir boss, ain't nobody around here gon' be neglectin' yo' chilin. "Kenneth, I would like to discuss this. Maybe we can come up with a solution that works for both of us." She stood up, scraped her plate into Kenneth's and carried them to the sink.

"Look, I've got to go." He picked up his briefcase and turned toward the children.

Elizabeth leaned against the sink and watched her family for a moment. Kenneth was in one of his Brooks Brothers suits. He looked good in navy blue. That yellow tie didn't hurt him none either. Erin was jumping up and down, begging Kenneth to pick her up. Danae was in her high chair happily playing with her food. The evidence of her delight was on the floor, the table and especially all over Danae. Kenneth gave Erin a big hug and kiss. He moved toward Danae and bent down to kiss her. She reached for his tie. Kenneth stepped back, patted Danae's head and looked at Elizabeth.

Elizabeth got excited. They had been in the same house again for a few weeks now. He had eaten breakfast with them almost every morning, but not once had he bothered to say good bye to her as he left for the day. He hadn't bothered to tell her when he would be back home, or even if he was coming home that night. Lord, please let today be a start of something new.

"Would you clean her up? I am sick to death of having to endure this mess just to eat breakfast with my children." He looked around the kitchen, mouth twisting like he had tasted some Ecoli in his beef patty and then chased it down with a glass of sour milk. "Part-time job. Mmph, you can't even keep this house clean. I've got a suggestion for you, Elizabeth. Before you handle somebody else's business, try handling your own!"

Each one of Kenneth's words was like a physical blow that cut deep into her self-esteem. Her shoulders slumped as she looked around the kitchen. Okay, the kitchen did look a hot mess, but they had just finished eating. Danae has more fun playing in her food, than eating it. Elizabeth didn't think she needed to stop her. But as she saw the results of the mess through Kenneth's eyes, she realized she had made yet another mistake. She balled her fist tightly, "You win, Kenneth. I don't need a job, okay." Giving in didn't feel good, so just to let him know that she was nobody's punk, she snippily added, "Are you happy now?"

"Smartest thing you've said all morning," Kenneth turned back to his girls. "I'll see you two later."

"Will you be home for dinner?" Elizabeth asked.

Kenneth's hand was on the doorknob. He turned around and stared at Elizabeth as if she had lost her mind.

"I... I was just wondering what you wanted me to fix for dinner."

"I have no idea what time I'll be back. Does that answer your question?"

Elizabeth turned her back on Kenneth and started snatching the rest of the breakfast dishes off the table. He opened the door and Elizabeth rolled her eyes.

Erin tugged Elizabeth's pajamas. "Mommy, is Daddy being a good-for-nothing again?"

Elizabeth closed her eyes real tight, *Oh God, help me, I have created such a mess*. She got on her knees in front of Erin. "Baby, your Daddy is a good man."

"But you said…"

"I was wrong, Erin. Your Daddy loves you and he works real hard for his family -- he takes care of us. Only a good man could do what he does for us, and I am grateful that he is a part of our family."

Erin hugged her mom, then quickly broke free and ran toward the back door. Elizabeth turned to see Kenneth still standing in the door with a bewildered expression on his face. "Daddy, guess what? Mommy's not mad at you anymore."

"I'll see you later, Erin," was all Kenneth said, but as he closed the door, he glanced over at Elizabeth.

***

By noon the house was clean and the kids bathed. She fixed a few sandwiches. They ate lunch together, laughed and joked about nothing in particular. They just enjoyed each others' company. At about one o'clock, Elizabeth put Erin and Danae down for their nap. She took a deep breath knowing that she had about an hour to herself.

She would spend it with the Lord. Elizabeth picked up her Bible and turned to I Peter. She read the first and second chapters of I Peter yesterday, and was determined to finish it today.

She turned to I Peter 3. The first thing that leaped at her was:

Wives, likewise, be submissive to your own husbands, that even if some do not obey the Word, they without a word, may be won by the conduct of their wives, when they observe your chaste conduct accompanied by fear.

Do not let your adornment be merely outward – arranging the hair, wearing gold, or putting on fine apparel.

Rather let it be the hidden person of the heart, with the incorruptible beauty of a gentle and quiet spirit, which is very precious in the sight of God.

Elizabeth closed the Bible and clasped her hands together. "Lord, You ask too much. Isn't it enough that I give You my love, and my life?" She remembered the way she talked to Kenneth during their discussion this morning. The things she thought about him, the way she rolled her eyes and slammed the breakfast dishes around. She was a long way from this gentle and quiet spirit that was so precious to God. She covered her face with her hands, and bowed her head in shame. "Oh Lord, why don't I have what is so precious to You? How do I get it, Lord?"

Submit.

Elizabeth's head jerked up, she looked around. The room was empty, but she knew she heard the word that had been haunting her since she accepted Jesus as her savior.

Why did the Lord have to ruin a perfectly good book by putting a word like submit in it? She gritted her teeth. How could she do what God wanted, when she was married to a man like Kenneth? "You see how he treats me. Why do You require this of me?"

For him, Beloved.

Why does Christianity have to be about self-sacrifice? It would be so much easier if Kenneth would bring himself to Christ without a sacrifice being laid on the altar. But instead, she was required to get something she did not possess.

Nina had a gentle and quiet spirit. Elizabeth remembered asking her how she could be so calm, and how she could keep taking nonsense from that wavy head she was carrying a baby for. Nina just smiled and said, "It's in God's hands. What can I do but wait?"

Waiting was one thing, but waiting without action, without retaliation for wrongs done, was too much to ask. "*Lord, You're going to have to help me. Though I desire to please You, I can't do this thing alone.*"

At six-thirty that night, the girls were sitting at the kitchen table eating fries and hot dogs. Danae was crying as Kenneth walked into the kitchen. "What's wrong with her?"

Elizabeth looked up. "She kept throwing her fries on the floor, so I smacked her hands."

Kenneth loosened his tie as Danae reached out for him. "Stop all that crying, girl. You shouldn't have thrown your food on the floor anyway." He bent down and placed a kiss on her cheek. "You'll be all right."

He turned to greet Erin. "Hey little one. I came home to eat dinner with you. Why didn't you wait for me?"

"I'm sorry, Kenneth," Elizabeth chimed. "I didn't know how soon you would be home. I made you some red beans and rice though."

Kenneth walked over to the stove. He took the lid off one of the pots and savored the aroma. "Mmh, mmh, mmh, smells like home."

"Well you go on up stairs and change. I'll bring your food up, so you can have a few minutes of peace and quiet."

There was that same bewildered look he had on his face earlier this morning. "You never used to care if I had peace and quiet around here."

Elizabeth pulled Danae out of her high chair. "I just thought you might want to unwind, Kenneth. That's all."

"Well I guess you thought wrong." He grabbed a bowl out of the cabinet. "I'll take some up with me. Have the kids come to my room when they're finished. Okay?"

***

Elizabeth had fallen asleep on the sofa in the family room. Her Bible lay open across her stomach, when Kenneth nudged her awake. She stretched and yawned. "Mmmm." She looked up at him and stretched again. "Is something wrong?" she asked, as she sat up.

"No. Nothing's wrong. I already put the girls to bed. I wanted to talk to you for a minute."

"What time is it?"

He looked at his watch. "Nine-thirty."

"What did you want to talk about?"

Kenneth sat down on the love seat opposite Elizabeth. "I need to know something."

Elizabeth rubbed her eyes and gave Kenneth her full attention. That's when she noticed he was wearing a pair of tan slacks and a white Polo shirt. She couldn't make out the fragrance, but one thing she did know, Kenneth smelled good, too good for an evening at home, and he definitely wasn't dressed for bed.

"This morning, when you told Erin that I am a good man, and that I provide for all of you. Why did you tell her that?"

"Because it's true."

"But you've never said anything like that to her before. When you get mad at me – like you were this morning, you normally tell the kids how rotten I am."

She reached out and touched his hands. "Kenneth, can you forgive me?" She shook her head, trying to clear the memories, but they wouldn't go away. They just sat there, in her mind's eye, accusing her over and over again. "I wish I could undo so many things. I wish I had been the kind of wife you needed from the beginning." She released his hands, leaned back on the sofa and sighed. "But... I'm learning to let my past go and move on. Most of all, I'm just trying to grow up."

Kenneth pointed at the Bible in Elizabeth's lap. "You've been reading that a lot lately. Is it helping you – you know, grow up?"

Elizabeth laughed. "In ways you couldn't even imagine." She thought back to the submission passage in I Peter and said, "At times, in ways that I don't even want to imagine."

"You never used to read the Bible at home. Why now?"

"Things are different. I'm a Christian now, Kenneth."

Kenneth gave her a quizzical look as he took the Bible out of her lap, perused a few pages then sat it on the floor. "You've always been a Christian, haven't you?"

Help me make him understand, Lord. "I've always been a church goer, Kenneth. But a few months ago, I accepted Jesus into my heart. It was the best thing I've ever done. Would you like me to tell you about it?"

Kenneth stood up. "No, not right now. I have plans tonight."

"This late? Where are you going?"

"Look Elizabeth, I came home for dinner, and I plan to be here for dinner with the kids every night I can. But once they go to bed, I'm on *my* time. Alright?"

Elizabeth stood up. "Exactly what do you do on *your* time?"

Beloved, not this way.

No, Lord, I'm not listening to You. Let him stand here and tell me to my face that he's still got his whore. I want You to hear how this man mistreats me.

"I'm going to be honest with you, Elizabeth. I am seeing someone." He turned away from her and picked his keys off the coffee table. "I'm just not sure if I want to be married to you anymore."

Hurt. Pain. *What else is in store for me, Lord?*

"You're going to have to give me some time to figure out what I want," Kenneth told her.

"Do I mean nothing to you? Good God, Kenneth. Does seven years of marriage mean anything? How can you treat me like this?"

"Don't cry, Elizabeth. I didn't…"

"I'm not crying!" She raised her hands to her face and felt the betraying wetness. *Lord, isn't my broken heart enough of a sacrifice? Why must I cry in front of this man too?*

"Look, I wasn't trying to hurt you, I just didn't want to lie about it."

"Well that's just great, Kenneth. Don't be a liar, be an adulterer."

Kenneth threw his hands up in the air. "I can't talk to you. I'm outta here!"

Elizabeth picked up the ceramic vase on the coffee table and flung it at Kenneth's head. The vase smashed against the family room wall as Kenneth slammed the back door. She fell back onto the sofa. Her Bible lay open on the floor, accusing her of not fulfilling I Peter 3. She defiantly looked to heaven and said, "*He started it.*"

21

Isaac was sloppy drunk. No other way to describe it.

He was at his usual table at his Friday night hot spot, getting his drink on, and barking orders at Keith and Valerie. "Y'all got to do better. We're losing money left and right!"

Keith tried to defend himself. "We make plenty money, man. What difference does it make if a new guy comes in and starts earning a little money too?"

Isaac tried to lean forward, but quickly fell back in his seat. Slurring every other word he said, "It's your job to make s-sure don't nobody else earn no money 'less we give 'em permission."

"What you want me to do, man? Shove a pistol down the throat of every guy that tries to earn a fast buck?"

Isaac slammed his fist on the table, his drink spilled. "That's right. That's exactly what I want you to do. You're supposed to be my enforcer, go enforce something!"

"You know what?" Keith stood up, and slung his chair back. "Forget it – I'm going to the bar and drink in peace."

"I'm not t-through talking."

"I'm through listening. Call me when you sober up."

Isaac was leaning, almost falling out of his chair. "I'm not drunk, boy. You can talk to me now!"

Keith looked at Valerie. "I'm going over to the bar. Can you get him home?"

"Yeah, Keith, I'll get him home. Don't worry about it."

Keith angrily stalked over to the bar, turned his back on Isaac and ordered himself a Whiskey Sour.

"Why you got to be so hard on Keith? You know he does a good job for you." Valerie told Isaac.

Isaac waved down a waitress and pointed at his empty glass. "If he's doing such a good job, why am I losing money?"

Valerie shifted in her seat and peered at Isaac. "Ain't nobody done business in The Promised Land but you, since the day you took it over, and you know it. If you're losing money, it's because people are going outside The Promised Land, and Keith ain't got nothing to do with that."

The waitress brought another drink over to Isaac, then looked at Valerie. "Are you taking him home?"

"Yeah," Valerie told her, then turned the evil eye back on Isaac. "What's the real reason you're drinking yourself unconscious? As if I don't know."

"What you think you know, girl?" Isaac sneered back at Valerie.

"I know plenty! Like the fact that you're upset over Nina."

"Why should I be upset about Nina?"

Valerie was silent, fuming, but silent.

Isaac leaned a little too far and almost fell out of his seat. He righted himself. His head began to bob back and forth. "Told me God was going to take care of her and *my* baby. Do you believe that? God! Like I didn't have nothing to do with it." He picked up his drink and gulped it down. "Nope, I'm not needed."

Valerie opened her mouth to scream, then closed it before any uncontrollable sounds could penetrate her lips. They sat in silence for a while, Isaac brooding and Valerie pouting. Finally, Valerie could stand it no longer. She left Isaac to his thoughts and went to the bar with Keith. "Oooh, he makes me sick!"

"You need to ignore him when he's like this," Keith told Valerie. They sat and talked for a while trying to take their minds off the drunk in the corner. The three of them had had many happy and eventful years together. Keith and Valerie could always round up a 'remember when' story. So that's what they did as they waited for Isaac to pass out.

Just when they thought it was safe to approach Isaac again, Ray-Ray walked into the Belante' Club with two of his boys. Valerie saw him as he hungrily searched the crowd like a lion crouching upon its prey. She nudged Keith. He turned to see Ray-Ray pointing in Isaac's direction. "I told Isaac that fool was gon' be trouble." He pulled out his gun. "You stay here."

"Oh no." She pulled up her right pant leg and grabbed her gun from her ankle strap. "It's on."

Ray-Ray's boys held watch at the door, while he advanced on Isaac. He pulled out his Glock and started blasting. A bullet went through Isaac's shoulder, his head jerked up, as the pain wrenched through his body. That sobered him up real quick. He grabbed his shoulder and stared at his assailant. He knew without a doubt that he was about to die.

What would they tell his son? Is death the end of everything? Or was Nina right, and some God was going to judge him for the wrong he'd done?

"Nooo!" Valerie yelled as she shot off several rounds, and dived on the table to cover Isaac. She took a bullet in her abdomen, pulled the trigger one last time, and then dropped the gun.

Ray-Ray fell to his knees and clutched his chest. Keith shot one of Ray-Ray's boys, as he tried to open fire on Isaac. The other gunman assessed the situation and made a fast break out the front entrance.

Keith turned and saw that Ray-Ray was still on his knees gasping for air. He purposefully trodded over to Ray-Ray, put his piece to his head and said, "I hope you prayed up, fool." Bang!

Ray-Ray's body made a big thud, as he dropped to the floor. His eyes were wide open, the horror of expected death painted on his face.

With blood gushing from his shoulder, Isaac stood over Valerie. She didn't look good. Her eyes raced back and forth. She was going in and out of consciousness. He looked around the room, nobody was moving. "Call an ambulance!" He screamed, then turned back to Valerie. "Come on, baby," he shook her. "You've gotta make it. Don't do this to me."

Her eyes fluttered, as she opened her mouth and whispered, "St... st... opped ... him."

"Yeah, baby, you stopped him." He reached out his hand to rub her hair and winced at the pain shooting through his left arm. "The ambulance is on the way. Just hold on, okay?"

Her eyes fluttered again, but she didn't respond.

"Isaac, come on man. We gotta get out of here," Keith told him. He looked down at Valerie, then at the crowd surrounding them.

"I can't leave her, Keith. That bullet was meant for me." He watched as blood trickled from Valerie's mouth. "If she dies, I'll be here with her. It's the least I can do."

Tommy Brooks, the bar owner, walked over to Isaac with a nervous look on his face. "The police are on the way. Y'all need to get on out of here."

Isaac looked from Valerie to Keith.

Valerie coughed up some blood.

Isaac knew she didn't have much time left. "Get out of here, Keith." He grabbed his friend's hand and squeezed it. "I appreciate everything you did tonight. Go – take care of that gun."

***

Nina and Lisa were on the couch wolfing down hot buttered popcorn and watching a somebody-done-me-wrong made for TV movie, when she heard the news break.

"Shots rang out at The Belante' Club. Two men and one woman were pronounced dead at the scene. Another man, Isaac Walker, age 31, was taken to Miami Valley Hospital. His condition is unknown at the moment," the announcer informed the listening audience.

Nina slowly stood up, one hand pointing at the TV, the other over her mouth.

"Oh my God!" Lisa said as she stared at the TV.

Nina clutched at her stomach and hunched over as a searing pain shot through her like a boulder tumbling down on an unsuspecting victim. "Aaaaah!"

Marguerite ran into the family room.

"Aaaaaaaaah!"

"What's wrong Nina? Is it time?"

She pointed at her belly and fell down on her knees, yelling and crying at the same time.

"Isaac's been shot," Lisa told Marguerite.

"Well don't just sit there, Lisa. Call for an ambulance!" Marguerite put her arms around Nina. "It's going to be all right, honey. Don't worry." *Lord, help us.*

22

*T*he entire Underwood family was in the family room.

They were stretched out on the floor playing Trouble together. Danae had fallen asleep in Kenneth's lap. Erin stretched and yawned. "I can't play anymore Mama. I'm sleepy."

Kenneth looked at Elizabeth. "Okay, you take Erin, and I'll put this one to bed."

Elizabeth smiled. "Alright – just remember who was about to win this game before you two chickened out." It had been two weeks since Kenneth left the house on one of his late night "me time" trips. He arrived home most evenings at six and ate dinner with the kids, just like he said he would. Tonight he was even playing games with the family.

"Who are you kidding? You know you can't beat me."

"All I have to do is pop a six and I'm home free."

"Yeah, but I'm only four spaces behind you, and you know I always come from behind to win."

Elizabeth picked up Erin and started to walk out of the room shaking her head. "No way you would have beaten me. There's just no way."

Kenneth stood up with Danae in one hand and the Trouble game in the other. "How 'bout we finish this little game in your room?"

Elizabeth stopped and turned to look at Kenneth. They hadn't been alone together in months. Was it wise to have him in her room this late? Shoot, this was her husband. "Okay, you're on!"

They put the kids to bed and met in Elizabeth's bedroom. Kenneth put the game in the middle of the bed and sat down. Elizabeth sat across from him and said, "Oh, it's on now." She pushed down the ball, praying for a six. The die popped up a three instead. She moved her man three spaces.

Kenneth popped up the six Elizabeth wanted. He smirked and moved his man to the slot directly behind hers.

Elizabeth started to sweat. She needed to pop up another three. Anything less or more would keep her on the board -- an unwilling target for Kenneth. "Hold on, it's hot in here. Let me change into my pajamas. I'll be right back."

"Yeah, buy all the time you want, but you know I've got you."

She ignored Kenneth's taunts and stepped into her walk-in closet. She took off her University of Dayton sweat-shirt, unhooked her bra and sighed at her liberation. If bra burning was still in fashion, Elizabeth would be first in line with a drawer full of 34Cs to fuel the flame. She looked on her shelf trying to decide what she wanted to sleep in tonight. Her eyes perused her nightgowns. They were all too sexy – no, not with Kenneth in the room. She had a pair of flowery flannel pajamas a friend had given her for Christmas. Kenneth always complained when she put those on, accusing her of putting up the "not open for business" sign. She definitely didn't want to bring up memories of their sex arguments. So, as she unzipped her faded jeans and slipped them off, she decided on the striped green silk pajamas.

"You've gained a little weight," Kenneth said.

Startled, Elizabeth jumped and turned to face Kenneth. She criss-crossed her arms over her breasts. Willing herself to act like there was nothing out of the ordinary about Kenneth talking to her while she was half-naked, she responded, "I was thinking about going on a diet, I - I just haven't had the time yet."

"No, don't lose weight, it suits you." Kenneth's eyes danced down Elizabeth's mocha sweetness and lingered in special areas that only he knew about. "You look good – real good."

"Kenneth, I'll be out in a minute, just let..." He looked longingly at her. Elizabeth read the hunger in his eyes, her stomach did the butterfly dance. "Is something wrong?"

Kenneth leaned against the wall, still appreciating the view before him. "What would you say if I told you that I want to sleep in here tonight, with my *wife*?"

"Kenneth, we haven't..."

He gently touched her lips to silence her protest. His eyes spoke volumes. "I want to be with you, Elizabeth. I've wanted this for some time."

Elizabeth didn't respond.

"Is that okay?"

Lord, how can I do this? He's hurt me so much. "Kenneth, I don't know – I mean, I'm – what if you..."

Kenneth walked over to his wife, uncrossed her arms and looked into her eyes. "You're gonna have to trust me." He hungrily kissed her.

She tried to back away from him. "I need time, Kenneth."

He pulled her back into his embrace. His hands trailed the plush curves of her breasts. "I need *you*." He nibbled on the soft flesh of her neck. And then, in a pleading tone he asked, "Please, baby?"

The butterflies were now in her throat as well as her stomach, so she answered by unbuttoning Kenneth's shirt and quickly tossing it on the floor. He smiled, and said, "That's right baby, drop it like it's hot."

Kenneth laid her on the floor of her walk-in closet, and gently removed her lace panties. His eyes danced over her body. "You're beautiful," he told her. Then he made hot, steamy, blow-your-mind love to the only woman God intended for him to have. His wife.

The game on their bed was completely forgotten, as Elizabeth and Kenneth entered into the game of love. Simple rules, winner take all. And since they were both in it to win it, by morning, a truce in favor of love would be called.

***

When Elizabeth woke, it quickly registered that she was snuggled up next to Kenneth – the way it used to be. She stretched and moaned trying to wake up. She turned over and looked at her sleeping husband. Remembering what they had experienced the night before, she prayed, *Lord, don't let us just enjoy each other in bed, and then not be able to hold a civil conversation outside this room. I want to adore this man. Help me to move beyond the hurt and resentment I feel. Help me to forget what went wrong, and concentrate on making things right between us again.*

Reluctantly, Kenneth opened his eyes, and gazed into his wife's face. He smiled, "Good morning."

"Good morning."

He yawned. "Mmm, what time is it?"

Elizabeth turned slightly to look at the clock on her dresser. "Oh, my God, Kenneth, it's seven-thirty!"

Kenneth jumped up. "I've got a meeting at eight. There's no way I'm going to make it," he told her, as he headed toward the bathroom.

"Will your people be upset?"

He turned back to his wife, kissed her on the forehead. "They'll get over it. And if not, last night was worth it."

Once Kenneth was off to work, Elizabeth woke Erin and Danae, fed and bathed them, then dropped them off at the babysitter's. She went back home, made some potato salad and a couple of sandwiches, threw it in a picnic basket with a 2-liter bottle of Cherry Seven-Up and drove to Kenneth's office. It had been a long time since she had surprised him with a picnic lunch. After his performance last night, Elizabeth felt that Kenneth deserved something special. She pulled into a space designated for visitor parking at TechStar and turned off her car.

Kenneth's secretary wasn't at her desk. That was a shame. Elizabeth knew that Kenneth replaced his old secretary about a month ago. Oh, well. Hopefully, she would meet the new addition to TechStar before she left.

She opened the door to Kenneth's office with a big grin on her face. She was just about to say, "Surprise!" when she saw Kenneth rearing back in his seat. A woman, in a too-tight fitting mini skirt had her hands on the arm of his chair. She was cheesing big time as she leaned into him.

Elizabeth dropped the picnic basket.

At least this one was a nappy head, albeit a completely gorgeous nappy head, Elizabeth thought as she cleared her throat. Kenneth and his strumpet turned and stared. Her wonderful husband jumped out of his seat and straightened his clothes. "Ah, Elizabeth, honey." He pointed at the woman standing next to him. "This is Cynda, my new secretary."

Elizabeth picked up the picnic basket, strutted over to Kenneth's desk and gestured to shake Cynda's hand. "Nice to meet you," she said, as she released her hand. "Tell me, Cynda, do you have a plan B?"

"Plan B? I guess I don't understand."

"Obviously your plan A was to sleep with my husband, move up in the company, and move me right out of my house. Since you are now fired, I guess you're in need of a plan B."

"Elizabeth!"

She turned to Kenneth. "What? I know you don't have a problem with me firing this woman!"

"I can handle this myself. I don't need you coming in here firing people."

"How dare you! You may have a short memory Kenneth Underwood, but I don't. I helped you build this lousy company. If it weren't for me, you wouldn't even know how to spell CEO."

Kenneth's hands balled into fists. Through clenched teeth he told Elizabeth, "I said, I can take care of things myself."

"That's just fine." She slammed the picnic basket on his desk. "You and Miss Upward Mobility, can enjoy the lunch I made, once you're finished with whatever you were about to do." She turned and stormed out of his office.

Driving down the street, she kept slamming her hands against the steering wheel and yelling, "Stupid, stupid, stupid." She knew not to let her guard down with that man. She knew he would only hurt her again, but like a fool, she fell for his mess anyway.

When Kenneth took her in his arms last night, she actually thought that maybe – just maybe, they would make it through the storm. But evidently Kenneth was just passing time, and any warm body would do.

"I can't let him get away with this." A convenience store was right up the street. Elizabeth decided to stop in and pick up a few supplies. "I'll show him."

She parked her car in front of the store, went in and bought a five-pound bag of sugar and a Snicker bar. She drove back to Kenneth's company and parked her Lexus next to his two-seater Mercedes. Opening the bag of sugar and the Snicker bar, she got out of the car. Locks on gas caps were probably invented for players like Kenneth. Fortunately for Elizabeth, Kenneth hadn't been smart enough to get his stuff locked down. She smiled as she pictured Kenneth's face when he realized his precious Mercedes would need a new engine. She twisted off the gas cap, sat the Snicker on top of Kenneth's car and lifted the sugar bag.

Beloved, not this way.

She firmly gripped the sugar. "Lord, how can You deny me this? You know how much he's wronged me."

Love does not keep track of wrongs.

She dropped the bag of sugar and flopped down on the ground between both cars. "Lord, I am such a failure at being a Christian. Why do You even bother with me?"

You are My beloved.

The tears flowed like Niagara Falls as she sat on the ground thinking over her life – her marriage – her walk with God. *Lord, Your love is so unconditional. It's too much for me to comprehend.* She rocked back and forth as the words to a worship song filled her heart – Speak to my heart. Change my life. Manifest Yourself in me. That's what the song said, and that's what she desperately needed. She bellowed, through the current of her tears, *"Change my life, Lord. I can't keep reverting to my old ways. I want to live for You -- I want to know that You are pleased with me."* She looked down at the trail of sugar that had spilled on the ground and cried harder. *"Oh, Lord I need Your help. I can't do this on my own."*

"Elizabeth." Snot and tears ran down Elizabeth's face as she turned to face her husband. He pulled his handkerchief out of his jacket pocket and handed it to her. "Are you okay?"

She wiped her face and blew her nose, "No."

"She took me by surprise, Liz. You've got to believe me. I called her in my office to go over my calendar – before I knew it, she was all over me."

Elizabeth didn't respond.

Kenneth sat down next to her. He put his hand under her chin and turned her face toward his. He stared at her, a look of confusion swept across his face. "Sometimes, when I look at you, you seem so different from what I know – I mean you look the same, but you act different."

"I don't feel so different. Look at me," she pointed at the bag of sugar. "I was getting ready to pour this down your tank."

He laughed, "Now that would have been the Elizabeth I know."

Elizabeth nudged him. "This is serious. Kenneth, I need help."

Kenneth tried to wipe the smile from his face. "Is this serious enough?"

She blew her nose.

"You know what I noticed?"

"What?"

"You didn't curse not once during this whole episode."

"I've been praying about my mouth. I guess Jesus heard me."

Her answer caught him off guard. He was temporarily speechless. When he opened his mouth, all he could say was, "You've really changed, haven't you?"

"God, I hope so."

He grabbed her hand and held it. He didn't look up, but she could tell that something was bothering him. Finally he said, "I just got a call from New Orleans. Mama's sick."

"Mama Rosa. What's wrong, Kenneth?"

He still wouldn't look at her, but she could hear the sadness in his voice when he responded, "Cancer. I've got to go home. I was hoping that you and the kids would go with me. This might be their last chance…"

"Excuse me."

Elizabeth and Kenneth looked up to see Cynda standing in their world with her three-inch high heels, too-tight mini skirt and a cardboard box in her hands. "What is it, Cynda?" Kenneth asked.

She tapped her heel and chewed on a piece of gum. "All of my stuff wouldn't fit in this box. When can I come back to get the rest of it?"

"I'll have your stuff mailed to your home address," Kenneth told her.

Cynda turned in a huff and strutted away from them.

"You fired her?"

"I told you I would take care of it."

"Why didn't you let me do it?" Elizabeth stood up. Her hands went straight to her hips. "I'm out here getting ready to put sugar in your tank because I thought you wanted to sleep with that, that---"

"Elizabeth, you've got to let me handle my own business."

"But – b---"

"I'm a man. Sometimes you're just going to have to back off," he told her, as he stood to be beside her.

"But this wasn't just your business. Don't you understand?"

"No, Elizabeth. You're wrong. It was my business to handle."

She clenched her fist. "Ooh, you make me sooo mad sometimes."

"Will you go to New Orleans with me?"

She relaxed her fist and looked at her husband. He hadn't said the words, but she knew he needed her. As mad as she was, nothing could keep her from being by his side at a time like this. "Of course we'll go with you, Kenneth."

23

*T*he swell of her belly was not completely gone, but there was no life there just the same. Nina could hardly believe how empty her belly felt. She found herself wondering, as she touched it, if life would ever exist there again. She turned her head slightly to the left and smiled. Life may not be in her belly – and maybe it won't ever be there again, but she was looking at the life she and Isaac had produced and he looked wonderful.

Her baby stretched his little arms and wiggled his body. He let out a wail that was much too big for his five-pound body. Nina picked him up. "What's the matter with the baby?" He continued to stretch and wail. "I know what you want." She opened her gown and laid him against her breast, he latched on and suckled until he was full. Nina laid the baby on her chest and rubbed his small back. He burped and fell back to sleep.

As she held her son in her arms, she closed her eyes and prayed. *Lord, I give him back to You. May he grow in the wisdom and knowledge of You. Help me to raise my son in the fear of You, Lord. May he forever keep Your commandments, my Lord, my King.*

"Praying again," Isaac said dryly as he opened the door. He walked over to the bed and looked down at the small bundle in Nina's arm. "My son, huh?"

Nina stared at Isaac. His left arm was in a sling, but other than that, he seemed no worse for the wear. He reached down and touched the baby's arm. At his touch, a small grin appeared on the baby's face. Pure joy showed on Isaac's face, as he looked at Nina. "Did you see that? He knows me."

Nina looked down at her baby and smiled.

"I wish I could hold him. Hopefully, I won't have this sling on for long."

"I heard what happened."

He had just spent three hours going over the events of last night with the police. They thought they could make him talk – roll over on Keith, but Isaac showed them. He sat down next to her bed and hung his head. "Valerie died."

"I know. I was sorry to hear that," she told him.

Isaac looked at Nina. Her eyes were moist. He knew she meant what she said, but couldn't understand why she would be sorry. Valerie was always doing stuff to Nina. If anything, he would have thought Nina would rejoice over Valerie's demise and he told her just that.

Nina laid her baby back in his crib. "I don't rejoice. My heart is sick over what happened to Valerie. I also mourn the deaths of those two men."

"Well, you can stop mourning for them. I'm glad that Ray-Ray is dead. If I'd killed that fat pig months ago, like I started to -- none of this would have happened."

Nina softly rubbed Isacc's cheek with the tips of her fingers. She looked into his dark cold eyes. "You carry around so much hatred, Isaac. You've got to learn to forgive."

Isaac knew Nina wanted him to forgive Ray-Ray, but he had never forgiven anyone their transgressions against him. And he wasn't about to start with the fat slob who murdered Valerie. Isaac had something else on his mind anyway, and he would have an answer. "What about me, Nina? Can you forgive me?"

"I already have."

Isaac stood up and walked over to the baby's crib. He stared at his son for a long while. "You know what the last thing Valerie said to me was?"

"What?

"I'll always love you." He looked up and she saw that the sadness in his eyes had returned. "She jumped in the way of a bullet that was meant for me because she loved me. You talk about God wanting us to forgive others, but tell me, Nina. How do I forgive myself for that?"

He put his right hand against his temple and rubbed. When that failed to soothe the ache in his head, he slammed his fist on the bed rail. "I never lied to her, you know – never promised her a rainbow – no crystal stairs. Shoot, my whole life, I never loved nobody but myself!" He looked down in the crib in front of him, let his hand move over his son's small body one more time. "But now…"

A mist clung to his eyes, but no tears fell. "Now I think I understand the type of love worth sacrificing for.

My Mama was the only person I'd ever been willing to die for… but she's been gone a long time now."

Nina lay in her hospital bed listening and watching. Isaac was battling with something. Something deep within himself. She didn't know what, and didn't know how to help him.

"Nina, we are family, you know. You've got to let me take care of you."

"We've already been through---"

"You don't have to live with me," he told her. "You've made it perfectly clear that your God is against any form of fun and happiness," he told her sarcastically.

She tried to sit up, but failed. "You've got it all wrong, Isaac. I didn't know happiness, until I knew Jesus."

Isaac flinched. "Anyway. I'll get you an apartment of your own. And if you're worried about living off me – you can manage the laundromat I own. You wouldn't even have to get a babysitter. You could just bring the baby to work with you."

She looked at Isaac. For the first time, she saw vulnerability in his eyes. She wasn't sure if it was because his girlfriend just died, or because his son was born. All she knew for certain was that he needed something. She knew Isaac believed that she and the baby could fulfill his needs. But Nina knew they would never be enough for a man like him.

"Will you let me help you?"

Sure, the situation would benefit her. She'd have a home for her son. She'd be able to take her son to work with her – all that sounds good. But once again she would be a taker. What could she give Isaac?

Give him Me, Beloved.

How, Lord? I don't know what to do.

Walk upright before him.

"I'll have to pray about it, Isaac. I'll let you know next week."

"Pray?" He waved his hand in the air. "Whatever," Isaac said, then pointed at his son. "By the way – what's his name?"

"I was hoping you would name him."

Isaac smiled. He thought about his little brother. His brother never got the chance to reach puberty. Dead before Isaac got out of that juvenile detention facility. He always said, if he had a son... "Donavan. His name is Donavan."

24

"*H*ow are you doing, Mama Rosa?"

Mama Rosa opened her eyes and frowned at Elizabeth. "You came with Kenneth, huh? I *must* be dying."

Elizabeth's smile turned upside down. She had hoped that this mean ol' woman could put aside her hatred of her now that she had cancer. She had hoped that she wouldn't play tug-o-war with her for Kenneth's affection this trip. But one look at Mama Rosa told Elizabeth that she had hoped in vain. Nevertheless, Elizabeth was determined not to cause Kenneth further pain by acting out her frustrations. "The nurse said that you respond well to having your arms and legs massaged. Would it be alright if I did that for you?"

A sharp pain went through Mama Rosa's body and she flinched. Her hands tightened around the iron rails on both sides of the bed. "Where's my son?"

"He'll be here in a minute. He's talking with the doctor." Elizabeth sat down and started massaging Mama Rosa's arms. She told her stories about the children and how excited they were to see her.

"You've kept those kids away from me."

Elizabeth didn't respond, she just kept massaging her mother-in-law's arms and legs.

"I told Kenneth you was no good."

"Mama!"

Elizabeth turned to her husband as he walked in the room. She put a finger to her mouth. "Shush. It's okay."

Kenneth walked around to the other side of the bed. "Mama, look who I brought to see you."

Mama Rosa opened her eyes, a smile crossed her lips. It was short lived. A shooting pain went through her body that left her panting and gasping for air.

Elizabeth thought she was about to pass out. It made her so nervous, she ran out of the room, found the nurse and pulled her back into Mama Rosa's room. The nurse calmly walked over to the bed and pulled out a tube which was connected to the bag over Mama Rosa's bed. "Rosa, can you hear me?" the nurse asked.

Mama Rosa shook her head.

"When the pain starts, push this button. This will give you some relief."

"What's that?"

The nurse looked to Kenneth. "It's morphine. It'll keep her comfortable."

The nurse left the room and Kenneth turned back to his mother. "Mama, why didn't you tell me you were sick?"

Elizabeth wiped the sweat from Mama Rosa's forehead.

"Son, I didn't want to bother you. You've got enough to worry about with your company and taking care of them kids."

"You still should have told me, Mama."

"I – I didn't want to add to your sorrows. With that s -- silly woman you married, I knew you already h--ad plenty." Her breathing was labored. Her words clipped, but that didn't stop her from getting another jab on his wife.

Kenneth looked to Elizabeth. He smiled half-heartedly, then gave her an apologetic shrug.

Elizabeth shook her head, and mouthed, "I can take it."

They stayed with Mama Rosa about two more hours. Elizabeth discovered that she had more restraint than she'd known existed on the face of the earth.

The woman hated her guts, but Elizabeth couldn't blame her. In the seven years she and Kenneth had been married, Elizabeth couldn't point to one occasion when she went out of her way to win the favor of her mother-in-law. They usually played tit for tat with Elizabeth giving as good as she got. Kenneth had never stood up for her. Never put his mother in her place.

Yet, Elizabeth felt ashamed that she had never allowed Kenneth to enjoy time spent with his mother. He was always busy breaking up an argument. She couldn't change the past, but today, she would give him this time with his mother. She not only endured her insults in silence, she went one better than that -- she grinned and took it.

Kenneth got a call on his cell phone, and the grinning stopped. She heard him say, "I thought I told you not to call me. I'm with family." He hung up the cell phone and turned to Elizabeth. "I'm going to get this number changed."

"If you hadn't given it out in the first place, you wouldn't have to worry about changing it now."

He changed the subject. "My cousin, Mark, wants us to stay with them. Is that alright with you?"

Elizabeth wondered if her dysfunctional family was ready to share living quarters with someone else. But hey, it was Kenneth's family. If he wasn't ashamed of all their drama, why should she sweat it. "That's fine."

***

Outside of Nina, Mark and Tina Smith had to be the nicest people she'd ever met. They were warm, friendly and inviting. It wasn't so much what they said, they just seemed to have a quality about them that made people feel comfortable. Elizabeth took her shoes off and walked to the kitchen to help Tina fix a snack for the family. In her head, she could hear her mother saying, "Girl, what's wrong with you? Where's your home training? Put those shoes back on." But, to tell the truth, even though Elizabeth had only been in the Smith's house thirty minutes, she felt like she was home.

"How long have you and Mark been married?" Elizabeth asked Tina, while she put mustard on a couple of sandwiches.

"Twenty-seven years," Tina replied with a big grin on her face.

"Wow! How'd you survive?"

"What do you mean?"

Elizabeth looked over at her husband. He was playing with the girls, and well out of earshot. "Kenneth and I have been married for only seven years." She hesitated for a moment. "Put it like this – some days, I'm glad we don't keep a gun in the house."

Tina laughed.

Mark looked up. "Hey, what's so funny in there?"

"You just entertain your cousin and leave us alone," Tina joked with her husband, then turned back to Elizabeth. "Every marriage has its ups and downs. Believe me, you don't go through twenty-seven years of marriage without going through the fire a time or two. You'll get through it."

Elizabeth's eyes moistened and a tear rolled down her cheek. Embarrassed, she turned away from Tina.

"Are you okay?"

Elizabeth shook her head.

Tina handed Elizabeth a paper towel, then asked, "Do you remember the Bible story about God telling Abraham that Sarah would conceive a child?

Elizabeth shook her head again, while blowing her nose.

"Remember how Sarah laughed at God?" Tina asked.

"Yes."

"Anybody with common sense probably would have laughed, right?" Tina leaned against the sink. "Sarah was looking at the situation for what it was. She knew her womb was dried up and that Abraham didn't have any function in his junction. So how on earth were they going to make a baby?

"God's response to Sarah's laugh is something I always lean on whenever I think I'm faced with a situation that seems immovable." Tina smiled. "*Is anything too hard for God?*' was all He asked Abraham."

"I don't know, Tina. I think our situation is beyond hope."

"I firmly believe that God likes to work in hopeless situations." Tina patted her on the back. "Just pray and obey God's Word, the rest is up to Him."

"But…"

"Elizabeth Underwood, is anything too hard for God?"

Elizabeth hung her head low, then answered, "No."

Tina handed one of the plates to Elizabeth. "You just keep praying. Let God handle the rest. Now let's get this food out there before they start a riot in here."

Elizabeth laughed and followed Tina out of the kitchen. Tina sat some chips and dip on the coffee table, then plopped down next to Mark. He put his arm around his wife and nibbled on her neck. "I think I'd rather have the cook than the food."

Tina giggled like a teenager at a high school prom.

Kenneth watched Elizabeth as she put the sandwiches down in front of him. He looked up at her questioningly.

She ignored the unspoken question in his eyes. "Well, eat up," Elizabeth told the group.

Elizabeth looked back at their hosts. They were hugged up on one corner of the couch – whispering, grinning and kissing.

"Kenneth, can you put the girls to bed when they finish?"

He was still staring at her. Elizabeth thought his eyes were trying to steal the secrets of her mind. "You're going to bed already?"

"Yeah, I'm tired," she turned to the others. "Goodnight everybody. I'll see you guys in the morning."

After several goodnight hugs, Elizabeth took a shower, and escaped into the sanctuary of the guestroom. She pulled a cream nightgown out of her suitcase and put it on.

Twenty-seven years and they were still lovey-dovey. Until interacting with the Smiths, Elizabeth had almost convinced herself that her and Kenneth's dysfunction was normal. NORMAL! What a joke. *I don't know how to fix it, Lord. So many things have happened. We've hurt each other over and over. How can we move past it, when it still hurts so much?*

She turned off the light and climbed into the modest, yet caressing bed, waiting on God to answer her questions. Hoping that it was not too late for her family.

Kenneth slid into bed with her about an hour later. He pulled Elizabeth close to him and rubbed up against her. "Mmm, you smell good," he told her as he kissed the back of her neck. His hands skillfully rubbing her inner thighs as he inched her gown up.

Elizabeth grabbed hold of her gown and pulled it back down.

Lifting his head off the pillow, Kenneth asked, "What's wrong?"

She started to tell him that on days when he wanted sex from his wife, he might want to turn off his cell phone. Instead, she told him, "I'm not in the mood."

"You're not in the mood?"

She scooted away from him. *Is he stupid or something? Come on, Lord. What man in his right mind would think that his wife would want to make love after his girlfriend tracks him down*

147

(right in front of his wife) all the way in New Orleans? "No, I'm not."

Kenneth plopped his head back on his pillow. "Have it your way, Liz."

Elizabeth turned into her pillow and cried. She tried to stop the tears but they flowed freely. Without her permission, she might add.

"Why are you crying?"

"I—I d-don't know."

He turned her around to face him. Snot drizzled down her nose. He grabbed some tissue off the nightstand and handed it to her. "I need to know, Liz. You were crying earlier too, when you were in the kitchen with Tina. What's wrong?"

She blew her nose, then said, "I just wish I could make you happy."

He hit his forehead with his palm. "Oh, so you think withholding sex and crying after I touch you, will make me happy?"

"There's no need to be a smart aleck," she smiled at him. "I just think we need to work through our problems before we make love."

"Okay. So what problems do we have?"

"Kenneth, let's see about your mother right now. We can discuss our problems when we get back home."

"I'm not going to get none tomorrow night either?"

Elizabeth expelled a heavy sigh and turned away from her husband. "Goodnight, Kenneth."

***

Mark took Kenneth to the gym to work off some steam. The tension had been boiling between Kenneth and Elizabeth the last two nights. Kenneth's mood was dark.

They were running on the treadmill when Kenneth opened up. "Man, I don't know what's wrong with that woman."

"Who? Elizabeth?"

"She won't let me touch her. As if I don't have enough to deal with."

"Didn't you tell me that your girlfriend called you while you were visiting Mama Rosa the other day?"

"Ex-girlfriend," Kenneth corrected.

"Does Elizabeth know that?"

Kenneth stopped the treadmill. He stood there to catch his breath. "Come to think of it, I don't think I ever told Liz that I broke it off with Denise."

"Well, cuz, what you waiting on?"

"I guess I was trying to hold out – leave myself a little escape room."

Mark turned the treadmill off, did a couple stretches then got off the machine. "Do you want room to escape?"

They got on the bicycles and started pedaling. "I don't know. Elizabeth is different now. She's not the same woman I wanted to escape from."

"What changed her?"

Kenneth looked embarrassed. "It feels weird saying this – but – well, Elizabeth got saved a couple months back."

"Same thing happened with my wife."

Kenneth looked at Mark, imploring him to continue.

"Yeah. We had just celebrated our twenty-first year of marriage. The kids were away at college. The house was always so quiet, and I started wondering – what's next? What do we do now?" Mark shook his head and smiled at the memory. "And then one day Tina came home and announced that she accepted Jesus into her heart. Well I didn't wonder what to do any more."

"What did you do?"

"Are you kidding, boy. I wasn't about to let my woman out do me. She was different when she came home – changed. I had always loved her, but man, after she received Jesus – I loved her more. I had to have what she had. So I went down to that church and accepted Jesus myself."

Kenneth hunched his shoulders. "How did that make your relationship better?"

"Well for one thing, whenever things aren't going right between me and my Queen, instead of thinking about leaving or finding a replacement – I pray about the situation. God is always there with an answer."

"Prayer, huh?"

"Yeah, and that's what I suggest you do. And when you get off your knees – wine and dine your wife. Help her to believe that she is the only woman in your life – for the rest of your life."

25

*O*n Christmas Eve, Kenneth brought Elizabeth an arrangement of roses.

Elizabeth smiled, "What's this all about?"

Kenneth put the roses down in front of Elizabeth, bent over and kissed her cheek. "These are for my baby."

"Don't you think Erin is just a little young to receive roses from a gentleman?"

"Not that baby," Kenneth snuggled up next to Elizabeth, "my other baby."

Elizabeth laughed. "Danae is really too young for roses."

He kissed her neck and slowly moved up to her ear. "Okay, then. I brought the roses for my woman -- my wife. What do you say to that, Mrs. Underwood?"

"I say, thank..." His mouth captured her "you", as he passionately kissed her. She was engulfed in his heat. She could feel his desire for her, his hunger. It felt good. She put her arms around his neck and kissed him back.

"Mmm, you feel so good." He pleasured her mouth again, and pushed her further into the sofa. His hands were delving into recently unchartered areas. "Oh, Liz, I need you."

"Kenneth, Kenneth." Elizabeth pushed at his chest. "Get up. We're on Tina's couch for God's sakes."

"So---"

"So, get up."

He moved off of her and tried to quiet the emotions that were running through his sexually deprived body. "Go get dressed. I'm taking you to dinner."

"What about the kids?" Why was he doing this?

"Mark and Tina are going to watch them."

"What about your mother? I thought we were going back there tonight." Does he really want to spend time with me, alone?

"I just left Mama. She told me to spend tonight with you."

Elizabeth looked shocked. "She did?"

Kenneth fessed up. "Well, I told her I wanted to spend Christmas Eve with you, and she said that was a good idea."

Elizabeth put on the red pantsuit she bought at Casual Corner. She decided not to worry about the reasons why, or what would happen tomorrow. She was going to enjoy herself tonight and let the chips fall where they may. And she had to admit; as she glanced at her reflection in the mirror, she looked good in red. Actually, she looked really good in red.

Kenneth whistled, when she walked out of the bedroom. "Mmh, I guess I'm going to have to be your bodyguard tonight."

Elizabeth smiled.

He took his wife to NOLA's, one of New Orleans' finest restaurants owned by Emeril LaGasse. Elizabeth watched him all the time on the cooking channel, so Kenneth thought she would enjoy visiting his restaurant.

Kenneth was right. From the time they walked into the restaurant, Elizabeth couldn't wipe the grin from her face. When the waiters seated them and took their order, Elizabeth put her hand on top of Kenneth's and rubbed it. "Thank you."

"No. Thank you. You've been wonderful with my mother and I know she can be a handful sometimes."

"Who, *your* mother?"

Kenneth laughed. "But seriously. I've never seen you so restrained. You're normally going at it with my mother the moment we walk in the door." He looked at her. She saw the pain in his eyes. "It means a lot to me."

She gently stroked the line of his jaw. "I am sorry about this thing with your mother." He looked away. Why men hated to let their emotions out, she would never know. "But I need you to know that I'm not the wonderful person you think I am. I've had to pray real hard so I wouldn't tell Mama Rosa off."

"But you did it."

"But I don't want you to think I'm special because of that. It wasn't me. Only God could have kept my mouth closed when your Mama told me she had been begging you to leave me for years."

"She said that?"

"She also told me, she was glad you had another woman."

Pain etched across Kenneth's face. "I'm sorry I hurt you."

"You know what they say, 'Time heals all wounds'." She looked away from him, her eyes glazed over. "I hope they're right," she mumbled to herself.

Kenneth turned her face back towards him. "I'm not seeing her anymore. You believe me, don't you?"

She shook her head. "Yeah." Tonight she was determined not to worry about it, but what about next month – next year?

Not one, but two waiters walked over to their table and placed a boatload of food in front of them. "Will there be anything else?"

Elizabeth looked at the waiters. She was impressed. "No, this is fine."

Kenneth ordered the grilled prosciutto-wrapped salmon with black pepper-parmesan grits. Yeah, he actually ordered grits and salmon. "This is good."

"Good? It's marvelous!" Elizabeth exclaimed as she bit into another Gulf Shrimp.

They continued feasting, then Kenneth said, "Mark told me that God helped him keep his marriage together for all these years. Do you think," he hesitated, "that if I gave my life to Jesus, it would help us?"

"Yes. But you can't do this just for me, or even for us. You have to get saved for yourself – that's the only way it will last."

"Yeah, I know that. I just wanted you to know that I'm thinking about it."

Finally, after months and months of shedding tears of pain and agony, she was able to shed a few tears of joy.

"I didn't mean to make you cry, Liz."

"I like to cry when I'm happy."

"I might be able to give you a few more tears of joy before the night is over." He shifted his eyebrows suggestively.

His eyes smoldered, while his loins yearned for the release that only she could give him. Elizabeth smiled. "You really want to be with me?"

He leaned over and kissed her. "You're the only one I want, baby."

***

Mama Rosa died the day after Christmas.

Elizabeth, Kenneth, Erin and Danae spent Christmas with Mama Rosa. They opened presents, laughed, joked and played around. Kenneth and Elizabeth did more playing than the kids did. Kenneth couldn't keep his hands off his wife, and Elizabeth wasn't complaining one bit.

She caught Mama Rosa looking at them a few times when she was lucid.

They ate dinner and the kids gave Mama Rosa a big hug. The next morning they were back at the hospital bright and early. The nurse called, she said that it wouldn't be long.

Elizabeth held Mama Rosa's hand. She didn't have much time, and she knew she had to talk to this woman about her eternal soul. *"Lord, forgive me for not doing this sooner."* She looked down at her mother-in-law. Her skin was gray and cold.

It's now or never, Elizabeth told herself. "Mama, have you accepted Jesus as your savior?"

"N" –cough- "never was much f-for church."

"Death is not the final resting place, Mama."

Mama Rosa gave her a quizzical glance. The best one she could muster in her weak state.

"No, Mama. It's only the beginning. When you die, you can be in paradise with Jesus."

Kenneth stood behind Elizabeth, listening.

"Re-really?" Mama Rosa asked.

"Yes. But you've got to make the choice. You have to accept Jesus into your heart. Do you want to be in paradise, Mama?"

Mama Rosa shook her head.

Whew! "Okay, I'm going to say a few words, and then I need you to repeat after me. I know it's hard for you to talk, so just repeat the words in your head. When you finish, blink your eyes, so that we know you've said the words."

"Say, I believe that Jesus is the Son of God."

A moment's silence. Mama Rosa slowly closed her eyelids and then reopened them.

"I believe that Jesus died and rose from the grave so that I might be saved."

Another moment's silence. Mama Rosa blinked again.

"I receive You now, into my heart Lord Jesus."

Silence. And then unmistakable joy erupted on her mother-in-law's face. Kenneth saw it too. His eyes filled with tears. He walked around to the other side of the bed and held his mother's hand. "You're going to be in paradise, Mama."

Elizabeth started singing. *"I sing because I'm happy. I sing because Christ has set you free. His eye is on the sparrow and I know He watches over you."*

"You have a beautiful voice," Kenneth told her.

Before Elizabeth could respond, Mama Rosa tugged on her daughter-in-law's hand. Elizabeth could tell that she was trying to say something.

"What is it, Mama Rosa?" Elizabeth bent down to get a little closer to her.

"I – I l-love you," she whispered, then lifted her eyes to heaven, jerked twice, and she was gone.

The flood gates opened. Elizabeth's tears gushed forth. "Oh, Mama, I'm so sorry. I wish we had more time."

Kenneth dropped his head and cried openly. He hugged this woman who had been good to him, and inhaled her scent one last time. This was his Mama. He was going to miss her everyday for the rest of his life.

"There's so many things I still need to say to you, Mama. So much I need to make up for." Elizabeth couldn't stop crying. She knew Mama Rosa was in heaven, but the guilt of how she had treated this woman wouldn't leave her.

Kenneth looked up at his wife. He grabbed her hand. "You've made up for it all, baby. I love you," he told her, and meant it.

Elizabeth grabbed some tissue and walked over to Kenneth. She softly wiped the tears from his face, their eyes locked. Kenneth pulled his wife into his arms and held her. For a brief moment in time, they stood at both the end of things and the beginning.

26

New Year's came and went. It was now 1999, and nothing changed but the date. Nina still had to earn a living, so she prayed and prayed about the situation. By the time she was finished praying she was convinced that God was okay with her working in Isaac's laundromat, and took Isaac up on his offer. Marguerite had a mild heart attack the week after Nina was released from the hospital, so she told Isaac that she did not need a place to stay. She and Donavan continued to live with Marguerite. Nina watched over her, and made sure she took her medication as the doctor instructed. Marguerite's house was only two blocks away from Isaac's laundromat. Nina walked to work every morning with her sweet son in her arms. Working at the laundromat wasn't bad. She wiped the machines down and called the repairman when something went wrong – which was often. She handled the budget and as an added bonus, to help moms get their work done, she did story time for the kids.

This morning three children accosted her as soon as she walked into the laundromat. "Tell us a story, Miss Nina. Come on, please."

"Okay, okay. Give me a second and I'll be right back." She unlocked the office door, put her purse inside her desk drawer and parked Donavan's stroller. She walked back out to the wash area, pulled up a chair, sat Donavan on her lap and yelled. "Anybody who wants to hear the story about the rich man and Lazarus come over here." Several children ran to Nina. "Sit down in front of me," she told them.

"Okay. Now there was a rich man who wore the best clothes from the best designers. He had anything and everything he ever wanted all his life. But there was also a beggar named Lazarus, who was full of sores. He laid on the rich man's porch begging to eat the crumbs that fell from his table. The dogs came and licked his sores. When the beggar died, he was carried by the angels to heaven. The rich man also died and went to hell..."

Nina continued her story. She told the children how the beggar now lived in comfort while the rich man lived in torment. Once she finished, one of the children asked, "Why didn't the rich man want to help the beggar?"

"Some people are just like that," she gently told him.

"Nina!"

She jumped, and turned to face the cold stare Isaac presented her with. What have I done to him now?

"I need to see you in the office," he commanded, then walked into the office without waiting for her response.

"Is something wrong?" Nina asked as she walked into the office and closed the door.

Isaac took Donavan out of her arms. "So, was the rich man in your story supposed to be me?"

"No, Isaac. It was simply a story about a man – any man who enjoyed all of what life had to offer, and was too selfish to share even a crumb with someone in need."

"Most of them beggars crying 'I need food. I haven't ate in three days,' just want some money so they can buy crack."

"And some are really hungry, and don't have a place to stay."

"Let 'em get a job. They can get all the food they need then."

Was Isaac some evil demon sent straight from the pit of hell just to cause her demise? He was never interested in anything that would help anyone else, only in the things that profited him. "Jesus said when we feed the hungry, it is as if we are feeding Him."

Isaac sat down behind the desk and bounced Donavan on his knee. "Which is it, Nina? Last week you told a bunch of kids that God don't want us to cast our pearls before swine. But this week, you say we should help every crack head on the street."

Lord, I need Your help. I feel like an utter failure when I try to tell people of Your goodness. "I'll be out front if you need me," she told him as she opened the door and left.

Nina moved through the laundromat, talking with customers, and unclogging washing machines. Once behind the counter, she concentrated on sorting through the clothes that needed mending. The seamstress would be at work in an hour or so and she wanted to make sure everything was in order.

Isaac walked out of the office without the baby. He looked over at Nina. "He's asleep. I put him in his crib." He locked the office door, then threw her the key.

"Thank you," she said, then went back to sorting the clothes.

"Excuse me, can you help me? I put six quarters in that machine." The customer pointed to the third washing machine in the row directly in front of Nina. "But it won't work."

"Sure, I can help you," Nina told her as she stepped from behind the counter.

27

*E*lizabeth was in bed, thinking about getting up to fix her family some breakfast, when the door to her bedroom opened. She immediately recognized the smell of bacon and eggs, sat up and smiled at Kenneth as he laid the tray on top of the bed. "Breakfast in bed huh, what'd I do to deserve this?"

Kenneth winked at her. "I'll never tell."

She bit into a piece of toast. "If you do, I'd have to kill you," she said, laughing at her own joke.

Kenneth sat on the bed, mesmerized. "I like to hear you laugh." He grabbed her hands and brought them to his lips and one by one he gave each finger a sweet, gentle kiss. "I want to hear that sound every day."

Elizabeth couldn't think of anything to say, so she started shoveling bacon and eggs in her mouth. It still amazed her that she and Kenneth had moved past the hurt of his affair. When they arrived home after Mama Rosa's funeral, they sat down and actually talked. Elizabeth told Kenneth about the feelings of rejection she'd experienced as a young adult. So many guys dumped her for this new girl or that girl. "I needed you to be different," she told him.

Kenneth told Elizabeth all that was in his heart. "The first day I met you, I knew you were someone I could love. You were so different from me." He held her hand and looked into her eyes. "You were confident, vibrant... ready to take on the world. I had never been like that, until you helped me to believe that I could accomplish more, do more."

She gave him a half smile as she said, "And still, that wasn't enough."

Kenneth let go of her hands and stood. He turned his back to her. "No, it wasn't. Because you were also overbearing, selfish and destructive." He shook his head, and turned back to face his wife. "I kept trying to figure out how one person could possess so many characteristics that I love, and still have so many that I hate."

She stood to move closer to her husband. "You gave up on me... on us."

Kenneth closed his eyes and released a heavy sigh. "Yes."

"How do I know you won't give up on us again?"

Kenneth looked at Elizabeth. He could see the silent plea in her eyes for reassurance. She was asking him about tomorrow, but the only thing he was sure about was right now. His hands softly stroked her face. "I can't make promises about a tomorrow that I can't see. But walk with me, Liz. Let's see what the future holds for us, together."

Kenneth did not promise her a life of eternal fidelity as she had hoped. He asked her to walk into the future with him, and see what was in store for them. Just then, she remembered the gentle words Tina spoke to her the night she cried in her kitchen, *"Is anything too hard for God?"* Her resolve began to build. She would walk into the future with Kenneth, but she would do it with her faith and trust in God.

The days evolved into weeks, and she continued to walk with Kenneth and trust God. And now, she was eating breakfast in bed. A breakfast that her husband prepared just for her.

"So what's on your agenda today? I was hoping I could hang out with you."

Elizabeth choked. Kenneth had to hit her on her back a few times before the bacon dislodged from her throat. She wiped her mouth and questioned Kenneth. "You want to spend the day with *me*?"

Kenneth rubbed her back. "Not just today, baby. Tomorrow, next week, next month, next year. Ah heck, let's just spend the rest of our lives together, and call it quits when we're so old and decrepit that no one else will want us. What do you say?"

"If you keep saying stuff like that, you're going to send me into cardiac arrest."

Kenneth smiled at her. "I love you, Elizabeth. I'll do whatever it takes to prove that to you." He lifted her chin, causing her to look directly into his eyes. "When I'm done loving you, you won't be able to recall a time when the loving stopped. That's my pledge to you, baby."

Tears. She was full of tears these days.

Kenneth wiped a tear from her face. "Some more happiness?"

Elizabeth embraced her husband. Oh, how she loved this man. *Please, God. Don't let this feeling end.*

"This might not be the best day. I joined the choir at my church, and we have practice this morning. I guess I can miss reh…"

"Hey, it's off to church we go. I'm on your schedule today."

Elizabeth dressed in a hunter green Jesus Sport jogging suit. She opened her dresser and pulled out a gray sweatshirt and handed it to Kenneth. "If you're going to hang with me today, you might as well dress like me."

He read the front of the sweatshirt, "Jesus Sport." He looked at Elizabeth. "That's cute, where'd you get this?"

"A couple at my church own a clothing line. SPORT stands for Sanctified People Of Righteousness and Truth. Nice, huh?"

Kenneth rubbed his hands over the shirt. "This is quality stuff."

"Do you think I would buy it, if it weren't?"

Kenneth smiled. He knew how picky his wife was. "Does my sweatshirt come with a pair of jogging pants?"

"I'll go online and order you a pair."

"They have a website, huh?"

"Yeah."

"Well, order me a couple more sweat suits while you're at it. This is comfortable," he told her after putting on the sweatshirt and a pair of jeans.

Kenneth tagged along with his wife the entire day. He sat quietly in the back as she practiced a few songs with the church choir. He was patient when they went to the mall to exchange a jacket that was too big for Danae, but ended up bringing home two other outfits. It turned out to be a pretty good day for the Underwood family.

By the time they made it back home, everyone was ready for bed, but not necessarily sleep.

28

"*I* need to get this stuff hemmed," the customer said as she slung some clothes on the counter.

Nina was just putting Donavan down for his mid-morning nap. She pulled the cover over her son as he lay in the bassinet behind the counter. Nina turned to greet the customer, and the smile that was on her lips vanished, as she recognized the woman. "Cynda. How... how are you?"

"Not bad." Cynda told her as she tossed her hussy blonde hair.

Cynda was wearing a hip length leather zip jacket, cotton ribbed turtleneck and black leather pants with Italian leather boots to match. Not only was she dressed well, but she was gorgeous, no mistaking that. Nina touched the collar of her gray swing dress. A Wal-Mart original, but she had purchased it second hand at the goodwill store last week.

"How long will it take to hem these pants?"

Nina picked up the clothes and examined them. "Two pair of pants – it shouldn't take more than a week."

"A week!" Cynda picked up a pair of red stretch pants. "I need these pants back by Friday. Isaac and I are going to Chicago this weekend." Nina's head jerked up. "And I intend to be wearing these pants when we leave."

Hurt registered in Nina's eyes before she could talk herself out of it. *Lord, take the pain away. I don't want to be hurt anymore by Isaac and his women. They shouldn't matter to me. I belong to You now.* "If you can try these pants on," Nina pointed to a dressing room, "I'll see how much of a hem you need – and we'll try to get them done for you this week." Cynda remained in the laundromat for a grueling twenty minutes. Nina prepared the hemline, as Cynda raved on and on about Isaac. She said that they were back together – and would stay together. Nina tried to imagine this woman as Donavan's stepmother, but shuttered at the thought.

Later that afternoon, another one of Nina's ex-wife-in-laws came into the laundromat. Nina was sitting at the desk behind the counter sorting through receipts and entering the daily totals into a spreadsheet. Keith helped her set up the file. He was good with computers. Isaac walked into the laundromat. A young woman in a baseball shirt and jeans laughed with him as they entered. Isaac went into the office. The girl stood by the counter tapping her long nails.

Donavan woke up with a shout. Nina put down her receipts and bent down to pick him up. "What's the matter? I know you're not hungry. You just want Mama to hold you." She swung him in the air. "Yeah, I know that's what you want."

"Where on earth did you get that homely dress?"

Nina stopped swinging Donavan. "Excuse me?"

"And look at those nails. Honey, you simply must take better care of yourself."

Nina put Donavan in the pouch she had strapped around her. It allowed her to work and carry him around at the same time. She looked at her nails. They did look bad, but pulling lint out of dryers and clogs out of washing machines didn't seem to be a conducive environment for salon-beautiful nails. "Do I know you?"

"I wouldn't waste my time getting to know the likes of you." The girl spat the words at her.

"Okay." Nina said, reminding herself to be calm. "Is there something I can do for you?"

She put both hands on the counter and twisted her shoulder in the direction of Nina. "Yeah, there's something you can do for me. You can get your baby's Mama drama out of this laundromat and go find somebody else to support you."

Nina looked in the direction of the office. She heard Isaac come into the laundromat, but was so intent on getting her daily log finished that she didn't notice his companion. Obviously, this woman must have entered with him. "Isaac doesn't support me." The girl gave her one of those 'yeah right' looks. "He does sign my paycheck, but I work hard for every dime I make. I pay my own bills." Donavan started kicking, she adjusted his position inside the pouch. "Believe me, the only thing going on between me and Isaac is the care of our son."

"And why would you feel the need to explain that to *this* chicken head?" Isaac asked Nina as he approached.

"Somebody needs to explain something. How am I supposed to know what's going on between you and Nina." She was talking to Isaac, but her head was doing the jerk in Nina's direction. "I mean, you got her working at your place of business and all."

Nina saw the cold blooded anger in his eyes, but couldn't tell if it was directed at her or this young woman on the opposite side of the counter. "Hand me my son."

Nina wasn't sure if she wanted her son mixed up in Isaac's drama. "He's a little restless…"

"I said, hand me my son!"

She pulled Donavan out of his pouch and handed him over to his father. Isaac smiled at his son and tossed him in the air a few times. Donavan laughed and threw out his arms for more. "You're getting big, boy." He cradled him in his arms, as he smiled down at the joy of his life. "Tell me Deanna, where else do you think Nina could work, and be able to take care of my son at the same time?"

She hunched her shoulders. "Nowhere, I guess."

Isaac kissed Donavan on the nose, then handed him back to his mother. He turned to Deanna. His eyes were cold and deadly. "Then I suggest you keep your mouth shut."

Deanna put her hands on her hips. "Now just wait one minute…"

Isaac took a step forward, grabbed Deanna's arm and squeezed, with his index finger in her face he said, "Nobody messes with my family. You got that?"

Deanna twisted her arm, trying to loosen Isaac's hold. It was unrelenting. "Let go of me!"

He released her with a shove.

Deanna stumbled, righted herself, then looked at Isaac with a surprised expression on her face. Without saying a word, she turned, and strutted out of the laundromat.

He turned his attention to Nina. "If Keith shows up, tell him to meet me at the house," Isaac told her, then left without a backward glance.

Nina sat down behind the counter with a heavy heart. She closed her eyes and silently prayed. *Oh Lord, will Isaac ever learn how women should be treated. I pray for him constantly, I tell him about You every chance I get, but nothing seems to work.*

"Praying for me?"

Startled, Nina opened her eyes and looked up. Keith was leaning on the counter, smiling, looking just as happy and carefree as ever. Nina stood up and shifted Donavan from one hip to the other. "You snuck up on me, Keith. I'm going to have to put a bell on that door. I didn't hear you come in."

"Let me see my Godson." Keith grabbed Donavan and started bouncing him up and down. Donavan cooed and giggled. "You were praying, weren't you Nina? Isaac says you pray all the time."

"Yes, Keith, I was praying." Nina came from behind the counter, picking up trash and checking the dryers for lint build up.

Keith walked behind her, still bouncing Donavan up and down. "Do you ever pray for me?" he whispered.

Nina was pulling an abundance of lint out of one of the dryers. She threw it in the trash, and looked up at Keith. "Not a day goes by that I don't pray for the peace of God to rule in your life." She softly touched his arm. "Every time I see you, you're smiling, but something, I don't know what, but something has hurt you. God will take the pain away."

Keith looked away, unable to respond.

"Miss Nina, Miss Nina, tell us a story." Four little girls ran toward Nina and Keith. "Please… come on, you tell the best stories."

"Donavan isn't sleep yet. Let me get him situated…"

Keith pushed her toward the children. "Go ahead, Nina. I'll hold Donavan while you entertain them."

She looked at Keith, trying to make sure he was okay with holding Donavan, while she told the children a story. He didn't seem to mind. "Okay, gather around." Four little girls eagerly sat down, as two boys and another girl joined the circle. Nina put her hand on her chin. "Let me think for a minute." Her fingers tapped her cheeks a couple times. "Yes. Okay, I've got one," she told the kids, then paused for effect before beginning.

"There was a woman who was a sinner. When she heard that Jesus sat down to eat at the Pharisee's house, she brought an alabaster box filled with fragrant oil, and stood at His feet crying. In fact, she cried so much that she began to wash His feet with her tears, and wiped them with the hair on her head. She kissed His feet and anointed them with the fragrant oil.

Now when the Pharisee who had invited Jesus saw this, he spoke to himself, saying, 'This Man, if He were truly a prophet, would know who and what kind of woman this is who is touching Him. She is a sinner.'"

"What type of woman was she?" one of the kids asked.

"Yeah, what'd she do?" another asked.

"She was a prostitute. But that doesn't matter. There are many sins committed by man that would cause people to think they are not worthy of forgiveness."

"Like what?"

"Well, like murder for example." Keith shifted in his seat, but kept playing with Donavan as if he was not the slightest bit interested in the story that was masterfully keeping six, seven, and nine year olds engaged while their parents washed, dried, and folded their clothes.

"Anyway, Jesus knew what the Pharisee was thinking, so He said, 'Simon, I have something to say to you.' Simon said, 'Teacher, say it.'

"Jesus told him, 'there was a certain man who loaned money to two men. One owed several thousand dollars, and the other only ten bucks. Neither of them could pay back his debt, so he freely forgave them both. Tell Me, Simon, which of them will love him more?'

"Simon answered and said, 'I suppose the one that he forgave the most.' Jesus said to him, You got that right. Then He turned to the woman and said to Simon, 'Do you see this woman? I came to your house. You did not give Me water to clean My feet, but she has washed My feet with her tears and wiped them with the hair of her head. You did not kiss Me, but this woman has not stopped kissing My feet since the time I came in. You did not anoint My head with oil, but this woman has anointed My feet with fragrant oil. Therefore I say to you, her sins, which *are* many, are forgiven, because she loved much. But to whom little is forgiven, the same loves little.'

"Jesus then said to the woman, 'Your sins are forgiven.' And those who sat at the table with Him began to say to themselves, 'Who is this Man who even forgives sins?'

"Jesus didn't pay them any attention, He looked at the woman and said, 'Your faith has saved you. Go, and sin no more.'"

Keith handed Nina the baby without so much as a goodbye or good riddance. He expeditiously moved toward departure.

"Keith, what's wrong?" Nina asked as she watched his swift exit.

"Nothing!" Keith yelled, already out the door. "I've got to catch up with Isaac."

Nina didn't see Keith again until a month later. She was in the office, kneeling in prayer before beginning her day, when the door to the office was yanked open. Isaac walked in, laughing and talking nonstop. Nina heard someone say, "Shhh."

"Man, if I had to be quiet every time she started praying, I'd never be able to talk."

Nina raised up and greeted Keith and Isaac. Donavan was asleep. She left him in the office, as she went into the common area of the laundromat to give Isaac some privacy.

She turned on the neon 'open' sign, got a rag and a bucket of soapy water and started washing down the washers and dryers. By day's end, they would look dusty and grimy again, but that didn't stop her from freshening up the equipment for today's users. She was diligent about her work, never wondering if anyone appreciated the love and care she put into making this laundromat a clean and safe environment. It was just her reasonable service.

Nina looked up as a woman in her late thirties walked into the laundromat. Her clothes were tattered and worn, her eyes hollow and lifeless. One look and Nina knew this was a woman acquainted with grief. And for a brief moment, when their eyes locked, Nina felt the pain this woman carried.

"Excuse me," the woman said as she approached.

"Yes?"

She tried to move a little closer to Nina but stumbled. Too weak to stand, she sat down on the bench next to a group of dryers. "I'm real hungry. Can you spare some change so I can get something to eat?"

Isaac and Keith walked out of the office tossing Donavan back and forth between them.

"Of course I can." Nina pulled some money out of her pants pocket and counted fifteen dollars. She hoped this money would last until she got paid on Friday. There were a few things she needed from the grocery store, but this was a much better cause than hoarding it for herself. "All I have is fifteen dollars, but you're welcome to it."

"Oh no you don't!" Isaac yelled as he grabbed the money out of Nina's hand before she could give it away. "Can't you read?" He snapped at the woman, then pointed at the sign on the door. "No panhandling!"

Nina was mortified. "Isaac, give me back that money!"

"No, I'm sick of this." He held the money out of her reach. "You're a sucka' for a hard luck story, ain't cha? You won't let me give you nothing, but you're about to give away money that I know you need."

"You don't understand, Isaac." Her eyes filled with water. "God would want me to do this."

"And I'm telling you that you won't throw your money away like this."

The woman stood up and started to walk out of the laundromat. "Wait... please, wait." Nina turned back to Isaac. "I will not obey you over God, Isaac. He is Lord, not you." She turned back to the woman and told her, "I don't have much food at my house, but all that I have is yours."

"Over my dead body!" Isaac exclaimed, then handed the money back to Nina. "Give her all your money if you want, but she will not enter the place my son lays his head."

"What's your name?" Nina asked the woman when she handed her the money.

"Theresa."

"Well Theresa, if you stop back here tomorrow, you and I can have lunch together – my treat."

Theresa hesitated, then asked, "Will he be here?"

Nina looked at Isaac. He was fuming. "No. He's never here during lunch time."

"Then I'll be back."

"See you tomorrow."

Donavan started to squirm in Keith's arms. Isaac grabbed his son, then stood in Nina's way as she tried to resume her cleaning. "Have you lost your mind? Why did you tell that derelict to come back here tomorrow?" Nina didn't answer, she just kept scrubbing the dirt and grime off the washing machines.

Isaac grabbed her arm. The rag fell to the ground. "Answer me!"

She looked Isaac in the face. She matched his anger with compassion as she told him, "She needs my help."

"She's taking advantage of your kind heart."

Nina shook her head. "You're wrong. No one can take advantage of what I do in the name of the Lord."

He let her arm go and stepped back. "I want you to stop all this God-Lord-Jesus, nonsense. Do you hear me?" He waved his hand in the air. "God is not sitting in the sky just waiting to do you a favor. Okay?" He handed her the baby, then told an awestruck Keith that they were leaving. Before leaving, Isaac turned back to

Nina and said, "There's no reward for being a good Samaritan, Nina. In this world, you get what you take.

29

*I*saac couldn't sleep.

His subconscious mind kept going over that awful night when Valerie was shot. To make matters worse, Cynda was in his bed. She took all the appeal out of 'loving the one you're with.' He threw back the covers and got out of bed. He went over to the window of the high rise apartment and stood there looking down at the city. Here he was, back in the windy city, his old stomping grounds. He loved coming home. He would round up his boys and whatever woman lucky enough to be on his arm that night, and they would get their party on.

But for the past two nights he had been with Cynda, and as usual she found a way to get on his last nerve. This was his second trip to Chicago in a month. The first trip with Cynda wasn't so bad. She was still in her grateful mode. Happy that Isaac took her broke butt back, after she got fired from that technical consulting firm.

He wanted to get out of Chicago, head back to Dayton, but he still had unfinished business. One more night and all would be done. One more night and he would be able to see his son again. He stuffed his hands in his pockets and leaned against the windowsill. Who was he kidding? There was someone else he couldn't wait to see again. Nina, the Jesus freak.

Just thinking about the situation caused Isaac to shake with frustration. He burned for Nina, but she burned for Jesus. She spent all her spare time with a dead man, and His friend the Holy Ghost. To hear her tell it, this Holy Ghost lives inside of her. And if that ain't freaky enough, her Holy Ghost is supposed to help her commune with this dead man. Who, according to Nina, is not dead at all. He's alive. "Hmm, show Him to me," Isaac mumbled.

Cynda rolled over in bed, stretched her arms out and squinted. "Huh?"

Isaac turned around. "Nothing, go back to sleep."

Cynda rolled back over and quickly obeyed. Isaac moved away from the window and flopped down in a wing-back chair. Depression overwhelmed him at times when he least expected it. Right now, he was in one of the sourest moods he'd known in a long time. He just couldn't understand why Nina had fallen in love with this God she couldn't see or touch. He used to be her god! He used to be the center, but now everything was about this God in the sky.

Last week, Keith had asked him if he thought all that stuff Nina was yapping about was true, as if he had some kind of truth meter or something. Besides, if he did have some kind of truth detector, he wouldn't have to use it. He knew Nina wasn't trying to run a scam. No, she believed every word she said. But Isaac didn't believe it. Not a word of it.

For one thing, if this God of hers did exist, He wasn't the forgiving God Nina was always going on and on about. He was a God that repaid evil with evil. If not, then what were cancer, AIDS, and a fast bullet to the head all about? What was his Mama's death about?

Cynda stirred.

Isaac let out an exasperated sigh. Now I'm going to have to deal with this conceited heffa, Isaac thought as he walked over to the closet and pulled out an off white velour-jogging suit.

"What time is it?" Cynda asked as she rubbed her eyes.

Isaac threw the jogging suit over the wing-back chair. He didn't look Cynda's way as he strolled into the bathroom to take a shower.

***

"You ain't ready yet?"

"I'm coming, just give me a minute. I need to finish putting on my makeup."

Isaac sat on the bed in a huff. If he didn't need Cynda to drive his shipment home, he'd leave her slow behind.

Cynda walked out of the bathroom with a smile on her face. "Perfection takes time, baby." She twirled around so he could view the snug fit of her red stretch pants, and her low cut straight-off-Manhattan-Street-costing-him-a-fortune drawstring top to match.

He pictured Nina in her hand-me-downs. He couldn't explain it, but she made those rags look elegant.

This tack head, with her three-inch high heels, made the best look a mess. "Let's go."

There was a chill in the air as they stepped out of the hotel. The bellhops scurried to get their cars. Two others brought down their bags. Limousines filled the entryway parking area. Isaac was once again struck by the beautiful landscape that graced the entrance of the hotel. A flowerbed surrounded four well manicured trees. He turned to check out the landscape on the side of the hotel and caught a glimpse of a bum leaning against the building, bottle in hand. The bell pulled Isaac's Cadillac and his Benz in front of them.

Isaac stepped away from the car, and walked over to the man leaning against the building. The closer he got, the more he wished for a gas mask. "Whew, dog, you stank!" Isaac told him.

The man put the bottle to his lips and took a swig. He wiped his mouth with the back of his dirty hand. "What's it to you?"

Isaac pulled a wad of money out of his jogging pants, took the clip off, and counted out five one hundred-dollar bills. He threw the money at him. "That ain't for booze. Go get yourself cleaned up, and get some food in your stomach."

Cynda's mouth opened and closed several times.

"What's wrong with you?"

She pointed at the bum. "You just threw all that money away. Do you know what I could have bought with that?"

He looked her up and down, and smirked. "Don't you have enough three-inch heels and skin tights?"

She put her hands on her hips. "If you don't like how I dress Isaac, just say so. You don't have to go throwing good money away on every bum in the street."

"Maybe it'll bring me luck." He watched the bum walk away with a little pep in his step. "Let's go."

Isaac jumped in the Cadillac. Cynda got in the Benz and followed him from Chicago's glamour to the ghetto. South of downtown along State Street used to be called the Black Belt. It was the ghetto he grew up in, and it was the place Spoony conducted his business transactions.

Every time Isaac drove through this place he got a bad taste in his mouth. He might be able to roll up to this city and sleep in just about any hotel he wanted to now, but he had not forgotten what his grandmother told him about the racial riots of 1919 and the restrictive covenants of 1923 that locked his people down in the ghetto with no hope of getting out. That restrictive covenant wasn't lifted until 1947, but Isaac knew that some landlords were still living by those old rules. "This place is worse than the South," he said as he pulled up to Spoony's small frame house.

"Spoony Davison, my man."

"What's up, player?" They clasped hands, but Spoony's snake eyes studied Cynda from top to bottom. "That you?" He asked Isaac, while nodding his head in Cynda's direction.

Isaac looked over at Cynda, but directed his comment to Spoony. "I see your woman hasn't settled you down yet. Still chasing every skirt in sight."

He lifted his hands and shrugged. "Don't hate the player, hate the game."

Isaac laughed. "So, you gon' let us in, so we can get down to business or what? I don't have all day."

Spoony opened the door and did a dramatic sweep with his arms. They went down to the basement where Spoony conducted business and sat down on Spoony's black leather sofa and relaxed.

"Heard about the drama that went down. I was real sorry to hear about Valerie."

Isaac stretched out his feet. "Yeah. I still wish I could change what happened. But it is what it is."

"She hung in there with you for some years."

Cynda twisted in her seat. Spoony's wife brought three glasses of iced tea. Isaac looked up at her as he took his drink off the tray. Her face was sunken in. She looked like she had been through sixty years of trauma. "Linda, why you still with this thug?" Isaac asked her, and meant it.

She hunched her shoulders and smiled, but didn't answer.

"Cause I'm the best deal she gon' get." Spoony answered for her, as she walked back up the stairs. He turned to Isaac and lifted his glass. "To Valerie. She died like a soldier, and for that, she has earned much respect."

Isaac wanted to tell Spoony that Valerie died like a sucka; loving a man who, at best, only liked her some. But he wouldn't say that about Valerie. No, he'd smile as their glasses joined in the air in salute to a fallen street heroine. And he'd continue to live with the guilt of her death.

"Has anybody ratted ya' boy out yet?"

"Naw." Isaac thought about Keith's actions lately, all nervous and preoccupied. He got the shakes every time they talked about things that needed to be taken care of for the business. He just wasn't himself, wasn't acting like the Keith he knew. "Sometimes I think he's gon' rat his own self out."

"Mmmh, maybe he don't have the stomach for real action."

"He's never flinched before. Something else is going on, I just don't know what it is."

Spoony wiped his hands on his pants, stood up and walked over to the pool table. "Let's get down to business." Isaac and Cynda joined him at the table. Spoony popped open a briefcase. "Ain't it pretty?"

"Sweet Isis," Isaac said as he picked up one of the bags of cocaine, and started counting the rest.

"Twenty kilos, just like you requested." He motioned with his arms. "What? A nigga can't be trusted, or what?"

Isaac looked over at his mentor and smiled. "A wise man once taught me to trust no one. He told me, 'keep your pistol under your pillow just in case you got to shoot the one you sleeping with'."

Spoony laughed. "Okay, okay. Count 'em. Matter-of-fact, let's sample the product." He walked over to the bar, opened one of the bags, threw a little snow on the counter top and lined it up. "Who's first?" He asked, while holding out a small straw.

Isaac waved him off. "Naw, man. You go head."

Spoony looked at Cynda. "What about you, beautiful?"

Cynda glanced at Isaac for approval. "Hey, you a grown woman. If ya' Mama never told you to 'just say no', far be it for me to try to school you now."

"All right," she said defiantly. "I think I'd like to try it." She grabbed the straw from Spoony, bent down and inhaled the coke into her nostril. She stood back up. White powder was around her nose. As she wiped her nose with the back of her hand, her head started spinning.

"Good stuff, huh?"

"Whew. It gives you a big time rush."

Spoony bent his head, and enjoyed the same rush. Oh what a feeling!

Isaac opened Cynda's Coach bag and pulled out stacks of cash. "Do I need to count it?" Spoony asked.

"Whatever helps you sleep at night."

Spoony came back over to the pool table. "Naw, dog. You got that wrong. My counting this stash will help *you* sleep at night."

Isaac turned to Cynda. "Take this briefcase and get back to Dayton. Hand this stuff to Keith. I'll call you when I get back in town."

Cynda picked up the briefcase. Spoony closed the bag of cocaine he and Cynda sampled and threw it in the briefcase. Cynda kissed her man and left without another word.

Spoony's eyes roamed over Cynda as she strutted up the stairs. "Man, let me know when you through with that."

"Do me that favor," Isaac told him.

Spoony sat down and rubbed his hands together. "How much you want for her? I know she's been running your stuff since Valerie died. I'm prepared to compensate you."

Isaac laughed. "Man, give me fifty cents, I don't care. Just take her off my hands."

Spoony ran his hands up and down his cheek. "You think she'd play around with Linda and let me watch?"

"If the price is right, she'll do anything."

Spoony smiled. "Oh, I'll pay for the play."

30

"*H*ey, Nina. How's it going?"

Nina was behind the counter folding clothes when Keith came in. She looked up and smiled. "It's going well, Keith. How about you?"

"Not too good." He put his hands on the counter. Looked around, then leaned over the counter a little bit and whispered. "Listen, Nina. Do you suppose I could talk to you for a minute?"

Nina looked into Keith's sad, withdrawn eyes, and saw the same despair she noticed every time he came into the laundromat. Maybe today, he would finally let go of the pain that's consuming his life. "Sure, Keith. You want to come behind the counter or talk in the office?"

He looked at the office door. "Naw, let's stay out here. I don't want Isaac trippin'."

"Oh, don't worry about him," she waved her hand dismissing the thought. "He took Donavan to the mall to get him fitted for a new pair of shoes. And you know he won't be able to stop with just one pair." Nina laughed as she opened the office door.

"That boy is getting big, he'll be walking soon."

They sat down, Keith on the sofa, Nina in the chair opposite him. "I know, I can hardly believe he'll be one next month." She shook her head. "Where does the time go?"

Keith didn't say anything. He looked at Nina. She caught that glimpse of despair again. He put his head down.

Nina was silent, determined to wait him out.

He leaned over and started tapping his fingers on the coffee table. He fidgeted in his seat. He put his hands on his head and started pulling at his hair, and rocking back and forth. "I can't get this stuff out of my head!"

Nina was silent.

"I am tormented day and night." He stopped rocking and looked at Nina again. "I keep seeing it over and over again – all the stuff I've done – I just can't push it out of my mind anymore." He turned an accusing eye on her. "And then I see you. And do you know what you said?"

Oh, Lord, please deliver him. "What, Keith?"

"He that is saved from much, loves much." Nina smiled. Keith rubbed his forehead with the palms of his hands. "Remember when you told that story about the prostitute crying at Jesus' feet? I was playing with Donavan, but I remember – I remember every word. How can that be true, Nina? How can God forgive so much sin?"

"I don't know how He can, but I know He will." She scooted up a bit and grabbed his hand. "I also know that God loves you, and He wants to take away your pain."

Keith snatched his hand back and stood up. "You don't know, Nina. You don't know the things I've done."

"God knows, and He still loves you."

Keith walked back and forth. Up and down, he rubbed at his face, and then stopped in front of Nina. "I paid for three abortions. Did you know that?" He threw his hands up in the air and started walking again. "I've stolen, dealt drugs. I've shot more people than I care to remember. But I had never killed nobody." He stood deathly still and looked Nina in the eye. "Until Ray-Ray. I killed him in cold blood. That fact has haunted me for almost a year." He slumped back in his seat. Nina sat on the edge of the sofa and rubbed Keith's back.

"Moses was a murderer," Nina said softly. "And God picked him to deliver His people out of Egypt. King David was an adulterer and a murderer. He was also the apple of God's eye. Funny how God chooses to forgive and restore whomever He will. And He don't seem to care one bit what the rest of the world has to say about it."

Keith looked up at Nina. His eyes filled with water. He opened his mouth, then closed it. He put his face in his hands and started rocking. Nina saw the struggle within, and started praying.

Keith jumped up. "I got to go. I need to think."

***

"What have you done to Keith?"

Nina was putting a fresh diaper on Donavan when Isaac stormed into the office. It had been a week since she'd seen Keith, so she hadn't the foggiest idea what Isaac was talking about, and told him so.

"He's over at his house crying like a baby, talking 'bout 'God forgives murderers'."

Oh, Jesus. Thank You. "Maybe I should go see him – make sure he's alright."

"No, you've done enough damage, with all them Jesus stories you tell around here." He grabbed her shoulders. "Just stay away from him."

Nina tried to pull away from Isaac, but his grip was unyielding. "Isaac, please. You're hurting me."

As quickly as his eyes burned with anger, they now smoldered with lust. He hadn't held Nina this close to him in a long time. And as much as it pained him to admit, he missed her more than he would have thought possible.

He bent his head. Just as Nina opened her mouth to protest, Isaac covered her mouth with his own. Desire spilled from him, as his body heated. "I want you, Nina. Don't you know that?" He rubbed her cheek. "Can't you tell how much I miss you?"

He brought his mouth back down to hers and Nina yielded. She put her arms around him and allowed herself to be swept away by his kiss. She forgot that he was a criminal and that she belonged to God. She forgot about not being unequally yoked together with unbelievers, and allowed herself to dream.

This moment, right here and now, she belonged to Isaac and he belonged to her. His kiss deepened and his hands caressed places Nina forgot could be ignited. She didn't know how it was possible, with Isaac's hands on her and his mouth claiming and devouring her – but just then, she remembered her vow to God.

She tried to push away from Isaac, but he had a firm grip. "Let go, Isaac."

"No." He whispered into her mouth.

"We can't do this."

"I ain't got no problem with it," he said defiantly.

"I belong to God. Fornication is sin."

He released her with a shove. "You and me," he pointed to where his son lay sleeping, "And Donavan are family. It wouldn't be fornication, Nina. It would be magic."

Nina lowered her head and stepped away from Isaac and his magic. In a barely audible voice she said, "I have decided--"

"What? Speak up!"

A boldness grew in her that she was unfamiliar with. She lifted her head and looked Isaac smack dab in the face. "I have decided to serve the Lord. All else is secondary or non-existent."

Isaac's body went cold as he took in her hurtful words. "Well, I guess I should thank you for making it clear that our relationship is non-existent. But are you actually telling me that our son comes second to this God of yours?"

Nina sighed. "The only way I can truly love my son is by loving God first."

"That's a bunch of bull. You are a naturally loving person. You've always been good, Nina."

Her eyes misted over as she asked Isaac, "Then why did I abort my first baby?"

He didn't have an answer for that. Better to just let that sleeping dog lie. "Nina, why do you hang your hopes on this God? What has He done for you?"

She smiled. "He's done everything."

"He can't save you, Nina. He didn't save my mother from my father."

"I'm sorry for what happened to your mother. But your heart has become filled with so much hatred over this – if you would only forgive." Nina softly touched Isaac's arm. "Please, Isaac, can you try to forgive your father?"

Isaac's lip curled. "I wouldn't piss on that man if he was on fire, and you ask me to forgive him? You might as well ask me to believe that this God of yours exists."

"God is real, Isaac."

He changed the subject. "Are we going to make love?"

"I can't."

Isaac clenched his fists and punched at the air. "Fine! Keep it. Matter fact, let it shrivel up and die from inactivity." He stormed out of the office letting every one of the customers in the laundry area know that he had a big ol' attitude problem. He turned back to Nina as she stood in the doorway of the office watching his departure. "I don't want to hear another word about God, Jesus, or whoever else you sit around here telling stories about. If your God is so great, let Him warm your bed, but He better never be mentioned in this laundromat again." He slammed the door, leaving several stunned patrons behind.

She tried not to watch as he walked to his car – tried not to miss him, tried not to hope for his speedy return. But it was like trying not to breathe. She didn't know what curse had been placed on her that she was destined to forever yearn for what she could not have. But through all of his unfaithfulness, his evil doings, and mockery of her God – she loved him still.

Maybe her feelings stemmed from the affectionate way Isaac treated Donavan. Yeah, that's it. Her feelings for him are only a reflection of his treatment of their son.

Lord, if You have increased my feelings for Isaac, then save his soul. If he will not come to You, then take away my feelings for him.

31

"*I* don't know what else to do. I've tried everything."

Nina sat in her living room listening to Elizabeth talk about the fact that Kenneth had been attending church with her for two months now, but had still not been converted.

She'd tried everything. She begged, she pleaded. Told him that she didn't want to go to heaven without him. Elizabeth even brought out the big guns. She told Kenneth that if the rapture happened before he was converted, he would be left on earth without his family. She showed him the scripture that said, "*In that night, there will be two in one bed: the one will be taken and the other will be left*". Kenneth just smiled and said, "Don't worry. I'm thinking it over."

"So what do you think, Nina?"

"Maybe he is thinking it over. He just needs a little time."

"No," Elizabeth told her friend. "Kenneth is one of the good guys. He doesn't lie, cheat or steal. He's an African-American man, who also happens to be president and CEO of his own company. He just doesn't think he needs God."

Nina shook her head. "Need I remind you that the effectual, fervent prayer of the righteous avails much." Nina stood, and pulled her friend up with her. "Let me show you how it's done."

Nina took Elizabeth to the back of the house. She got down on her knees while Elizabeth stood, watching. The next thing Elizabeth knew, Nina was wailing out to the Lord on Kenneth's behalf. Elizabeth was amazed. The mere thought that someone could pray with such hunger and authority was something she had never considered. Nina, who was not bold by nature, boldly claimed Kenneth's salvation in the name of Jesus. She cast down the strongholds that were holding Kenneth bound to the world and rebuked Satan's hold on his life. When she finished, she stood up and looked Elizabeth straight in the face. "You cannot badger and harass Kenneth into the Kingdom. Pray, and get out of God's way."

***

Elizabeth walked into her house. Kenneth was on the floor playing with Danae and grinning from ear to ear. Just then, Elizabeth thought she glimpsed perfection. Light-bright-freckles-and-all. He was her Adonis. "Hey, baby."

Kenneth turned to his wife. "Hey yourself," he said as he opened his arms to her. "Come join us on the floor."

Elizabeth obeyed. "Where's Erin?"

"Upstairs, sleep." He grabbed her in a bear hug as he watched Danae dance around the room. "I still can't believe Danae is three-years old already."

"Well, birthdays come every year, ya' know."

He rubbed her nose. "Yeah, I know smart aleck. It's just that time passes so fast. Before I know it I'll be an old man with grandkids." He squeezed her tighter. "I guess I just want to hold on to all of you forever."

Elizabeth opened her mouth to tell him that if the rapture came, he'd be holding onto nothing, but she heard the still small voice of

Nina telling her to 'get out of God's way.' She kissed Kenneth full on the mouth and let her love speak volumes.

Later that night, when Kenneth made love to her, the passion inside him burned deep into her soul. She rode the tide of their love on the sea of unforgettable passion. And at that moment, even though she was ashamed to think it, she knew that she would fight anyone that tried to claim this man's heart, even God.

Sunday morning was an unwelcome invader. Elizabeth stretched and yawned. Light peaked through the bedroom window. She turned away from the loud morning sun, and got reacquainted with her friend, Mr. Sleep.

Kenneth jumped up. "Oh, my God, we're going to be late."

She rubbed her eyes. "Late for what?"

Kenneth laughed. "The choir, babe. You sing this morning, remember?" He picked up her nightgown and tossed it to her. "Get out of bed! I'll go work on the kids."

By the time Elizabeth came down stairs, it was eight thirty. Erin and Danae were happily seated at the kitchen table gobbling down Pop Tarts and orange juice. She shook her head and looked to Kenneth.

"What? It's nutritious."

She walked over to the counter, yawning as she went. "Just let me get a cup of coffee, and we can go."

Kenneth gave her a sheepish grin. "Good Lord, why are you always so tired lately?"

She poured the coffee in her cup. "It's not my fault. This crazy man comes to my room every night, whispering sweet nothings and – whew! The things he does to my..."

Kenneth covered Erin and Danae's ears with his hands. "My children shouldn't have to hear all this filth," he smiled. "And you, a Christian woman."

She turned around to face her husband as she sipped on the coffee. Kenneth released his children and walked over to

Elizabeth. He cupped her face in his hands and looked her over for a moment. "Your eyes, babe. I can see a smile in your eyes again."

She blushed, then turned from his inspection.

"No, don't turn away." He turned her back to face him. "I don't think I ever told you this, but one of the reasons I married you was because when you smiled at me, I didn't just see it on your lips, but your eyes lit up. It made me feel like I was home. Like I was safe with someone who loved me."

"I do love you."

He kissed her. "And I am home again." Elizabeth's smile grew bigger. He gently touched her face. "Babe, you smile with your heart. Don't ever change."

They arrived at The Rock at nine o'clock on the nose. Elizabeth kissed Kenneth, then ran up to the choir stand. As she sat down, she remembered that she forgot to do that effectual, fervent prayer thing Nina told her about. She found Kenneth in the crowd. He'd found seats for him and the kids. Elizabeth saw two sistahs checking out his ring finger. Kenneth didn't even notice. *He seems all right to me, why mess with perfection?* Elizabeth asked herself.

Beloved, not this way.

She bowed her head in shame. *I'm sorry, Lord.* She silently prayed. *I know that Your way is the right way. And that Kenneth needs to know You. He needs to feel Your unconditional love, as I do. But, Lord, as I pray for Kenneth to come to You, can You please make sure that he doesn't get so wrapped up in You that he forgets about the love he has for me? I need him, Lord.*

Elder Woodlow welcomed the congregation to the first service of the day. The praise team stood behind the podium and ushered the people into the Lord's presence. The congregation joined in as they sang to the Lord. Whether loud or soft, melody, or some 'what in the world is that noise?' type stuff, it was all sweet music to God's ears. This was the time His people came to worship and sing songs to Him. Not all the time, but when the crowd really poured their hearts out to God, and laid their troubles at the altar, God would sweep through the sanctuary like a mighty rushing wind. Several people would fall to their knees. The power of the wind was so strong that some were stretched out on the floor. Healing was in the room.

Sometimes the spirit in the sanctuary was so awesome the members were sure that the day of Pentecost, when the Holy Ghost filled the hearts of thousands, couldn't have been much different.

Elder Hardison informed the crowd that it was 'Happy Grace Giving Time!!' A time to worship God through giving. As each member came to the front of the sanctuary, they put their money in the basket and walked back to their seat.

Corey, the Music Director, looked at Elizabeth. She stood before the congregation and grabbed the microphone. Butterflies were doing the jitterbug throughout her stomach as she opened her mouth and sang:

"There is no one like the Father,
there is no one like the Son,
there is no one like the Holy Ghost."

A hush went over the sanctuary floor. Kenneth smiled, enjoying the moment when the world found out what he already knew. His baby could blow.

Elizabeth continued:

"The Father took His time and made us,
the Son came down and died for us,
the Holy Ghost came like a mighty rushing wind,
so we could repent, be baptized and freed from our sins.

"Sing girl!" one of the men in the sanctuary hollered.

"All right now," a woman in the back said.

Half the congregation stood up, and began to wave their hands in praise to the Lord, as Elizabeth's angelic voice serenaded Him.

"Listen, the world did not know the Father,
and the Son came to teach us about His love,
the Holy Ghost came to reveal all three,
how they work together just to set us free."

Pastor McKinley received the microphone, as Elizabeth took her place back in the choir. "Yes, you can be set free today. God is looking down on you right now saying, 'Come brother, come sister, wash and be clean.'" Pastor McKinley went on for another hour, imploring the lost to come to Jesus. By the time his sermon was finished, several worshipers stood at the altar repenting and crying out to God.

Kenneth squirmed in his seat. He had been attending this church with Elizabeth for a few months, but every time he thought he was ready to commit, something would remind him of his adulterous past. He desired to be a better man than his father, but when the chips were down he followed in the way of his father anyway. Kenneth was having a hard time forgiving himself for that.

Did God forgive adulterers? Could he wash and be cleansed of his sins? He wanted answers, but didn't know who to ask.

Finally, he just bowed his head and started praying. *"Lord, I know I'm no good. I've done things that I am truly ashamed of. I don't know if You can forgive me. But I want to come to You – I want to be a part of Your family."*

Come.

Kenneth looked around. No one met his stare, so he knew that only God had said, "Come" to him. A tear rolled down Kenneth's cheek, as he stood up. He threw off the curse of his natural father and took the walk of faith down the aisle. God does forgive adulterers, he thought. With tears barreling down his face, he whispered, "Now I can let your memory rest in peace, Daddy. I've won. I'm finally going to be a better man than you were."

Elizabeth looked over at Michael. He winked. Her heart filled with joy and the tears were endless. The Bible says that the angels rejoice, when one sinner comes to repentance. Elizabeth rejoiced with the angels, but she knew anxiety over the fact that this man no longer belonged exclusively to her. *I'll deal with my feelings, Lord. I am truly happy for Kenneth.*

After service, Nina hugged Kenneth and congratulated him on his new journey with God. She turned to Elizabeth. "I know you must be ecstatic!"

Elizabeth's smile was strained. *I'm working on it, Lord. You're going to have to give me a little time to adjust to the fact that I will be sharing my husband again. At least it won't be with some tack head woman.* "I'm thrilled." She hugged Nina, then looked to the gentleman standing next to her.

"This is Keith. He gave his life to the Lord last week." Nina looked at Keith. "Excuse his nervousness. This is the first time he's been in church since he was a kid."

Keith smiled at Elizabeth. "I enjoyed your song. It really touched me."

"Thank you."

"Well, we'll see you later. I want to introduce Keith to Elder Michael."

Kenneth put his arm around his wife as Nina and Keith walked away. "So, hon. I'm finally saved, just like you wanted."

She smiled at him.

Kenneth frowned. "No, with your heart. Smile at me with your heart."

"Oh, Kenneth, I'm so selfish." She hugged him tightly. "Of course this is what I wanted. You're saved, and we will both see the King. That's the way it should be."

***

At the same time, Isaac was on the highway coming back from Chicago. He had just picked up another shipment. Cynda had already become part of Spoony's harem, and Keith had too much Holy Ghost to transport drugs. Isaac simply didn't have the patience to train another girl or find another right hand man. So, here he was, traveling with several kilos, on the highway back to Dayton.

Isaac needed some down time. He had this incredible urge to be by himself, no business to worry about, no people clamoring around him, and no Nina shoving her God in his face. It was just Isaac and his kilos out on I-70 and that was how he wanted it.

Just one problem. Five-o was on his back, and had been for the last two miles. Isaac looked into his rearview mirror and watched his nemesis radio in. He assumed it was to trace his license plate. Good luck trying to pin a stolen car on me, Isaac thought. The car he was driving was rented and had been paid for in advance.

Isaac checked the speedometer. He was doing sixty-seven in a sixty-five. Not bad, just two over the speed limit. Just to be on the safe side, he lowered his speed down to sixty-four. Isaac smirked, "Now what, fool?"

The police officer hung up and continued his pursuit. Isaac snarled. He was a Black man in a Bentley. That's the only reason Five-o was hot on his trail. Isaac cursed himself for his own stupidity. When he was at the rental place, he started to pick a less conspicuous car. But the Bentley was calling his name – so he took it. Now, you would think, more than thirty years after Martin Luther King, Jr. had his dream, a Black man would be able to ride the highway in a Bentley without the police suspecting he was doing something illegal.

Yeah, okay. He *was* doing something illegal, but it was the principle of the thing that made Isaac mad. He slammed his fist down on his dashboard. Was anybody listening to Rodney, 'Can't we all just get along?'

Colors flashed him, telling him it was time to pay the piper. Isaac was tempted to floor it and take his chances. Just ride the wave, and see if it dumped him on dry land. But running took energy, and he was kind of tired right now. So he pulled over and waited. The police officer kept his chicken-butt in his car, until back up arrived. Then he got out of the car and drew his gun. Yeah, he was walking tall now.

"Get out of the car with your hands in the air," a bull horn from the second police car instructed Isaac.

Isaac did as he was told. "What's the problem, officer?" He asked with a sneer. "I wasn't speeding, was I?"

"Are you Isaac Walker?" The police officer asked, ignoring his question.

"Yes, I am."

"Turn around, I need to cuff you."

"What's the charge?"

"You're not under arrest – I need to search your car."

Did these people think he didn't know his rights? "Don't you need a search warrant for that?"

The officer in the second car got out waving a piece of paper. "Got it right here Mr. Walker. We received an anonymous tip that you were transporting illegal drugs."

Isaac exploded. "You received WHAT?"

"Just turn around so we can cuff you, sir. This won't take but a moment."

That's what you think, Isaac thought to himself, this will take years.

PART 2

32

Two years later - 2001

*M*arguerite passed away last year. Her heart finally gave out. Nina thought her own heart would shatter from the sheer pain of having to face the loss of yet another loved one. Somehow life kept going, even when you thought you couldn't possibly face another day. You grew stronger from the pain. That old saying must be true, 'Whatever doesn't kill you makes you stronger.'

Nina put her hot chocolate on the coffee table and stretched out on the sofa in the tiny apartment she shared with Lisa. She had a few hours before she needed to be at church so she decided to spend the time relaxing and reading some letters.

The first letter was from Keith:

Greetings to my sister in the Lord,

I hope this letter finds you and Donavan doing well. I know it has not been easy for you these last few years, but my prayer is that you keep trusting in Jesus. He has not forgotten you, nor will He ever fail you.

My parole hearing went pretty well. I will be released in six months. Can you believe it, Nina? After being locked up for only two years, I'm getting out. God must be in this. I'm anxious to get out of here, and discover the ministry that God has given me. I don't regret turning myself into the police. Once I gave my life over to Christ, it just didn't feel right, not owning up to my sins.

Thanks for the pictures of you and Donavan. That boy is getting big! I sure hate that Isaac has missed these last years with him. Do you ever hear from him? Has your financial situation improved any?

Tell the brothers in the prison ministry that I really appreciate their support. I can't wait to get back to the church. I've been away a couple of years, but I believe this time has helped me grow stronger in the Lord. My life is very different from the way it was when I was on the streets. I am ready to be used by God. Whatever His mission.

Peace and grace to you and yours,

Keith

Nina smiled as she placed the letter on the table. It was always a joy to hear from Keith. He had a way of making her feel like everything would turn out right. She picked up the next letter, and her smile vanished. This would not be a joy to read. If it was anything like his previous letters, it would be down right insulting. Nina bucked up, and opened the letter from Isaac anyway.

Nina,

How many times do I have to tell you to stop writing to me about Jesus? I am sick to death of hearing you go on and on about how Jesus can save me from my sins. Well guess what, I like sinning. So why in the world would I want somebody to take away something I enjoy?

And while I'm on the subject, let me just clue you in. If this Jesus of yours really existed, do you think I'd be in jail right now? Or would I be out on the streets taking care of my family, like I'm supposed to? You and Donavan are the ones suffering because of my incarceration. Now you tell me why a loving God would allow you to work two jobs, hardly ever see your own son, and then you're still barely able to put food on the table. It don't make sense, when I could be out there earning enough money so that you and my son wouldn't have to worry about nothing.

But no, your sorry-good-for-nothing-so-called-God, let the White man lock me up. And now my family goes hungry while you praise Jesus. Well, I won't praise Him. I don't see what's so worthy to be praised about this Jesus anyway. If He's so all-powerful, let Him open my prison doors and free me! And to answer your question, yes, I have been reading the Bible, but not for the reason you hope. I intend to find every contradiction in this book of lies and throw them in your silly-God-believing face. I am putting together quite a list right now.

Give my son a kiss and tell him I love him.

Isaac,
     Your man, if you would quit being stupid!

Nina set the letter down and prayed. She prayed for Keith's strength in the Lord. But more fervently, she prayed that Isaac's hard heart would be softened.

33

The ordination service was tonight.

Elizabeth searched her closet for something dignified to wear. After all, the wife of an elder would have to be an example for other women. Isn't that what they told her? As if she didn't have enough to worry about already, now she had to make sure she didn't offend anyone.

She took a black dress off the rack and frowned at it. Red, yellow, and orange looked so much better with her complexion. But no, Kenneth wanted her dressed the same as all the other elders' wives, who would be in black. Did somebody die, or what? Why did everybody have to be in black? Or maybe that was just the point, maybe the other wives felt just like she did. That this appointment to Elder, meant *more* work for the church and death to her marriage.

Elizabeth sighed. She hated that she felt this way. But in the two years since Kenneth gave his life to the Lord, she had not been able to shake the feeling that she and her children were being cheated out of time with him. She looked at the dress again and shook her head. "This submission thing is going to kill me." She threw the dress on the bed and sat down at her vanity.

Kenneth had taken the girls out for some ice cream to give her some *me* time before the ordination service. He was a good man, no doubt about that. She had no doubts about the fact that Kenneth loved her and was devoted to her. But she also knew that he loved the Lord with all his being, and this love took more of Kenneth's time than any extra-marital affair ever did.

The door to her bedroom opened and Kenneth peeked his head in. "Hey, beautiful."

"Hey yourself." She smiled up at him as she pulled the remaining rollers out of her hair.

"Just wanted to let you know we're back. I'll keep the girls downstairs. We're ready to go whenever you are." He closed the door.

Elizabeth's smile evaporated as she remembered that in the month since she had known about Kenneth's appointment to Elder, she had not yet congratulated him. She pounded her forehead with her fist. "What is wrong with you?"

***

The ordination service took about an hour. The deed was done. Her husband now had more responsibility to the church and less to his home and family. Erin and Danae gave their dad a hug and ran off to join their friends. Elizabeth stood by her husband's side. She felt too guilty to look at him, but she grabbed his hand and squeezed it. "Congratulations, honey. You deserve this," she told him.

Kenneth put his index finger under her chin and lifted her face so that she looked him in the eye. "Now was that so hard?"

"Honestly, Kenneth, I don't know what's wrong with me sometimes."

"I do."

She gave him a sharp look. "What do you mean?"

"You're still afraid that I'm going to abandon my family. At one time you feared another woman would drive me away. Now you've got it in your head that my service to God will cause me to abandon you and the kids."

Elizabeth's hands went to her hips. "I think no such thing, Kenneth Underwood."

He sighed. Elizabeth saw a look of sadness in his eyes that tore at her heart. "I destroyed your trust, I know that. But I have worked so hard these last few years trying to rebuild what I tore down."

"Kenneth, I do trust you, I don't know what you're talking…"

He pressed his finger against her lips. "Every time I'm called away to do something for one of the members in the church I see the fear in your eyes. Elizabeth, it must be terrible to wonder if your husband's coming home each time he leaves the house." His finger fell from her mouth, as he turned and walked away.

"Kenneth, I --. Oh, what's the use." She balled her fist and looked around for something to smash. Finding nothing, she sank into one of the pews and buried her head.

After what felt like an eternity of silence, Elizabeth heard Nina say, "Hey, there's a party going on in the fellowship hall. Why are you in here moping?"

Elizabeth looked up and gave Nina the best smile she could manage.

Nina grabbed the tissue box on the window seal and sat down next to Elizabeth. She rubbed her back and handed her the tissue. "You're supposed to be happy today. What's wrong?"

Elizabeth blew her nose. "Kenneth thinks I don't trust him."

Nina kept rubbing her friend's back. "Do you?"

"Well of course I trust him. With most things – I mean, there are some things -- well, you know what I mean."

"No, I don't. Explain it to me."

Elizabeth gave Nina the evil eye. "Ooh, you make me sick sometimes."

"Yeah, I know, now answer the question. Do you trust your husband?"

Elizabeth was silent.

"Well?"

"I trust him. All right?" She stood up and looked back at Nina. "I... I guess I'm just scared. Ah, who am I kidding, I'm scared to death – I keep thinking I'm going to lose him. Is it a crime to love somebody so much that you don't want to lose them?"

"Have you told Kenneth how you feel?"

"No. How can I?"

Nina stood up and grabbed Elizabeth's hand. "You simply open your mouth and tell him," she told her friend, then pulled her in the direction of the fellowship hall.

Kenneth looked up as Elizabeth and Nina walked into the room. He smiled and pointed to the empty seat next to him.

"I'll talk to you later. I'm going to sit with Kenneth." Elizabeth told Nina.

"Keep your chin up."

"Yeah. Thanks." She hugged Nina and sat down next to her husband.

"Nina talked you into joining the celebration?"

"No, Kenneth. I wanted to be here with you. Nobody would ever have to convince me to celebrate my husband. You are everything to me."

He leaned closer to her and whispered. "But do you trust me?"

She looked into his eyes and saw his need for the truth. She heard Nina say, '*Tell him.*' "Kenneth, I am learning to trust you more and more each day. It's just that I'm so scared of losing you. I don't know what I'd do if I had to live without you."

"Well you can rest easy, babe. Cause you'll never lose me."

***

The celebration dinner was over and Nina was getting ready to walk out of the fellowship hall when she heard, "Nina, can I talk to you for a minute?"

She inwardly groaned, but stopped anyway. She tried to put a smile on her face. Harold Bunsford was staring down at her like she was Peaches to his Herb. "Yes, Herb – I mean, Harold."

His smile grew wide. "I've got two tickets to the ballet. I was hoping you'd be interested."

A man who liked ballet, how refreshing, but Nina had resolved not to date just for the sake of dating. She had Donavan to think about, and besides, dating had long since lost its luster.

Nina knew first hand that dating the wrong man could break your heart, and bring a lot of unnecessary trouble. "Thanks for asking, but I'm not interested."

Nina turned away from him. Her only thought was to find Donavan and leave the church as quickly as possible. Harold gently grabbed her arm and turned her back toward him. "Nina, what's wrong? I've asked you out a dozen times. You keep saying 'no'. Is there something wrong with me?"

Nina looked at Harold. He wasn't a bad looking man. He could use a little help bringing his wardrobe into the new millennium, but all in all, not a bad guy. He just wasn't *her* guy. Nina couldn't explain how she knew, she just did. And she didn't feel like wasting precious hours on a date to discover what she already knew. "There's nothing wrong with you, Harold. I'm just not interested. That's all."

"Nina, I know at least five other guys at this church who have asked you out. You've turned them down also. Why?" His tone was not angry, just inquisitive.

"Do you mind if we sit down for a moment?" Harold grabbed two chairs, people were filing out of the sanctuary. Nina and Harold waved their good byes to a few of them, as they sat down to continue their conversation.

"So why don't you date?" Harold asked.

"When I got saved almost four years ago, I told the Lord that I didn't want to date." She put up her hands to ward off Harold's objections. "Believe me, I've had plenty of dates in my life. So, I asked the Lord to send my husband. He alone will I date."

Harold looked puzzled. "How will you know who your husband is, if you refuse to date?"

Lord, how do I make him understand? Please give me the words to say. "I believe that God will bring him to me. My spirit will know that he is the one."

He lifted his hands in the air and shook his head. "I don't understand, Nina. What are you looking for?"

"Love."

He touched her cheek. "But, Nina. Surely you know that you could have love with me. If you would only give me a chance."

"Love is not as simple as you think, Harold." She took his hand and stood up. "Come with me." The fellowship hall and the sanctuary were nearly empty by now. The few remaining worshipers gave Nina and Harold nosey stares as they passed by.

Nina ignored them. She and Harold stood in front of the baptismal pool. She pointed at the picture above the pool. "It's Jesus on the cross. Nina, I see this picture every Sunday. What?"

"This is the man I will marry," Nina told him.

"I hate to break it to you, but Jesus ain't coming back in the flesh. And even if He did, I don't think He would be interested in marriage."

Nina laughed. "Not Jesus, silly. I will marry a man who is dead to the things of this world, dead to his own will." She looked up at the picture of Jesus on the cross and smiled. *"Not my will, but Yours be done,"* she said to no one in particular.

"What?" Harold asked.

Nina turned back to Harold. "Remember the prayer in the Garden of Gethsemane, when Jesus said, *'Let this cup pass from me, but not my will, but your will be done.'* He was making a declaration that He would follow God, even if God's will conflicted with His own. The man I'm going to marry will be submitted and obedient to God, even unto death. There's no greater love.

"And if he loves God that much, he can't help but love and care for me as well, that's what I want. It's what I need."

Harold looked at her with a sad expression in his eyes. "The man you're waiting on doesn't exist," he told her, then walked away.

Nina stayed at the altar looking at Jesus on that cross for a while longer. "Oh, he exists. I don't know where he is, but I trust You, Lord."

34

*I*saac stretched out on his bunk and started reading some more Bible mumbo-jumbo. Actually, he was still tripping off the last bit of hogwash he read in the fifth chapter of Matthews. Some mess about, blessed are the punks and suckas, cause they will inherit a butt whuppin. And blessed are the merciful, the reward for their good deeds will be a bullet in the head. Isaac remembered his dad saying, "Son, no good deed goes unpunished." Ol' usually-wrong, got that right, Isaac thought as he remembered giving a pocket full of money to a bum on the streets of Chicago. "Lot of good that did me."

If all that blessed mess wasn't bad enough, further down the fifth chapter of Matthew he read:

You have heard that it was said to those of old, 'You shall not commit adultery.

But I say to you that whoever looks at a woman to lust for her has already committed adultery with her in his heart.

"What?" Isaac sat up. "How can a man be held accountable for the thoughts in his mind? If he don't touch the woman, what difference does it make?"

"Man, you arguing with that Bible again?"

Isaac looked up as Pete walked in. "This crap don't make no sense."

"Isaac, man, you cool people and all, but I can't get involved with no blasphemy."

Isaac grabbed his Bible. "Okay, then listen to this:

"You have heard that it was said, 'An eye for an eye and a tooth for a tooth.

But I tell you not to resist an evil person. But whoever slaps you on your right cheek, turn the other to him also.'"

Isaac stared at Pete for a second, then said. "Now what cat up in here you think gon' turn the other cheek? He'd get knocked out. And what's this trash?" Isaac pointed at the offending words in the Bible. "If somebody takes your tunic, give him your cloak also. Well, why not give him your butt too? Cause that's what's next. You gon' straight be some man's woman up in this place."

Pete was silent. It was clear to Isaac that he was trying to think of something to say that would change his opinion, but couldn't think of anything.

"That's what I thought." Isaac said as he flung the Bible across the room. "You don't agree with this mess either."

"Look, Isaac, I might not be able to explain everything in the Bible. I might not agree with everything I read." Pete bent down and picked up the Bible and placed it on Isaac's bunk. "But I've come to believe that the Bible holds the Word of God. And God is truth, so when I don't accept something in the Bible, I pray about it and ask the Lord to increase my understanding in that area."

"Whatever, man." Isaac got up, getting ready to walk out of the cell, when T-Bone stepped to him.

He pointed at Isaac. "I want your spot, boy."

Isaac gave T-Bone a menacing look and posed himself for business. "Come over here and take it, fool. Ain't nothing between us but air."

T-bone had a shard piece of glass in his hand. He tightened his hand around his weapon and advanced on Isaac.

Pete moved out of the way.

"T-bone, this ain't your block. What are you doing over here?" A guard rushed to defuse the situation.

T-bone turned to face the guard. He hid the glass in the palm of his hand. "Nothing. I'm just visiting my boy, Isaac."

The guard turned to Isaac. "You want his company?"

Isaac thought about the shank in T-bone's hand. "I can do without it."

"You heard the man," the guard told T-bone, "Out."

"I'll catch you later, man." T-bone told Isaac as he moved out of his block.

"Can't wait." Isaac turned back to Pete. "See what I mean. Turning the other cheek in this place will get you a toe tag."

"Did you see what he had in his hand?"

"Sure did." Isaac rubbed his chin. "Pete, you connected with somebody in the kitchen, right?"

"Yeah, Joe."

"Tell Joe to make me a shank. I'm going to gut that fool and send him to his just reward."

35

"*S*ay what?" Kenneth exploded.

Elizabeth was at the kitchen table paying bills. The sound of her husband's angry voice caused her to put down the checkbook and look up.

"Yeah, well, you don't have to worry. I'll be there on the first plane smoking." Kenneth slammed the phone down and looked at Elizabeth. "They think something's wrong with my financial statements."

"Who does?"

"Bank of America." Kenneth flung his arms in the air. "Accused me of *creative accounting*. Can you believe that?"

Elizabeth stared at Kenneth. "Now honey, you haven't been cooking the books, have you?"

"Elizabeth, this is not funny. My integrity is at stake here."

"Okay, you're right. I'm sorry, honey." She walked over to Kenneth and gave him a hug. "So when do you have to go to New York?"

"Next week."

"Kenneth Underwood, you are not going to be in New York the week of our anniversary without me."

Kenneth kissed Elizabeth on her nose. "I wouldn't dream of it, babe. Our anniversary is next Wednesday right? Well, I've got to meet with Bob on Tuesday." He pulled her closer to him. "I'll handle my business, be out of that bank in no time flat – then take my beautiful wife on a 10th anniversary adventure in New York she'll never forget."

"Sounds good to me."

Kenneth snapped his fingers. "I need to call Rick."

Elizabeth shook her head and handed Kenneth his briefcase. "No, baby, you go on to work. I'll call your accountant. And believe you me, if he's done anything funny with our money – I'll make him wish he was still sucking his thumb and being serenaded by his Mama."

36

*W*hether in his body or out of his body, Isaac did not know.

But one thing was certain, he was definitely not in prison anymore. The blackness of this new place made him long for his three walls and government mandated iron bars.

A man stood next to Isaac. He was clothed in vibrant and wondrous colors. Colors that were unlike anything Isaac had ever seen. A hood hung over his head, so Isaac could not ID him. "Who are you?" Isaac asked.

The man looked at him. "I am Truth."

The air was gaseous and polluted, dry and tainted. Isaac put his hands up to his nostrils. "What's that smell?"

"It is the smell of decay, death, and dying. Come, let me show you."

As Isaac followed Truth he watched as a black slimy substance oozed down the walls of this – this – it had to be some type of deserted cave, Isaac thought. Then he heard the screams. It was unlike any thing he'd ever heard. "What in the world?"

"You're not in the world right now," Truth told him as he stretched forth his arms. "This is hell."

No dah, Isaac thought.

Truth continued, "It is a place where lost souls are tormented day and night, minute by minute – forever. You seem to enjoy sending people here. I thought you might like a tour."

A little further into the tunnel and they came to an opening. The very essence of evil sprang forth. Rejected and tormented souls were encased in the walls of the tunnel, anguishing their misery, as their silhouettes attempted to pierce through the muck and mire.

Hundreds of menacing spirits stood, growling and snarling, waiting for their captain to unleash them on the world. The demons were of varied shapes and sizes. Some were as big as a grizzly bear with heads like bats and ten-inch fangs. Some were small and monkey-like, with big hairy arms. Still others had large heads, large ears and long jagged tails. The most dreadful of all were the smaller piranha-like imps. They infested their victims in swarms and gnawed at their flesh. The shadow of their leader swallowed the darkness, as he towered over them. Green slime dripped from the tips of his flesh devouring fangs. He received his orders directly from Satan. It was his duty to send these evil spirits forth. He marched back and forth in front of his troops, preparing them for the battle to come. His beady eyes glared at his troops one last time, then with a shout, commanded, "Go!" The ominous beings flew up and out, as the doors at the top of the belly of hell opened to spew these evil spirits out. Their captain continued shouting, "Destroy lives! Do evil! Confuse minds! Distort the truth! Go!"

Isaac grabbed Truth's arm. "Didn't you hear them? They're going to destroy the earth. Why aren't you stopping them?"

"The earth has been given to Satan. He that will be saved, let him come to the Lord."

Truth took him into an area of hell that housed prison cells. It looked just like the cell Isaac was locked in every night. Same concrete floor, same iron bars, same filthy cot.

Truth told him, "These prison cells are readily available for those that served Satan, rather than the Lord, when they walked the face of the earth."

"Why are we here? I could have stayed where I was if all you wanted me to see was some prison cells."

"There is much you need to see here."

A man tightly gripped the bars of his cell and started screaming, "Help – help me, please. Come on Isaac. I know you hear me."

Isaac fixed his eyes toward the noise and saw a man in one of the cells. There was something familiar about the man. And that voice... Isaac stepped closer to the cell. "Leonard?"

"Help me, man. Get me out of here. I can't take it anymore."

Isaac smirked. "Why they got you in a cell? What'd you do – rob somebody down here too?"

Leonard's eyes rolled back in his head. He lifted his hand to his hair and pulled at it, as gut-wrenching screams bellowed from his mouth. But it wasn't Leonard's mouth anymore. Leonard was transforming into a deformed animal right in front of Isaac.

The creature reached out. "H-help me!"

Isaac jumped back. This was too Poltergeist for him. "What's happening?"

Truth touched Isaac's shoulder. "The drugs he sold while on earth caused people to become things they were never meant to be. As punishment, his body now changes form frequently. It will continue for eternity." He sadly shook His head and moved Isaac away from the cells. "We have more to see."

Isaac was horrified. He had no wish to see more of this place and he told Truth so. Truth kept walking. "Where are we going?"

"To the Fun Room."

Yeah right, Isaac thought. There's about as much fun as a train wreck to be had in this place.

The Fun Room had also been created for those who once enjoyed the pleasures of sin and all its trappings. Isaac held his nose as they walked into the room. A stank bomb must have exploded in this mug, Isaac thought.

In this room, demons watched as tortured souls tried to recreate the fun they partook in on earth. Crap games were going on. Con artists recited their street hustle over and over again. Former CEOs and executives discussed business ventures.

They were permitted to do anything they wanted in the Fun Room, anything but leave. And that was the rub, because there were also demons in the Fun Room. These demons taunted and tortured the souls. Every hour on the hour a bell would ring. The inhabitants of the Fun Room would tremble with fear and cry out for someone to save them. Isaac wondered why these people had such a problem with a bell ringing – their bodies didn't change form or nothing horrifying like that. Then the demons grabbed a few unfortunate souls and brought them to the center of the room.

Isaac recognized Ray-Ray immediately. Six demons marched around him like he was fresh meat. They hissed and cackled – spit and laughed. Ray-Ray looked real scared.

Initially, Isaac wanted to cheer on the demons. But then they started poking Ray-Ray with the long spears they carried. They pulled at his flesh. Ray-Ray let out a God-awful scream of agony that tore at Isaac's heart.

Isaac turned to Truth. "They're going to pull him apart."

"They often do."

"What do you mean?"

Truth pointed to a pile of discarded limbs. "The demons enjoy mutilating these people. They will pick them apart until there is nothing left."

Isaac looked back to the center of the room. Ray-Ray was crawling away from the demons. His left leg had been violently pulled from his body, but there was no blood. Isaac watched as the demons brought another group to the center of the room.

He closed his eyes to avoid the pain. His brother Donavan was in this group. He looked at Truth. "Why are you doing this to me?"

He didn't answer.

One of the demons put his spear in Donavan's flesh. Isaac heard his little brother scream and beg for mercy.

Isaac ran to the center screaming, "Noooo!"

The demon lifted his spear again. Positioning it for Donavan's chest cavity. Isaac grabbed the spear and tried to yank it out of the demon's hand, but its grip was much stronger than anything Isaac had ever known. The demon swatted Isaac to the ground. Venomous fluids oozed from his mouth as he hissed. His beady eyes centered on Isaac. With his lip curled and fangs fully exposed, he lunged.

Isaac was dead. He knew it would only be a matter of seconds. As soon as those fangs cut at his flesh, he was a goner.

Truth held up his hand. "Halt. You cannot have him."

The demon hissed as he looked at Truth, but he obeyed.

Isaac was forced to witness every painful moment of Donavan's torture. Two demons grabbed Donavan's arms and stretched him out crucifixion style "Donavan, run!" Isaac called out to his brother, as another demon lifted his spear. The spear pierced Donavan's left shoulder.

"Aaarrhhh!"

"Nooo!" Isaac yelled as the demon pulled the spear from Donavan and lifted it to impel him again. Isaac was no punk, and he wasn't about to take this mess lying down. He pulled himself off the ground and ran full speed toward the offending demon. He jumped on its back and tried to pull the spear from his hand.

The demon hissed and cackled, as he shook Isaac off his back. He picked Isaac up like he was a Raggedy Andy doll and threw him across the room. Isaac hit the wall –whoosh– his breath exited his body, as he slid down the wall and landed on a heap of limbs. Dazed, Isaac shook his head.

The nine-foot tall demon turned jaundiced eyes in Isaac's direction and pointed at him. "Stay there."

Isaac climbed down from the pile of limbs and ran back to the demon.

Jaundiced eyes was waiting for him. He put his spear down. Isaac advanced, the demon spat green slime on the ground. He picked Isaac up by the collar and pimp smacked him.

Isaac wanted to retaliate, but he couldn't make out which one of the three moving faces was the one that hit him. As soon as he could get the room to stop spinning and make out one head rather than three – he would smack that demon back. Before he could reconcile his vision, he was thrown against another wall.

Isaac didn't get up.

Donavan looked at him. His eyes were full of pain. "Don't come here," he told Isaac as another spear penetrated him.

"Why won't he run?" Isaac yelled at Truth. "Why don't you let these people defend themselves?"

"They made their choice," Truth told him. His voice was sad, but resigned. "Come."

"I can't leave Donavan."

"You can't do anything for him," Truth told him. "Come, I have more to show you."

"Oh, God, no! Just leave me alone."

Truth walked out of the Fun Room and headed toward a dark tunnel. Isaac quickly ran to catch up with Truth. As they walked, Isaac could hear more howling and cackling, and the cries of the lost souls. He came to a dead stop, mouth gaped open, as he pointed at a man crumpled and shaking in a corner. "He can't be here."

"For more than a century now."

"But he was a great man. The history books are full of his exploits."

"Even great men must serve the Lord."

Isaac remembered the story Nina recited years ago, about the rich man in hell. Great men must be no different from rich men, thugs or thieves. We all have to pay the piper, Isaac mournfully thought.

He looked at Truth. There was fear in his eyes. "Where are you taking me? Please tell me I'm not going to see my mother, am I?"

Truth turned to Isaac. "Your mother worshiped and served the Lord..."

"Lot of good that did her."

"Your mother lives in peace," Truth continued. "For eternity, she will only know goodness and joy. We're here."

The tunnel ended and the blackness of the great abyss gave way to pits of fire. Within those pits were souls. "These people once served the Lord, but they turned back to sin like a dog turns to his vomit."

"No!" Isaac screamed and turned his head away from the unbearable sight before him.

"She served me until she was sixteen-years old. But one man after another turned her away."

Isaac walked up to the pit that held the frame of Valerie. Her shrilling cries of agony penetrated his heart. Years of unshed tears gushed from his eyes as the flames from the fire licked at Valerie's skeletal form. Decayed flesh hung by shreds from her bones. It burned and fell into the bottom of the pit. She had no hair left. It had long been burned from her skeletal frame. Her face was as a hollow mass with out eyes, just empty, neglected sockets.

When the flames died down, Isaac could see the worms crawling through the bones of her skeleton. "Why do you torture me?" Isaac cried.

"She died before she could be restored back to the Lord."

The flesh crawled back onto her skeletal frame and the fire started at her feet again. Small flames at first, but they grew, and climbed up her body. Heavy tears flowed down Isaac's face as he said, "I'm sorry, Valerie. I should have loved you."

When the flames subsided, and the worms were crawling up her body again, she looked at Isaac, "Even if you had loved me, you still wouldn't have been worth this."

"I know," Isaac sobbed. "Oh, God. I'm so sorry. I'm so, so sorry. God, do You hear me? I'm sorry."

"Isaac man, wake up."

Someone was shaking him.

"Isaac, man you're just dreaming. Wake up!"

Isaac opened his eyes and stared at his bunkmate. "Where am I?"

"Same place as the rest of us. Erndale State Prison."

Isaac looked around a few times. "I'm not in hell?"

"Call it whatever you like," Pete told him. "I'm going to get some grub. You coming?"

Isaac jumped off his bunk. "Yeah. Yeah, I'm coming."

The chicken was half done as usual. The shriveled up potato wasn't worth baking once let alone twice. Isaac tossed the food around on his plate. It was sickening, but anything was preferable to his cell right about now. "What's the word?" Isaac asked Pete.

Pete was chomping down on his chicken, he swallowed then told Isaac, "T-bone's been telling everybody to start paying tribute to him, cause you won't live through the night."

"Is that so?" Isaac shook his head. "I don't know what's wrong with that knucklehead."

"I don't know eith..." Pete looked up. "Look, here comes Joe. Maybe he's got something for us."

Joe sat down next to Isaac. "Hey."

"Hey." Isaac and Pete answered back.

"Heard T-bone is sharpening up his shank – getting it ready for your neck," Joe told Isaac.

Isaac took a bite of his potato. "Is that so?"

"This otta even up the odds." Joe pulled a stick out of his pocket. It had a sharp piece of metal taped to the top of it.

Isaac looked at the shank, and the blood drained from his face.

"What's wrong, Isaac?"

"N-nothing." Isaac took the weapon. "Thanks man."

"Yeah," Joe smirked. "That fool gon' bust hell wide open when you get through with him."

Isaac's eyes bucked, his mouth hung open. A look of pure terror swept across his face. He shook his head back and forth. "No, no." He put the shank on the table.

Pete picked it up. "Isaac, what's wrong with you? You better put this in your pocket."

Isaac shook his head. "I can't send T-bone to *hell*."

"The way I see it. It's either him or you." Pete told him.

Isaac weighed his options. After what he had witnessed in hell, there was no way he would volunteer for a seat down there. Naw, that wasn't happening. He took the shank out of Pete's hand and stood up. "I need to make a phone call."

Isaac walked away from Pete and Joe mumbling something about finding a way to keep T-bone out of hell.

"What's up with ya' boy?" Joe asked Pete. "You think he's scared of T-bone?"

Pete waved his hand. "Joe please, I ain't seen nothing that could scare Isaac."

"You saw his face didn't you?"

"Yeah. I saw it."

37

"*B*oy, you better get back on that toilet. I'm not playing with you."

Donavan looked at his Mama. He shook his head. "No, I'm too tired."

Nina pointed at the toilet. "Yes. Now."

Donavan shook his head in opposition again.

"Donavan Jerome Walker, you are almost four-years old -- I'm tired of you peeing in the bed." She picked him up and sat him on the toilet. "Don't get up until you pee."

Donavan cried. The phone rang. Nina wanted to pull her hair out. Instead, she picked up the cordless and listened as an operator informed her that she had a collect call from Isaac. Isaac respected Nina's money situation. He had been in prison over a year and Nina could count on one hand the number of times he'd called collect. "Yes, I'll accept the charge."

"Hey, what's going on with you?"

"Nothing much. What's wrong with you?"

"Why something always gotta be wrong?"

"I can hear it in your voice. Now what's bothering you?"

Silence swallowed the air. Nina could hear Isaac breathing, so she waited. Finally, "There's this cat here name T-bone."

"Who would name their child T-bone?"

"Anyway. He wanted to go round with me, which means, one of us ain't gonna be living when we finish."

Nina gasped. "Isaac, no. You can't do this. Will you please think about Donavan? He needs you."

"Hold on Nina. I don't plan on dying. But I've got a problem with killing T-bone – that's what I need to talk to you about."

Nina pulled the receiver from her ear and stared at it. Was this man actually calling her to get advice about killing someone? "Isaac, I cannot condone..."

"Girl, ain't nobody asking you to condone nothing. It's either him or me, it's that simple. I'm not interested in going to hell, so it definitely ain't gonna be me." He paused. "I need to know how to keep T-bone out of hell though. I couldn't bare to send someone else there."

"Let me get this straight. You're telling me you are going to kill this T-bone guy, but you don't want to send him to hell."

Isaac yelled, "Exactly!" As if to say, finally, someone gets me.

Nina was stunned. "Excuse me?"

"I don't think T-bone could handle those demons. Shoot, I couldn't even handle them."

"Isaac, what are you talking about?"

Isaac exhaled loudly, "I'm talking about the fact that I've lost one fight in my life, and that was in hell. I can't send anybody else there to be tormented by those demons."

"Demons?" Nina scratched her head. "Isaac, what are you talking about?"

"I was there, Nina, in hell."

Nina thought she was going to have to call the Warden's office. Maybe the cooks are putting something in Isaac's food. Or maybe it's the confinement. He probably can't take being locked up. He might need to talk to someone.

"It was hideous, Nina. I saw Leonard, Ray-Ray, Valerie; and oh, God I even saw my brother Donavan." Isaac lowered his voice to a whisper. "They were all being tortured, Nina. You can't imagine the type of torture I was forced to witness. They don't have pitch forks like the movies show, Nina. They've got spears – and those demons plunge their spears into the flesh of..."

"Isaac, stop it!"

"Oh. Nina I'm sorry. Look, just tell me how T-bone can avoid going to hell when he dies."

Nina wanted to tell Isaac, don't kill him. That will certainly keep him out of hell. But she knew that was a waste of her breath. She let out a sigh and told him, "The Bible tells us that the only way to heaven is through Jesus Christ."

"I'm not talking about getting to heaven. I just want to know how to avoid hell."

No use telling him that it's either one or the other. "The 10th chapter of Romans says that *if you confess with your mouth the Lord Jesus...*"

"What do you mean, 'confess with your mouth?'"

Nina smiled. *Lord, is this You? Are You at work here?* "You have to say that you believe Jesus Christ is the Son of God."

"Oh. So you've got to believe in God in order to get out of going to hell?"

"Well of course." Nina rolled her eyes. "May I continue?"

"Yeah, yeah. What else?"

"Then once you believe in your heart that God raised Jesus from the dead, you'll be saved."

Isaac made a disgusted sound. "I'm not interested in salvation, Nina. I just want to know how not to go to hell."

"Well, you've got to be saved from sin in order to be saved from hell."

"Hmmm." Isaac said, clearly thinking things over. Nina could almost see him rubbing at his chin.

"If it's that simple, why are there so many people in hell?"

How did he know how many people were in hell? Nina wondered. "Isaac, this is not an easy thing. You can't just say that you believe Jesus is the Son of God and that He died and rose again and expect poof, pow, now I'm saved! You have to believe it with your heart, and that's very different from lip service."

"I see what you're saying."

He was rubbing that chin again, Nina just knew it.

"So how do I make sure that T-bone doesn't just say the words, but means them with his heart?"

Donavan walked over to Nina. "Mama I pee-peed."

Nina bent down and kissed Donavan. "Good job!"

Donavan beamed up at Nina, then turned and ran back to his bedroom to continue playtime.

Nina smiled, then told Isaac, "Your son better stop peeing in the bed."

"I miss him, Nina – didn't know I could miss someone so much."

"I know you do. I'll try to bring him out there next week."

"If the Feds hadn't confiscated everything I owned, we wouldn't be so tight for money."

Nina wanted to tell Isaac that if he hadn't been selling drugs and had a real nine-to-five he wouldn't be in jail, and would be able to provide for his child. She let that one go. "If you really want to make sure that T-bone means what he says, you can take him through the Roman Road to Salvation."

"The Roman what?"

"There are several verses in the book of Romans that we share with people, before discussing the passage in Romans 10."

"How many other verses?"

"Four or five if you count the salvation verse in Romans 10."

"That's going to take too long."

Nina was fed up. I mean really. First Isaac calls her house and tells her he's going to kill someone. Then he has the audacity to say he didn't want the guy to go to hell. And now he tells her he's not interested in the information she gave him because it will *take too long*. "Do you want the guy free from hell or not?" Nina demanded to know.

Isaac rubbed his chin. "Okay, okay. Just give me the scriptures – I'll read over them, and then I'll discuss it with T-bone."

Nina smiled. "Great. Now I want you to read these scriptures in the order I give them to you, okay?"

"Alright."

"You got a pen?"

"I'm ready."

"Romans 3:23, 3:10, 6:23, 5:8, and then you have him read Romans 10:9-11 and allow him to confess Jesus as his personal Lord and Savior."

"Thanks, Nina. Give Donavan a hug for me," he told her then hung up.

As she put the cordless back in the cradle, she thought about this bizarre conversation with Isaac. She went to her room and fell on her knees. She needed to pray for T-bone – Isaac was in need of some prayer also. And she most certainly couldn't forget Donavan. Her prayer for her son would be that he would be able to break the generational curse passed on from his father.

38

*I*saac couldn't sleep.

Or, it was probably more correct to say, Isaac wouldn't sleep. His eyes were blood shot red. He drooped in and out of consciousness, but he was determined not to take another trip to hell. Sleep deprivation was the only way to guarantee he did not experience a repeat of the other night.

Okay, he was a believer. Hell is not a fictional place – it is as real as earth. Isaac rubbed his chin. If hell is real, wouldn't the opposite also be true? Heaven would have to exist also, wouldn't it? Maybe that was the place Truth was talking about, when he told him that his mother lived in peace.

Isaac's thoughts turned to T-bone. He still couldn't believe what had happened. Or was it just that he didn't want to believe it? Isaac kept picturing that scene with T-bone.

"Hey T-bone, let me holler at you."

T-bone strutted over to Isaac like he owned half the world and had the other half on layaway. "What's up?"

"You want to go round with me, right?"

T-bone nodded.

"The only way I'm granting you a fight is if I can be sure you won't end up in hell when I kill you."

T-bone glared at Isaac. "What? Boy, you ain't 'bout to kill me, and you don't dictate fights around here. I could slit your throat right now."

Isaac smirked. "But you won't. I know you, T-bone. You don't want to simply slit my throat. You want to show everybody that you beat me down and then slit my throat."

T-bone hunched his shoulders.

"Well, I'm willing to give you the opportunity, but on my terms."

"What terms?"

"Sit down." Isaac pulled out a chair for T-bone. "I need to go over a few scriptures with you."

"Scriptures?" T-bone asked as he sat down.

"Yeah. This is information you need to know, so you can think about accepting Jesus into your heart so you don't go to hell."

"Why are you so concerned about me going to hell?"

Isaac's eyes glazed over, his shoulders dropped. "Man, I've been there. Trust me, you don't want to go." He turned the Bible to the third chapter of Romans and searched for verse twenty-three. "Here," Isaac handed T-bone the Bible. "Read this."

For all have sinned and fallen short of the glory of God.

T-bone looked up. "And?"

"Okay, well read this one." Isaac pointed to verse number ten in the same chapter.

As it is written: There is none righteous, no, not one.

"Don't you get it?" Isaac asked as he grabbed the Bible and flipped a few pages. "The Bible is trying to tell you that just because the sin you did has landed you in jail, that don't make it no worse than the sins them fat cats in corporate America commit everyday."

"Yeah, they just don't have prisons for the mess them cats do," T-bone added.

Isaac shook his head. "Something has been created for all kinds of sins. And if they go, they will wish for the prison we know, rather than the torment they will receive."

"What kind of torment? What are you talking about?"

Isaac's eyes misted, as he once again pictured Valerie in that pit. "Those demons, man, they pick at your body – and there is a consuming fire that jumps out of pits. It burns off your flesh." Isaac's head rolled back and he shut his eyes. "Ah, man, that place is indescribable. It's your worse nightmare, magnified – it's constant and unending. Trust me, you don't want to go."

"You're serious, aren't you?"

"Dead serious."

T-bone turned his attention to the Bible. "Okay, what else you got?"

Isaac pointed at the twenty-third verse of the sixth chapter of Romans.

T-bone read, *For the wages of sin is death, but the gift of God is eternal life in Christ Jesus our Lord.*

Isaac then turned to the fifth chapter of Romans and pointed at the eighth verse.

But God demonstrates His own love toward us, in that while we were still sinners, Christ died for us.

T-bone raised his head. "What you think that means?"

Isaac rubbed his chin. "Well I – well I actually think this scripture means that even if you were the only person on earth – even if you had done all the stuff you've done, Jesus would have still come to earth and died for you."

T-bone's eyes widened. "You really think so?"

Naw, Jesus wouldn't waste His time on slime like T-bone. "Yeah, I really think so."

"Okay, so what's next?"

"Well," Isaac stalled as he turned the Bible to the tenth chapter of Romans. "Now you need to accept Jesus into your heart. The ninth through the eleventh verse of this chapter will explain that to you."

"Are you ready to accept Jesus?" What was he saying? Good God, was he, a sinner, actually getting ready to lead someone in the sinner's prayer?

T-bone gave Isaac a thoughtful look. "I'm not sure," he said. "Do you mind if I borrow your Bible for a little while?"

Isaac moved his Bible out of T-bone's reach. "How long?"

"Not long, man, an hour or two."

Isaac handed the Bible over to T-bone.

A couple hours later, during the dinner rush, T-bone came into the mess hall and gave Isaac back his Bible. "Thanks, man. If I can ever do anything for you, let me know."

"What's that supposed to mean?"

"Means I'm in debt to you. Jesus saved my life." He clasped Isaac on the shoulder. "I won't forget what you did for me."

Isaac's mouth hung open as he witnessed a tear forming in T-bone's eyes before he hurriedly turned and left the mess hall.

***

Isaac was now back in his cell, still trying to figure out what happened to T-bone. Not only was he saved from hell, he didn't want to fight anymore – even apologized. What was that all about? Someone laughed. Pete was in the hole, so Isaac knew it wasn't him. He looked up, and one of the big grizzly demons he saw in hell sat across from him. Isaac scooted as far back on his bunk as he could, and literally started clawing the walls trying to get further away. "No, no," he screamed. "I can't be in hell again."

Two security guards walked by Isaac's cell and looked in. "Somebody done gave that boy some bad drugs," one said, while the other shook his head. They kept walking down the block.

"Hush up, fool. You ain't in hell," the demon told him.

"Wh – who are you?" Isaac asked, trying to calm himself down.

The demon shrugged his shoulders. "I'm you."

Isaac got off the wall, and sat down on his bunk. "How can you be me? I'm me."

"I'm the one that makes you do the things you do so well," he laughed. "Who do you think instructed you to kill your good friend, Leonard? When you beat on poor Nina, I was there – matter-of-fact I was helping you kick her. We almost got rid of that baby." He shook his head and snapped his scaly fingers. Grayish debris flaked off and drifted to the ground. "Missed that one. Hey, what about how I told you who to kill when you were claiming your territory? We made a good team, didn't we?"

Isaac snarled. "Nobody tells me what to do. I'm my own man."

"Yeah, right. You wouldn't know how to come in from the rain, unless I gave you instructions." Isaac's demon stood up and strutted up and down his 8-foot cell. He turned back to Isaac with a thoughtful look on his face. "Now, of course, I didn't have anything to do with you getting T-bone saved. What was that all about?"

Isaac yelled, "He's free from hell!"

The demon grabbed the iron bars and looked through the corridor. "Yeah, well, now his demon is walking up and down this place trying to find another house to reside in." He angrily turned back to Isaac. "Do you know how hard it is to find an empty house in a prison?" Slime dripped from his mouth as his nostrils flared. "Forget it. It's useless talking to you," the demon told him.

Isaac watched in horror as this monster climbed back inside him. His body jerked, as he felt the evil that once again resided within him. Isaac threw up – right there in the middle of his cell.

That did it. Isaac had reconciled himself to the fact that not only were hell and heaven real, but demons were also real. And if demons exist then angels must also exist. And if all that is true, then there must be a God.

Isaac closed his eyes. There couldn't be a God – look how the world is. But then there has to be a God, how else did this other world exist? "Why don't you ever look out for nobody?" Isaac screamed at God.

He stood up and punched his fist in the wall. "Why didn't you look out for me?"

Isaac, I have loved you with an everlasting love.

Isaac swiftly turned around to see if he had another unwelcomed guest in his cell. It was empty. He knew someone had spoken to him, and instinctively he knew it had been the voice of God. He turned his face toward heaven and asked, "Is this what You call love?" He waved his arms around the cell. "You were never there for me. I remember Mama making me recite that stupid prayer, *Our Father, who art in heaven. Hallowed be Thy name.* It's hollow all right," Isaac told God. "You're worse than a dead-beat dad. The courts outta lock *You* up for failing to support Your children."

No answer.

He stalked around his small cell trying to come to grips with his newfound knowledge. He thought about the pastor at his Mama's church, and how nice he had been. He even visited him a few times in Juvee. Every time Pastor Young came to visit, he would tell Isaac that God had not forgotten him, and whenever he needed help, all he had to do was look up and begin to pray. Isaac used to feel sorry for that man. He wasted so much time on him. There had to be others who would have gladly received such news.

Isaac found no joy in it. He had already given up on God. But, maybe that was God's way of showing His love…

Isaac shook his head trying to blot out all thoughts of God's love. Then he remembered all the times he had narrowly escaped death. He thought he was one of the luckiest men on the face of the earth, but maybe that was God again. Isaac sat down on his bunk and guilt filled his soul. He had brought harm to many. He had cared less about a human life than an animal ripping its prey to shreds. He lifted his head to heaven once again. "How can You love me? Don't You know what kind of man I am – the things I've *done?*"

Isaac felt strong, loving arms wrap around him and rock him back and forth. Kind of like his Mama used to do when he hurt himself and came running to her for comfort.

Isaac then heard a still small voice say to him, *My grace is sufficient for you.*

Isaac jumped out of Love's embrace. *Grace.* "No! no! no!" God was offering him forgiveness. He wanted to pour grace over all his transgressions. But how could he accept such a thing knowing that Valerie, Leonard and Donavan were in hell. He closed his eyes and put his hands over his ears. "I am the one who deserves to be in hell. Not them, ME!"

39

*G*etting their luggage and getting out of JFK Airport was a job in itself. That airport was entirely too crowded. By the time they got out of the place, Elizabeth was so tired all she wanted to do was go to Chinatown, grab some of that scrumptious shrimp fried rice and crash in their hotel room.

Kenneth had other plans. He hailed a cab and they drove to Chinatown and picked up the shrimp fried rice Elizabeth was craving. He then escorted her to their suite, dropped the bags and then left the room. Returning with a single red rose.

"I love you Mrs. Underwood." He bent down and devoured her lips.

"Ah, baby you're so sweet to me."

He looked at her greedily. "Have you had enough to eat?"

"Yeah, why? You want the rest?" She tried to hand him the carton.

"No." He lifted her out of her seat. "I want my wife."

Elizabeth laughed. "Okay, let me shower and change into something a little more comfortable first."

He kissed her ear lobe. "Don't make me wait too long."

Elizabeth fanned herself, as she walked to the bathroom. "Whew!"

No sooner had she opened the bathroom door, and reentered the bedroom, Kenneth was on her. Kissing her, moving her closer to the bed.

"What's gotten into you?"

They fell on the bed and he met her question with a hungry, sensual kiss. "You're mine," he told her. "Forever, and always."

Elizabeth's pulse began to race. His kiss burned into her soul, and she hungered and thirsted for more of him. As their love ruptured over the horizon of the passion they possessed for one another, Elizabeth heard Kenneth say, "And I'm yours." This is it, she thought. Now I have everything.

***

All day long, Nina had been bothered by this nagging feeling that something was about to happen, and that her prayers were needed. Donavan was extra needy and clingy.

She put him down to bed, went to her room and got on her knees. She didn't know what to pray for, so she prayed in tongues. Her unknown language was known to God. Nina stayed in that position most of the night. This was no time to get weary. In her spirit, she knew that this was one of those weeping and wailing nights. So that's what she did, long into the midnight hour.

***

Kenneth yawned and then reached out for Elizabeth. He pulled her closer to him and kissed the back of her neck. "Good morning, beautiful."

She stretched. "Mmm, good morning yourself, handsome." She looked at the clock on the dresser. It was 7:40 am. "What time do you have to be at the World Trade Center?"

Kenneth growled, "8:30."

"You better get up. You're going to be late."

Kenneth snuggled up a little closer to his wife. "Maybe, I'll see if I can meet with Bob a little later this afternoon."

Elizabeth sat up in bed and put her hands on her hips. "Kenneth Underwood, if you don't get your lazy butt out of this bed, I'm going to hurt you. The sooner you get this accounting business taken care of – the sooner I can drag you from store to store and spend your money."

Kenneth laughed. "Alright, alright." He drug himself out of the warm, cozy bed and got into the shower. By ten minutes after eight, Kenneth was dressed and on his way out the door.

"Hey, aren't you forgetting something?"

He moved away from the door with an insatiable grin on his face.

"That's right, baby. Bring it to Mama."

He kissed his wife with the passion possessed by a newlywed. But hey, ten years, ten days, what's the difference when you're in love? "I should be done with this meeting at about 9:30."

"Hurry back."

"Baby, I'm going to run back to you." He kissed her one last time and was out the door.

Elizabeth lay in bed a little while longer. She turned to look at the clock. It was 8:30. She stretched and moaned one last time, then pulled the cover back and got out of bed. She put her hair in a ponytail and jumped in the shower.

Kenneth's fragrance was still in the bathroom. She inhaled and smiled. This was going to be a good day. Elizabeth already knew which stores she intended to drag Kenneth through. She made a reservation at Sylvia's for dinner, and then the night belonged to him. Whatever he wanted to do, Elizabeth didn't care, as long as she was with him. She'd even sit through a boring opera. Although she couldn't figure out for the life of her what a black man saw in a bunch of funny singing, overacting White people. She turned off the water and got out of the shower.

It was 8:50. She would have to get a move on if she was going to be ready when Kenneth got back. She turned the TV to the news channel. A little drama always put some pep in her step. She grabbed her Juniper Breeze lotion from Bath & Body Works and sat down on the bed to apply it.

She was rubbing lotion on her shoulder, when she saw a picture of the World Trade Center. An airplane was protruding from the side of it. "I thought this was the news channel." She was not interested in seeing some science fiction movie this morning. She got up to change the channel, when she heard the anchor say, "This just in. A 757 just crashed into the north tower of the World Trade Center."

She sat back down. She couldn't breathe, couldn't think. Her hand stretched out as if she were trying to pull something or someone back to her. She opened her mouth and a guttural, "Kenneth" escaped her lips.

She was still breathing irregularly as she stood up, pulled on a pair of jeans and turtleneck. She threw on a pair of tennis shoes and ran out the door. The hotel was five blocks from the World Trade Center, but Elizabeth didn't care. She just kept running and running until someone stopped her. "You can't go in there," the officer said.

She was at the corner of West Broadway and Barklay, one block north of the Trade Center. She pointed at the building. "My husband."

"I'm sorry, lady, but you'll have to wait here. It's for your own safety."

And then it happened again. An airplane flew into the south tower of the World Trade Center and exploded. Both buildings were burning now. People were falling out of the windows and plummeting to their death, as the sky gave way to fire and smoke.

Elizabeth heard screams coming from every direction. "We're under attack! We're under attack!" They screamed. Try as she might, Elizabeth couldn't feel what was happening to the rest of civilization. She only knew that her husband was in one of those buildings, and if he didn't come out alive she didn't know how she was going to make it. *Lord, please let him come out of that building safe and sound.* She screamed, *"Pleeeease!"*

Several minutes later, when the south tower collapsed right before her eyes, she went from horror to hell on earth. The tower fell in perfect symmetry, one floor after another, and then another. And then it went up in a cloud of smoke like a giant mushroom.

"I'm under attack," Elizabeth said to herself as she crumbled to her knees.

40

"At 8:45 a.m. a hijacked passenger jet, American Airlines Flight 11 out of Boston, Massachusetts, crashed into the north tower of the World Trade Center, tearing a gaping hole in the building and setting it afire," the newscaster informed his audience.

"At 9:03 a.m.," he continued, "a second hijacked airliner, United Airlines Flight 175 from Boston, crashed into the south tower of the World Trade Center and exploded." He turned slightly and swept his arm in the direction of the Twin Towers. "As you can see, both buildings are now burning and people are falling and jumping from the buildings."

The newscaster turned back to his audience and continued his chronology of terror. "At 9:43 a.m., American Airlines Flight 77 crashed into the Pentagon. That building has been evacuated and President Bush now believes that the country has suffered an apparent terrorist attack."

Isaac, Pete, T-bone and as many inmates as could fit in the recreation room, stood stunned, watching as the events of 911 unfolded before their horrified eyes. Pete pointed at the screen, but could not form any words. As they listened to the newscaster the south tower crumbled.

The newscaster jumped. "Oh, my God," he screamed.

Isaac could take no more. He walked away from the TV, composure shattered. Tomorrow is not promised to any of us, Isaac knew that. Many people were discovering that hard lesson today, but God had preserved his life. He was willing to face that fact now. It had to be grace, cause he certainly wasn't worthy of any special treatment from God.

In the face of this tragedy, how could he deny the awesome power of God's grace any longer? He was in prison. They had confiscated his money, his houses, cars, and his business. He had been to hell and back, but he was alive. Isaac thought about his Mama, Nina, and Keith. Things they said to him over the years came rolling back like an unexpected thunderstorm.

His sweet Mama always told him how awesome God was. Isaac never witnessed any of God's awesome power. But then again, every time he looked at Nina, he saw how strong she had become. How she no longer bent to his will. *That was awesome.* And Keith, he totally turned his life around. Isaac couldn't even finish some of Keith's letters. They were too full of God's love. *That was awesome also.*

Maybe God was in the rain, Isaac thought as he entered his cell. His life flashed before his eyes. He saw the tragedy and pain as he always did, but this time he also saw God. Standing right in the midst of his sin filled life. Isaac fell down on his knees. He was tired of fighting this awesome God. Tired of kicking against the prick. Tears streamed down his face as he begged, "Oh God, please forgive me. I've been so wrong – so wrong."

He was prostrate now, before the King. Not caring who walked by, or what the inmates would say about the great Isaac Walker crying like a baby. He felt like a baby again. No, that wasn't quite it. He felt... he felt... free. Yeah, right at that moment, he was receiving forgiveness and being delivered from his past.

Instinctively he knew that the life he once knew was gone. From this day forward, even surrounded by bars – he was free.

Arise Isaac, for I have called you. You shall preach My gospel to nations.

Isaac worshipped the Lord. He wasn't sure about this preaching to nations thing, but he knew without a shadow of a doubt that he had been saved from much. Therefore, he set his heart on loving much.

41

*P*eople were still running and shouting. Elizabeth heard from some distant voices that the Pentagon had also been attacked.

A huge piece of debris flew over Elizabeth's head and landed about twenty feet in front of her. It was about the size of a truck. Elizabeth was covered with soot and ashes. People were pulling at her saying that she had to get out of there. Elizabeth ignored them and continued to wait. Kenneth would come out of the north tower, she just knew it.

Right then, as the north tower collapsed as if a giant hand smashed it, Elizabeth knew what it was like to have your hopes and dreams dashed. An overwhelming cloud of debris and smoke spilled into the air.

Elizabeth beat the ground with her fists. Screaming and crying she asked, *"What am I supposed to do now? How can I go on?"*

Lean on Me, beloved.

Elizabeth shook her head. *"You ask too much. You've always wanted too much from me."*

Lean on Me, beloved.

All Elizabeth could do was moan and wail. She laid her head on the ground and let the tears flow. She had no one. Kenneth had promised that they would grow old together. He told her that he was going to run back to her today. How could this happen to them? She looked up to heaven and angrily told God, *"He was everything to me."*

I am the first and the last, the beginning and the end.

"You ask too much!" She screamed, then flung herself back on the ground amongst the dirt and wreckage. Tears. She would cry a river. Agony. The pain of this day would never leave her. Let the mob trample over her, she didn't care. Her reason for living, her everything, was gone. She would never love again - death would be a merciful friend.

EPILOGUE

*T*wo angels stood outside the most magnificent pearl laden gates shouting, "Behold the Glory of God!"

Directly behind the pearly gates was a massive space where a cushion of snowy white clouds caressed the feet of its occupants. The tree of life stood bold and beautiful in the middle of the outer court. Its leaves were a heavenly green, and its fruit was succulent and enjoyed by all. Sweet blissful music could be heard throughout the great expanse of heaven. It was the harp, but it was better than any harp on earth; it was the guitar, but it was better than any guitar on earth.

There were thousands upon thousands of saints moving through the joys of heaven, clothed in glistening white robes, and bare feet. Many had crowns on their heads with various types of jewels embedded in them. A woman named Marguerite Barrow stood, surrounded by the most beautiful array of flowers, colors without name. Heaven was the great garden of love, so these flowerbeds could be found all over this glorious place. As Marguerite stood in the midst of the splendor, the diamond in her crown sparkled brightly. She earned this diamond because of Nina, the girl she loved, sheltered and watered with the Word of the Lord.

To the right of this flowerbed stood a man with too many jewels for one crown to hold. For him, a glorious purple outer coat had also been made, and it glistened with the jewels of thousands of souls that had been won into the Kingdom. On earth he had been a great pastor, one who believed in making disciples of God's people, rather than cripples. He didn't want his congregation to believe they could only find Jesus through him, but that they could find Him within their own hearts; and share Him with others. Because of this, many souls continued to be won into the Kingdom, even well after his death. Maybe that's why his earthly congregation still remembers his teachings, and their eyes still mist at the thought of his great memory. His name was Willie E. Mitchell, Sr. He was the founder of The Rock Christian Fellowship. He had been loved and respected by many, a modern day Job some might say. And now, as he walked in the midst of his friends, a dazzling smile would cross his lips every now and then. His friends all knew this meant that God had just added another jewel to his coat. Just God's little way of saying, "Thanks for making disciples."

On the opposite side of the outer court stood a great multitude of warrior angels. Their appearance was that of beauty and majesty. They wore white radiant garments with gold edged trim that embellished the front of the garment. At their waist, hung a huge golden sword, and large white wings flapped from behind. The outer court was like a waiting room. The saints were waiting to be admitted into the inner court and some, the Holy of Holies. The warrior angels waited for their next assignments. Right now, a great commotion was going on amongst the angels. They were anxious, something big was about to happen, they just knew it. Some asked if Michael would greet them today. To this day, the angels in heaven remained in awe of the one angel that was able to meet Lucifer in battle and come out victorious every time. Even Gabriel had needed Michael's help when Lucifer had attacked him. They all greatly admired their general and longed for a glimpse of him. The captain of these angels lifted his hands to silence them. "Brothers, I will have news for you momentarily, I am on my way to meet with the General now."

"Captain Aaron," a familiar voice among the angels called out to him.

"Yes Nathan?"

"I think I'm ready, I would really like to go back out sir."

"We'll see. I'll talk to the General about it."

Wih that, Aaron disappeared from the heavenly hosts in the outer court. He was now walking through the inner court on his way to the Holy Place. There were unnumbered mansions in the inner court, room enough for everyone. Sadly enough, the beauty and splendor of heaven would only be enjoyed by the few that served God. As he passed by the room of tears, he glanced in and shook his head in wonderment. It still amazed him that humans had tears so precious that God would bottle and preserve them in a room as glorious as this.

He opened the door of the Holy Place and stood in the back, as he heard the voice of thunder and lightening. He then heard a multitude of praises saying, "Holy, Holy, Holy." And as the voices became thunderous, Aaron also joined them. In this place, where God sits high and is lifted up, praises are sung to Him forever. His glory lovingly fills the atmosphere and joy spreads throughout His Heavenly court.

Thunder and lightening sparkled from the throne of Grace once more, then Michael's glorious nine-foot form stood. His colorful wings glistened as they flapped in the air. "Yes my Lord," he said, as he took the scrolls from the Omnipotent hand that held it.

Michael stood in front of Aaron. Michael's sword was longer and heavier than the other angels. Jewels were embedded throughout the handle of this massive sword, a symbol of his many victories. The belt that held his sword sparkled with the gold of heaven. Michael had defeated the Prince of Persia more times than he cared to remember. But the enemy was getting stronger as his time drew near. Michael eagerly awaited their next meeting. It would be their last. "Here is your assignment."

Aaron took the scrolls, then said, "My General, my Prince, Nathan has asked to be assigned to this mission."

"Are you sure he's ready? He was pretty shook up when he lost his last charge."

"In all fairness General, he did expect her to live once she had given her life to the Lord."

"I know he did, but he needs to understand that he is not responsible for changing the plan of God, just helping it along."

Thunder and lightening danced from the throne of grace once more. Michael excused himself and then returned with another scroll. "Give this one to Nathan."

Aaron, now back in the outer courts, shouted to the legions of angels, "If I call your name, come up here and take a scroll."

"Davison. Manuel. Brogan. And... Nathan." The four angels hurriedly grabbed their scrolls, anxious to see who they were given charge over. Their wings swayed in the gentle heavenly breeze as they prepared for their journey. "You have been given charge over men and women who will do great exploits for the kingdom."

Nathan stood in front of Aaron with a confused look on his angelic face.

"What's the matter, son?"

"Well, I don't understand why I was given charge over Kenneth Underwood. He didn't make it out of the World Trade Center, did he?"

"Go see about your charge. God's mercy is far reaching." Aaron told him, then put his hand on Nathan's shoulder. "Just remember, God is sovereign and there's no changing that."

"I understand that. But why must I go if there is no hope?"

Aaron put a stern look on his face before answering, "We do what we are called to do." He nudged Nathan. "Now, go!"

This story isn't over…!

Don't miss the exciting and moving conclusion of the story of Elizabeth and Kenneth, in *Abundant Rain*, Book Two. And the conclusion of the story of Nina and Isaac in *Latter Rain*, Book Three of Vanessa Miller's exciting Rain trilogy.

Watch for book two and three in 2004!

About the Author

Vanessa Miller of Dayton, Ohio is an author, playwright, and motivational speaker. Her stage productions include: **Get You Some Business, Don't Turn Your Back on God** and **Can't You Hear Them Crying.**

Vanessa is currently promoting the novels in the Rain Series; **Former Rain** and **Abundant Rain,** and **Latter Rain, Rain.** Vanessa believes that her God-given destiny is to write and produce plays and novels that bring deliverance to God's people.

Vanessa is a dedicated Christian and devoted mother of Erin. She graduated from Capital University with a degree in Organizational Communication. She is very active in her church (Revival Center Ministries), serving as Director of the Singles Ministry, Director of the Drama Team and member of the Women's Ministry Committee. A perfect day for Vanessa is one that affords her the time to curl up with a good book. She is currently preparing a promotional tour and writing the stage production for the **Abundant Rain** novel.

A Reading Group Guide

Former Rain

Vanessa Miller

Reading Group Guide

by: Valerie Coleman

Discussion Questions

Nina

1. When Nina accepted Christ into her life, she was forgiven for the abortion she had at the age of seventeen. Do you think she ever forgave herself? How would you minister to her on self-forgiveness?

Read:

    Psalms 103:12   Isaiah 43:25-26
    Philippians 3:13-14   Philippians 4:6-8

2. What biblical principles apply to Nina's ability to overcome her natural affection for Isaac as evidenced in Chapter 19?

Read:

    Romans 8:6-13   I Corinthians 6:18-20
    II Corinthians 6:14-18 Galatians 5:24-26
    Colossians 3:1-7   James 1:12-16
    I Peter 1:18-25

3. How did Nina exemplify the characteristics of Christ, when dealing with her "wife-in-laws?"

Read:

Proverbs 24:17-18   Matthew 25:35-44
Romans 12:17-21 I Corinthians 13
Galatians 5:22-23 Colossians 3:22-25

Isaac

1. Although God told Isaac that He had loved him with an everlasting love (Chapter 38), why was it not evident in Isaac's life?

Read:

Proverbs 6:16-19   Proverbs 15:29-33
Proverbs 28:7-10

2. Why did Isaac have such deep-rooted anger toward God?

Read:

Psalms 14:1-4   Lamentations 3:1-20

3. Isaac was surprised to see "the great man" in hell. What did Truth mean when He said, "Even great men must serve the Lord?"

Read:

Isaiah 5:13-15   Matthew 7:13-14
Luke 16:19-31   Romans 10:9-13
Ephesians 2:8-10 I John 1:8 10

Elizabeth

1. Why did Elizabeth have difficulty submitting to her husband?

Read:

      Job 33:17-18   Job 41:15-34
      Proverbs 16:18-19   Proverbs 29:23
      Ephesians 4:25-32   Ephesians 5:21-24

2.   In Chapter 20, Elizabeth said, "Things are different. I'm a Christian now, Kenneth." What did she mean by that statement?

Read:

  Ephesians 4:23-24 Colossians 3:10-14
  II Timothy 3:5-9   James 1:19-27
  II Corinthians 3:12-17, 4:3-6

3.   How do you feel about Elizabeth's determination to reclaim her marriage? What were the effects of her steadfastness?

Read:

      Isaiah 40:29-31   Isaiah 43:18-21
      Matthew 18:21-35 I Corinthians 7:13-14
      I Corinthians 15:58

Kenneth

1.   Why did Kenneth go outside of his marriage for companionship?

Read:

      Proverbs 12:4   Proverbs 15:1-2
      Proverbs 19:13   Proverbs 21:9, 19
      Proverbs 25:24   Proverbs 27:15

2. It was clear that Elizabeth and Mama Rosa had unresolved issues. What role should Kenneth have played in healing the breech between his wife and mother?

Read:

> Genesis 2:24   Matthew 19:3-9
> Mark 10:1-9   Ephesians 5:25-33
> Colossians 3:19

3. Chapter 27 illustrates Kenneth's devastation when he realized that the woman he admired and loved, also possessed characteristics that he abhorred. How do married couples overcome this transition?

Read:

> Amos 3:3   Song of Solomon 7:6-7
> I Corinthians 13   Philippians 2:2-4
> I Peter 3:1-7

The Group

1. The salvation experiences for Nina and Elizabeth were quite different. Both were converted, upon accepting Jesus as their personal Lord and Savior, however, Nina was more committed to her vow. Explain the difference between Elizabeth's conversion and Nina's transformation.

Read:

> II Chronicles 7:14-16   Psalms 27:4-14
> Psalms 51   Romans 12:1-2
> I Peter 1:13-16

2. Exodus 34:7 refers to generational curses as the iniquity of the fathers is passed down to the children. How did Isaac

and Kenneth live out this curse? What can they do to overcome this destructive legacy?

Read:

Exodus 34:7	Numbers 14:18
Proverbs 4:1-9	Proverbs 30:11-14
Ephesians 6:4	Colossians 3:21

3. Why was it difficult for Isaac and Kenneth to accept the grace of God in their lives?

Conclusion

The Roman road to salvation is discussed in chapters 37 and 38. The scriptures from the book of Romans lead a sinner to Christ. The history behind the road to salvation is based upon the industrialization of the Roman people in Biblical times. They constructed roads to encourage travel between cities. These roads were paved and patrolled to allow safe passage – the first of their kind. Because of these roads the gospel was spread faster and easier.

For answers to these questions

Visit: www.vanessamiller.com

OTHER OFFERINGS

From Butterfly Press, LLC

Abundant Rain

by: Vanessa Miller

Elizabeth Underwood. Bold. Vivacious. Confident. Her life was about to be turned upside down.

As far as Elizabeth was concerned, the Underwoods were the poster family for God's blessings. But when the storms of life interrupt Elizabeth's world, will she become entangled in her struggles or will she rest in the promises of God?

Read, enjoy, and find peace for your soul.

ISBN: 0-9728850-1-3

Release date: March, 2004

Visit our website at: www.vanessamiller.com

OTHER OFFERINGS

From Butterfly Press, LLC

Latter Rain

by: Vanessa Miller

Hustling wasn't easy, but Isaac did his best. He ruled the underworld like a predator – a self made CEO of the streets. But one woman dared to show him a better way. Her way changed all the rules. Now, all Isaac wants is to live for God and win back his baby's mama, Nina Lewis. But when the past catches up with Isaac, and tragedy creeps in his back door – all bets are off.

ISBN: 0-9728850-2-1

Release date: April, 2005

Visit our website at: www.vanessamiller.com

THE RAIN SERIES

by Vanessa Miller

If you have enjoyed FORMER RAIN and would like to order other books in the Rain Series, please fill out the form below.

■■■

Name: _____

Address: _____

City: _____ State: _____ Zip: _____

Email: _____

Former Rain   # Bks ____ x $13.95 =$_____

Abundant Rain   # Bks ____ x $13.95 =$_____

Latter Rain   # Bks ____ x $13.95 =$_____

Ohio residents add 7.5% sales tax ($1.05 per book) $_____

Shipping and handling:

First book is $2.99. Each additional book is $0.99 $_____

Total Amount Enclosed $_____

Please return this order form with your check or money order payable to:

Butterfly Press, LLC
PMB 257
5523 Salem Avenue
Dayton, OH 45426
(937) 248-9211